ORDER
OF
DRAIC

CW01498001

BY J S ALDRIDGE

First published 2024

ISBN 9798876505514

Independently published

Contents

Acknowledgements

This is my first attempt at this writing lark, and, depending upon the reviews, it could be my last. With that in mind, I would like to say a few thank-yous.

To kick off, thank you to Ann M and Andrew P who both took the dive into authoring long before me and whose kind words and encouragement led to you reading this.

Miranda R, what can I say, your attention to grammatical detail has given my ramblings a sheen.

Big love to Sonia and Sophia who are my world and told me to go for it. So I did.

Finally, thank you, reader. Thank you for giving this a chance; for diving into something from an author called 'Who?' Hopefully, you'll enjoy it. If you did, tell everyone.

Peace out.

Prologue: AD293

Sixtus sat under a palm tree, shaded from the Cyrene afternoon sun, patiently waiting. The dry heat baked a constant layer of fine dust onto his exposed arms and legs and dulled his chainmail. Brown skin turned beach. His neck was chafed where cloth and chainmail met skin and grit. His feet were sore from the journey, and he was constantly hungry. They had been marching for days, his centurion pushing the *centuria* hard to reach the town. The cool air from the sea brought a light breeze up the valley giving welcome relief from the heat. Sixtus bit into the last of his dry bread as he watched his commander's cuirass rhythmically flicker in the sun to his horse's gait as he rode up the hill to their camp.

His commander was unlike any other man he had met.

Georgius was as fierce as a lion in battle but carried himself with humility. He was a good man. He would tell stories of the one called Christ. His faith was unpopular within the army, but although Sixtus didn't follow it himself, he would patiently listen and nod when Georgius would regale them with stories of miracles.

Sixtus did as he was ordered and was waiting for this last year of his conscription to finish. Over his twenty-four-year career he had walked across most of the Empire, from the green and cold North to the arid South. He had seen much violence and carried the scars upon his skin as evidence of battles he had fought and won. He was one of only a few who still lived so close to the end of their service, and he hoped that this commander would see him safely to his discharge and the promise of his own land and the handsome endowment that would follow.

He rose as Georgius approached, unsaddled from his horse, and, smiling, patted him on the shoulder.

'The reports are true. I have scouted out the lair which is to the south. The beast takes rest in a cave at the rear of the wadi, the entrance is narrow, and I am told it is the only one. It is a fine day, so, what say you that we fight?' Georgius smiled warmly. 'I will pray. Make ready, Sixtus. Bring together the *contubernium*. We shall leave as the sun's shadow lengthens.'

Georgius savoured hunting *dracones*. It was a sought-after quarry, pursued by the elite as a symbol of warrior heroism. Sixtus and the other men of the *centuria* had been led by Georgius in what seemed a constant hunt, to the exclusion of all other duties, and they had experienced much success. In the beginning it would take up to thirty men to overcome a *draco* and very few would survive to tell the tale. The beasts were fierce; the largest they had seen was the length of five men from snout to tail-tip and a wingspan of double that. *Dracos* flew with the agility of a bat and speed of a horse. Their talons could split a man from neck to waist, even in chainmail. The fire from their mouths would stick like tar, igniting cloth, leather, hair and skin. It was an ugly, noisy death. The body would contort in such forms not before witnessed and all that would remain would be a stark charcoal statue of pain. Sixtus had seen men torn apart, dismembered, or decapitated by a bite, crushed between tail and rock, popped between claws like a man might crush a snail and even taken high in the air and dropped, as though the *draco* was also treating the battle as its own game.

With each *draco* defeated, Georgius' understanding of his adversary grew. He would study them as other commanders would gather intelligence on their opposing army. He would take a knife to the corpse and look at the form inside. He often explored their lairs, picking around at the remains of its prey and even examining its foul waste. He said that to defeat a *draco,* it was necessary to know them.

The hunt was profitable. The beast's corpse had value. Leather made from its skin was thicker and more durable than any other animal, and its head and tail could be sold or given as trophies. Sixtus had seen one *Censor* have a helmet fashioned from the skull of a smaller quarry. The meat was bountiful and rich and sold quickly to merchants. Very little of the vanquished animal remained. Bones were fashioned into tools or ground for medicine. Even the entrails were bought by prophets or other spirituals and used in rituals. The scales that covered its breast, wings, back and thighs were as strong as any iron, but weighed much less. They had retained enough to make *lorica squamata* and leather tunics to dress a *contubernium* of soldiers. Each of the squad received a share of the coin and Sixtus guessed that his commander had already gathered great wealth, along with notoriety.

The time came to leave. Sixtus had a regular and reliable squad, and his selection process was simple; the men had to have nerves of steel and be proved in battle. He had been handpicked by Georgius as one of thirty for the first hunt and subsequently made responsible for the unit.

The first hunt had been disastrous for Georgius and his men. The *draco* came charging down from the sky—those that were not burned where they stood were quickly dispatched by talon or jaw in the panic and fear that followed. Only he and Georgius survived.

Georgius took it as a sign from his God that they were both chosen for this path. They had learned quickly and each of the current squad had survived the last five hunts. Now they were beginning to act as one in the hunt. Georgius took the most personal satisfaction from single combat, therefore standing orders were not to attack the *draco* unless commanded. His proficiency was such that over time the unit of soldiers was reduced to from thirty to ten. Georgius had become skilled in the hunt and, in truth, the *dracos* were reducing in size as much as their rarity was increasing. The unit was beginning to treat the hunt as though they were merely observers and as an opportunity to gather several years' wage in one day.

Georgius came out from his tent wearing fine battle armour made from the best *draco* scales and emblazoned with a cross and *draco* etched on its chest. Each of the highly polished scales had a slightly different shade of grey and the light danced off his armour, glinting green tones, like the skin of a snake. He kissed a cross tied around his neck, tucked it under the collar of his leather tunic and mounted his horse.

Turning to the *centuria* which had gathered for their departure, he shouted, 'We go with God's blessing to defeat this beast which has caused much pain and grief to this city. We are the weapons of our Lord, and we do His work today. We shall dispatch this unholy of beasts and return peace to the city, the region and the Empire.'

He held his lancea high and his centuria roared and stamped their feet. Sixtus felt his blood rush and his heart beat louder with pride and anticipation. Georgius looked like a statue of Jupiter and Sixtus and the others of the ten felt like champions as they headed away from the camp to the battle.

The crowd had started to form as they approached the wadi. The high sides of the horseshoe-shaped valley created a natural auditorium and to Sixtus it seemed all the city had amassed around its edge, vying for a view of the spectacle promised. Georgius' reputation had grown with each victory, and where once there were no spectators, now it seemed like a festival. As they marched along the dusty path, sweat running down his forehead and middle of his back, Sixtus saw families smiling, children playing; the best vantage points had been claimed by the nobles and stalls had been hastily erected by opportunist merchants, selling food and other goods. It was the atmosphere of the Colosseum, but thousands of miles away. He made a mental note to bring more soldiers for the next battle to control the crowd, but for now he needed to prepare his mettle.

The unit stopped where the valley narrowed around the wadi to form a pool. The sun was low and cast long shadows towards the mouth of the cave that faced them. Ahead of them was a natural arena, edged on one side by the wadi which fed the cool, clear pool in front of the cave. Trees and rich vegetation thinned as the hillside rose to the crest and crowds above. The space was tight, which would restrict the *draco*'s movement, and it would have to come out of the dark cave into the sun. Sixtus nodded to himself. Georgius had planned well.

Georgius rode to the centre of the clearing where a sacrificial post stood, dismounted and knelt. He was some distance from his unit, alone. He prayed, made the sign of the cross, and then, rising, took his bow and quiver from his horse. The crowd fell silent. One of the soldiers ran forward with a torch, planted it at Georgius' feet, and retreated. Georgius lit an arrow tip and launched it in a high arc into the centre of the cave mouth. It was quiet enough that the clatter of arrow against rock from within could be heard. Georgius drew back and let loose several more arrows. His horse nervously pulled at its tether and stamped its front legs. Then it came forth.

The *draco* slowly slunk from the darkness on its haunches and surveyed the gully and skyline. It let out a guttural growl that Sixtus felt to his stomach, and he thought he saw Georgius step back slightly and glance over his shoulder to Sixtus and the other men. It was a mighty beast, not yet fully out in plain sight. Sixtus judged it to be the largest they had encountered. He hands gripped his pilum. *[handwritten: javelin]*

Georgius swiftly mounted his horse and nocked an arrow. *[handwritten: ?]* Sixtus watched. The first objective would be to disable the wings, preventing, or at least limiting, flight. The first arrow bounced harmlessly off the *draco*'s body. It was a poor shot and missed the softest flesh around the shoulder that needed to be pierced to disable the wing. A second and third swiftly followed but failed to find their target. The *draco* was now fully exposed, a truly magnificent beast and it looked angry.

It rose on its hind legs, unfurling its wings and expanding its chest. Georgius recognised the motion and let loose an arrow, deliberately aiming lower down the beast's body in anticipation of the impending movement. Upon release he dug his heels into his horse's side and pulled hard left on the reins, just as the *draco* lunged down and exhaled flames of such heat that the ground where Georgius had stood upon exploded in a ball of blue fire. The *draco* beat its wings and forced itself up, preparing to fly. But the last arrow had hit its mark.

The *draco* came down and looked at its wing, surprised by the injury.

Georgius had not hesitated a second and was now galloping towards the *draco*'s side, tucked down with his lancea raised slightly so that its full weight was not yet braced. Sixtus watched anxiously as the *draco* refocused on its assailant bearing down on him, lancea now level ready to be driven deep. The *draco* swung its tail and twisted its body, its full weight catching horse and rider. Both cartwheeled through the air, the horse letting out a sound that he knew was death. It landed, lifeless in the pool, shattering the mirror-like water. Georgius crumpled into the ground, throwing a cloud of dust into the air. He lay motionless.

Sixtus shouted, 'We go, now!'

He ran forward shrieking loudly banging his pilum against his parma, making as much noise as he could. The *draco* turned towards him, cocking its head almost quizzically. At that moment several pilum past him overhead. The *draco* was around an actus away—out of effective range, but close enough to worry the beast which easily brushed the pilum aside in flight. Sixtus and his unit were now in its sight.

The *draco* tried flight again and roared as one wing would not open. Instead, it hunkered down and edged towards him. His unit had now formed an arc around the beast and those that had not yet released their pilum were primed. Sixtus was in front of the arc; he was low on his feet, his pilum held like a javelin, resting over his shoulder and shield, behind which he took as much cover as he could. The vulnerability of his position seemed obvious to both.

There was a pause as the opponents assessed each other.

'Be ready!' Sixtus shouted. He could see the beast's powerful hind leg muscles twitching. 'He is going to strike!'

At that moment, the *draco* breathed flame. The flame path was wider than the last, but with less intensity. Still, it found its mark and he could hear the screams of several men. He took the chance to roll in the opposite direction to the flame's path and retreat to take formation in the arc. Two of his unit had been caught in the flames and lay contorted and engulfed in orange flame, black smoke billowing up from the charred ground.

The unit was well drilled and upon Sixtus shouting 'SIX!' the remaining men started to rotate their arc, forcing the *draco* to move around and backward. This gave the unit an opportunity to reclaim pilum and get closer to the prone Georgius. Sixtus could sense the *draco* was deciding what to do, weighing them up. It was looking for weakness. It was hunting them.

Suddenly it launched, using its one good wing to propel itself forward. It landed and in one motion snapped its jaws around one man and caught another under one of its hindlegs. Nothing compared to the sounds and smells of battle: the crunch of bone, the slice or tear of tissue, the smell of excrement. Sixtus knew death would have been swift.

'THREE!' called Sixtus.

On his command, the remaining six men threw their pilus and retreated into a new formation. Several of the spears found their mark, burying deep into the *draco*'s flesh. It roared and sent out a wide arcing flame in the air above the soldiers.

'That's vexed him!' shouted one of the soldiers. The others cheered and bashed their gladii against their parmas.

'Focus!' called Sixtus. 'To Georgius.'

The men started to crab around as one in an attempt to move the *draco* back, but it seemed to sense their objective and stepped forward—into their planned path. It snorted, as if in contempt.

'TEN!' yelled Sixtus.

With no ranged weapons in hand, he knew the odds were now in the *draco*'s favour unless they could rush-attack and overwhelm it somehow. The command of ten had split the unit into two which would work to flank the target. The *draco* would need to commit to one defence and in that moment the other unit would attack. When this strategy was conceived, the unit was twenty strong, giving two units of ten. However, they hadn't used this strategy since they had been reduced to a ten strong squad. In this moment they were two units of three not ten. But it was all he had left.

As they moved around the *draco* moved backward, trying to keep both units in its sight. It worked back until it hind legs were in the water. Its tail tip was twitching like a cat studying its prey and readying to pounce. It had come to position over the prone body of Georgius, as if guarding a prize. Foaming drool was dripping on to his body. Sixtus could smell the foul aroma.

'WE ENGAGE TOGETHER! ON MY MARK!' he shouted.

The remaining men hit sword against shield in unison.

'CHARGE!' and Sixtus ran towards danger.

Time slows in battle. Georgius would say that you would see a hummingbird's wings beat if you could find one in the melee and noise of a battlefield. As he ran towards the *draco*, Sixtus could hear each man's breathing beside him. He could see the muscles contract in the *draco*'s neck as it turned towards him. He could see its black pupils constrict as it focused on him. He saw it begin to lunge towards him. He thought it looked amused.

***

He smelt new scents. He felt soft material against his skin. Then he felt the pain. He heard a distant voice saying, 'He stirs. Go, send news.' He fell back into sleep.

Sixtus opened his eyes and tried to move, but his ribs pained him sharply. The ceiling was highly decorated, and as he gained focus, he could see it was depicting a hunt of some kind. He fell asleep again.

'There are you, you old fool.' He opened his eyes to see Georgius was sitting on his bed. His jaw was purple, and one eye was blood-shot. "It seems God has not yet finished with us, dear friend. Come, let us help you sit. You will not manage it alone at present."

Two female servants gently helped to lift Sixtus up and back so that he was sitting almost upright. The pain from his ribs distorted his vision for a moment, but he had experienced worse and was still grappling with the idea that he was alive. Light muslin drapes were slowly dancing to the tune playing on the breeze that came through the grand balcony and the blue sky beyond.

'What happened?' he croaked. He went to rub his eyes, but only found his right eye with his right hand.

'First. You must know that your fighting days are done. There is not a way to tell you this gently, but your left arm has gone. Well, it was taken. Bitten off, actually. You have many broken bones, but you will walk, and your bones will heal. We are guests of Felix Marcellus, whose daughter we saved from sacrifice by defeating the *draco*. You are his guest until you are convalesced. I have arranged for your early discharge and free passage to anywhere in the Empire for you to settle and live out your days. With your endowment and your share of our endeavours, you will be able to enjoy a life of comfort. I owe you my life and I am in your debt.'

'I have no recollection of the end of the battle. What happened?' asked Sixtus. He looked to his left arm and saw a bandaged stump just below his shoulder. The bandage was clean and to his great relief there was no odour. He thought to himself that it was better to be mostly intact and alive than complete and dead.

'Once again, only you and I had the protection of our Lord and survived our greatest battle.' Georgius was now pacing the room, highly animated, as he told the tale, 'As you know, I was knocked senseless by the beast. When I came to, it was standing over me and I heard you call for Ten Formation. There was half a chance that the *draco* would have turned the other way and faced the other unit, but God guided him towards you. He caught the three from the other flank with his tail, just as he had unhorsed me. However, they took the full force of his mighty tail, and they were mortally wounded, chests caved in, arms and legs shattered.

'Now if you recall, I have been studying these beasts with great care and I had a theory that there was exposed soft tissue area just here.' Georgius pointed to his own sternum. 'We have never been in battle close enough to test until that time. When I looked up, I was directly underneath this area, as if God had willed it. Once I had gathered my senses and mustered my strength, I crouched and then thrust my gladius with all my might upward. The blade slid straight and true and I felt little resistance until, to my surprise, I was almost half an arm deep. There followed a push of pressure that forced my arm back and out and so much blood came forth I was coated before I had chance to roll free of the collapsing beast.

'Felix, who witnessed our battle from his vantage point at the crest of the hill, says that the *draco* then lunged forward towards you and your cohort. It had spat flames from its nostrils, creating two intense flares which caught both of the men either side of you. It was bearing down to engulf you, but as it bit, it gave a great spasm and collapsed. In that moment it clamped only your shield arm, taking it cleanly from your shoulder. That must have been as my blade found its mark. It is a miracle. God be blessed.'

Sixtus felt a phantom itch on his left arm and went to scratch it. 'I am pleased to be mostly alive,' he said. Georgius gave a great laugh and slapped Sixtus' leg, which hurt, greatly making him yelp and Georgius laugh even harder.

Their host was generous, and in the weeks that followed, Sixtus became quickly accustomed to the comfort and abundance that surrounded him. He enjoyed the attention that he attracted and there were many visitors to the villa seeking to meet him and Georgius. Gifts were offered and there was great interest from female nobles who were seemingly attracted by his physical appearance as well as his celebrity. Georgius had arranged for a craftsman to fashion an arm that was fitted with strapping around his chest. He had instructed the arm to be made from brass. It was highly polished and carried a carving of a *draco* breathing flame. It was the most beautiful thing Sixtus had ever seen, and he wore it with great pride.

***

The two rode out on a cool evening to the site of their battle. The peace of the location concealed the violence that had recently taken place. The sacrificial post had been removed. The cave had been cleared of discarded animal bone and the faeces collected. It turned out that *draco* faeces burned well and hot and were now fuelling fires across Cyrene for those with the coin to buy it. A share of this revenue was even given to Georgius, and he shared some with Sixtus.

NE
Libya

(Kyrene)

Sixtus walked to where the *draco* had fallen. The ground was stained dark, the earth turned to rock. He knelt, and as he had done at each victory previously, collected several rocks that lay, coated and sun-baked in the *draco*'s blood. The rocks had no value other than to him. For Sixtus they were a symbol that we all return to soil no matter how mighty. He also felt connected to each of the vanquished through these stones. He had gained respect for those mighty beasts. They were more than fire and fang.

He returned to his horse, mounted and rode to Georgius who had remained silent since their time by the wadi.

'The city is to build a great statue celebrating my victory. I shall be shown in dominance over the beast, spearing its chest from my mount. I think it will be magnificent!' Georgius was only half-talking to Sixtus. He regained his focus. 'You are recovered, and I sense your impatience to leave. Where will you go?' he asked.

'I think I shall return to Britannia. For all its cold and rain, the soil is rich, and it is a land of abundance. I have seen enough dust to satisfy the desire of any man. My coin will go far there. I am minded to build a fine villa, take many wives, and pass my time gambling, drinking and making a large family. What of you?'

Georgius smiled. 'We will head east, to Nicomedia. There, I will settle. I will learn more of my Lord's teachings and share what I have learned with others. *Dracones* are fewer now, and I am tired of the search. Like you, I yearn for the comforts we have recently enjoyed, and, unlike you, I wish to remain whole to enjoy them.' He tapped Sixtus's brass arm with his horsewhip and smiled. 'You will gain much attention with that adornment, and it may not always prove to be a blessing. So, go with God's peace and know that we will part as friends. If you find God within you and are baptised, we will meet again in Heaven where we can share stories of our adventures. I leave tomorrow with the centuria, who have grown fat and weak over the past while.'

Sixtus saluted. Georgius held out his hand and they clasped forearms for a moment. No more words were spoken as they parted company and rode away separately.

1993

He woke coughing, wearily sat up from the sofa and checked his watch. He tapped a key on the IBM ThinkPad that was open on the coffee table in front of him amongst the chaos of well-thumbed gossip magazines, soiled ashtrays, and a half-eaten takeaway. The laptop chimed to life, and he checked his email's sent folder to reassure himself that he had managed to file before the deadline. The dumb bitch's agent had heard that he was writing a story and had spent the night before, and a large amount of money, trying to convince Anker over dinner, drinks, and a gentlemen's club not to go to print.

She was a bright young thing, pretty, talented, who would go far, and she had just broken through. To ruin her promising career before it had started would be devastating, blah, blah, blah. Anker had heard it all before, no doubt would hear it again, but he was simply doing his journalistic duty. If she hadn't had shagged a married TV presenter on the night of the Brits and if he wasn't seen as wholesome family man, there wouldn't be a story to write. Besides, the 'family man' was a swordsman who would have a stab at anything he could. It was a well-known secret that needed to be unveiled, and the girl was just collateral damage. It might actually make her more bankable. If he remembered, he would call Andy who had started at a new lads' mag; they were always scouting for pretty, talented, bright young things for glossy shoots and it would be lucrative for her.

Anker showered, and after checking several shirts, found one that was clean enough. As he scooped his door keys from the bowl of loose change by the front door, he finished off the remains of a vodka and Coke that had been forgotten on the table and started off to Wapping. Fortunately, he didn't keep 'office-hours' as his journey from his one-bed flat in South London to his office meant using the Northern Line, which he thought smelt of sweat and cheap perfume during rush hours and alcohol and fast food at night. That was, of course, when it worked. He timed his commute so that he could guarantee himself a seat. It was ten stops before London Bridge and some days he would manage to squeeze in a powernap, but the noise in the tunnel and the shrill beeping of the door alarm at every station insistently reminded him of everything he had consumed the night before. Sleep stubbornly evaded him.

The half-hour walk from London Bridge along the riverside to Wapping refreshed Anker. He sat at his desk with his bacon roll and black coffee, reviewed his inbox and retrieved his voice messages. He had a voice message from Plod, a private investigator who had become a reliable and regular source of leads for him.

The message was curt as usual. 'Will, it's Colin, meet at me at five in the Chippy. I have something.'

Colin 'Plod' Brown had left the Metropolitan Police a few years earlier, having had a distinguished career in the CID and then taken advantage of early retirement. His wife, Carol, had become irritated by his increased presence at home, exasperating their already strained marriage, which he had resigned to accept would probably end once his children had finished university. He had a full pension but supporting his children through further education was a strain. Soon after retirement he grew bored of golf on weekdays and weekend pilgrimages to Brisbane Road and realised that there was demand for his specific set of skills, which would devalue if he left it too long. He was very good at networking and information gathering. He was particularly adept at phone hacking which was a skill he had learned towards the end of his police service. He could not believe what people would say freely over mobile phones and even allow to be recorded in a voice message.

In the Met, it was the general view that criminals were not very clever, which is why so many were caught. From the intel he effortlessly gathered from phone messages over the years, his belief in that statement was absolute. His conviction record during the last five years of his service was impressive. He had known at the time that he was just ahead of the curve. Now he could see that email was going to be a new source of golden information and was working hard on ways to gain the same access.

The Chippy was the local name for the Carpenter's Arms, which was on a lesser-walked side-road in Soho. It was a proper boozer. London had become overrun with anonymous chains, family friendly pubs and Irish themed bars. The Chippy looked like it had not seen a lick of paint or had its carpet cleaned since the 1970s. It had a dart board, billiard table and booths. It was dark and needed the wall-lighting constantly on to lift the gloom slightly during the day, and at night it felt moody and Victorian. It smelt of stale smoke and alcohol, and the shoppers and tourists that wandered that part of London would open the stained-glass doors, peer into the unwelcoming interior and decide to move on. As a result, it was a discreet place to meet, and it felt like home to Anker, who had been drinking there since his first boss had bought him in to meet another source some years before. It was where he had first met Plod.

The landlord suited his pub; he always wore an aged, whitish short-sleeve shirt and a clip-on black tie, the latter being a necessity from his bar-keeping days in Manchester, when he worked in some of the rougher neighbourhoods as an interim manager. He was probably in his sixties, but his thick neck and the way he carried himself showed that in his prime he was a man of some physicality. He wasn't unkempt, just a bit past his sell-by date.

He looked up as Anker walked in.

'Bishop's Finger is off, just changed the barrel on the Guinness.'

'Two of those then, Guv,' ordered Anker as he claimed the first booth he passed by, dropping his copy of the Evening Standard on the table. 'Meeting Plod for a catch up,' he said, picking up the drinks and returning to his table. 'I'll settle up when I leave.' Guv grunted and returned to reviewing the Racing Post.

Shortly after, Brown walked in, sat down and took a gulp from the pint of stout in front of him, before greeting him with 'Wanker.'

Anker rolled his eyes.

'Plod,' he replied in an unimpressed tone.

'It never gets old, Will. Your parents must either have been really stupid or had the nastiest sense of humour.' Brown picked up the newspaper and started thumbing through the pages. 'I get a rise out of you every time I say it! It's too good to let pass.'

typo

'But every time?' asked Anker.

'Go on, admit it gets under your skin. Okay, I'll stop. Maybe. Wanker.' Brown winked.

'How's Carol?' asked Anker with a slight cock to his head and a subtle smirk.

'Doing better than your victims from today. Nice work, that. No slimy rock left unturned. How does it feel to push out those stories when your mates from whatever-fucking-university you went to are reporting on ecological disasters off Shetland, the murder of that lad in Merseyside, and two IRA bombings in as many months? You're the pride of your trade, aren't you? Hovering around looking for shit, like flies around a horse's arse? How many relationships have you ruined, careers bought crashing down?' Brown, seeming pleased with himself, took a long drink as a reward.

'It's in the public interest. I expose the hypocrites, uncover things people want to keep hidden. I'm a part of democracy.' It was a well-rehearsed response. Most of the time Anker's main interest was to have enough source evidence for his paper to fend off any libel claim. He had cared a while ago, but, if he was being honest with himself, he was more interested in the career opportunities brewing with each story picked up by other papers—or, even better, in other countries. 'Enough poking each other with a stick—what've you got for me today?'

Brown folded the newspaper back on itself and in half, spun it around and pointed at a picture.

'It's him.'

He's Block

'That's Peter Blackwood, the new Home Secretary!' Anker smiled and leant forward. 'Tell me more.'

'Get another round in first,' said Brown, and he downed what remained of his first pint. 'When you get back you can listen to this.' Brown took out a small Dictaphone from his coat pocket and placed it ceremonially in the middle of the table as Anker stood up.

When Anker returned, Brown pressed the clunky play button on the Dictaphone.

'It's me... I don't know what do.' The girl's young voice *Jenny* was cracking as though she was crying. 'I haven't told Mum and Dad. I'm pregnant. I don't know what to do. Please call me.'

The call ended, and a beep announced the next one. 'I'm really scared. What will my mum think? I really need you. You said you would be there for me.'

Beep. 'Peter, I can't do this. I can't be a single mum. It'll kill my mum. I'm twenty-three, I want to live some. Please, please come.'

'Blackwood has infant twin boys, right? Where did you get this from?' Anker passed over the next pint and instinctively reached into his pocket for his notebook. 'Who is she?'

'That's from Blackwood's mobile. I have him down to three at the moment; his government phone, his general mobile that he's had for a few years, and this one, which he picked up about six months ago. It's such a cliché that I'm struggling to believe it. The girl is Jenny Foxton, LSE graduate—she did three months' internship in his office, and they've kept in touch. Good kid from what I can see; family in North London, parents are both teachers, active members of their local Catholic church, all paid up Party members. Very middle-class and unextraordinary, all in all.'

'What does she look like?' Anker was already picturing the front page.

'For fuck's sake, Anker, she's 23 years old. Here, judge for yourself.' He slid over a thin brown envelope.

Anker pulled out a slightly out of focus, black and white photograph that showed a young woman getting out of a small hatchback, dressed for the gym.

'Don't blame him. I would. What a dirty bastard. He gives it all the beans about being an upstanding family man, an example to the black community of what can be achieved, and there he is slamming his doe-eyed free labour.' He paused to drink and lit a cigarette. 'This is great work, Plod.'

'There's more. I should have access to her messages in the next day or so. I'll keep tabs on both and let you know what I find. In the envelope is her mobile number, home address, and address of the gym where she works out. Usual fees?'

'Sure—bonus if we get the front page with this one. I'll head over tomorrow and have a mooch around—are you free? Actually, the night's young and I'm meeting up with Andy. He's got dinner at The Ivy with some wannabe and their agent. He said to tag along; we'll probably end up in the Pussy Cat Club. His publisher has an account there these days.'

'I don't have your energy or appetite for the hard life these days, so I'll slip off home after this one. I'll book the day out to you tomorrow. The nearest tube is Cockfosters, so I'll pick you up from there around four. I'll show you the neighbourhood and we might catch her at the gym.'

'I should be up by then,' replied Anker as he winked. 'It's generally a late one with Andy.'

Wednesday

Traveling North on the Tube was slow. As the train made its way through London, Anker could see the pockets of society it passed through. Afro-Caribbeans, Asians, Eastern Europeans, Jewish; they all had their neighbourhoods. The central part of the journey was full of commuters, tourists, occasional foul-smelling down-and-outs sleeping in the corner of the carriage, and a few tradesmen hauling their tool bags back home after a long shift. The time of day changed the mood of the tube: commuting hours were angry and rammed (he tried to avoid those), late evening until the last tube was full of drunks and also rammed. He was generally still out then, but during the sweet spot from around 2 PM to 4 PM it was almost pleasant.

London was the mixing pot of the world and most of the time cultures rubbed against one another without friction, merging to create a vibrant and varied environment. His line of work had tainted his early naivety, and it wasn't hard to find the friction points and darker lives that existed beneath the obvious. His job was to look past the skin-deep. On the tube Anker could people-watch, making up life stories of those brief anonymous travel companies he was drawn to noticing. Once the tube was in the 'burbs, the atmosphere lifted, and when the train was above ground, London would betray its hidden plush greenness that few people had the time or interest to notice.

He was still recovering from all the champagne, brandy, and cocaine that had been lavished on him until the early hours of that morning under the shallow disguise of hospitality. His skin was slightly clammy, and because he was coming down, he was easily irritated.

He left the post-war architecture of Cockfosters tube station and headed into the middle-class suburb that felt airy and spacious compared to the less affluent area where he had been living for the past few years. The beep of Brown's car horn snapped his attention and he climbed into Brown's Ford Mondeo.

'Jesus, you stink of alcohol, Will. Wind down the window.' Brown started the engine and they set off through the leafy roads and rows of well-kept 1950s semi-detached houses.

Brown drove steadily and within the speed limit, annoying Anker.

'You drive like my fucking granddad. What time is our appointment?' Anker blew his nose. A small amount of blood coloured his tissue, his mucus membrane being damaged from snorting cocaine. He smiled as he remembered racking a line off a lap dancer's thigh in full view of the bouncers who apparently couldn't see past the VIP rope separating them from the riff-raff. He felt flushed and a little sick.

The gym they were going to was a large up-market chain that had tennis courts—and more importantly a bar, so Will could grab a livener when they got there. Brown had booked in a show-around with the club membership manager so that they could join if prolonged surveillance was necessary. These tours generally ended up in the restaurant/bar to show off the amenities; if Anker was lucky, they wouldn't have to pay.

'I've confirmed the appointment and we'll be there in around ten minutes. Jenny usually does an aerobics class, which she finishes around 6:30. By my reckoning, she'll be passing through the bar as we're wrapping up,' said Brown.

There was space in the car park when they arrived, the time being the customary change of shift between non-working parents and retirees and after-work-trainers. Anker could only see BMWs, Audis and Mercedes in the car park, making their dark blue Ford conspicuous in its mundaneness.

They were greeted by an overly enthusiastic, wholesome-looking 'Membership Executive' whose name badge said 'Holly', but Anker thought she was more a 'Chelsea' or 'Porsche' type. As they were taken around the building and its impressive facilities of racquet courts, gyms, saunas, hot tubs, and clean changing rooms that smelt of pine, her accent slipped occasionally from private school to North London, and he wondered how many B52s it would take for her carefully composed façade to slip. A few times he had to nudge Brown, who probably didn't get to see so many young athletic people in one place. As he had predicted they finished the tour in the bar and Holly didn't seem at all fazed when Brown asked for black coffee and Anker asked for a pint of Stella and a pint of water.

The clock over the bar showed the time as 6:30 PM, and neither of them were paying too much attention to Holly's sales pitch on the different rare metal levels of membership available. Brown kicked Anker, with slightly more purpose than intended.

'What the fuck?' said Anker before he realised. He followed Brown's eyeline and saw Jenny Foxton walking towards the exit, bag shouldered and apparently on her own. 'Excuse me Holly, Colin was reminding me I have a call to make.' He downed the last of his Stella, ignoring the water. As he was leaving, he said, 'It looks great. I'll leave Colin to discuss the details around corporate membership and we'll speak soon.'

As he walked with speed to catch up with Jenny, he was running through the approach he might take. He knew he was acting hastily; they would usually have more information before approaching a target, but this felt like too good a story for him. He could use 'accidental acquaintance'—finding an opportunity to befriend the target. It was effective in helping gain trust and uncovering the facts, but it took time. If she was carrying a senior cabinet member's illegitimate child, he didn't have the luxury of time. He thought perhaps he might follow her and see where she went, but by the time Brown caught up, she'd be long gone. He looked around for something that may distract her and slow her exit. The anxiety side effects of cocaine were affecting his judgement and he felt himself become angry with the possibility that Jenny was going to slip by and be picked up by another journalist.

'Miss Foxton!' he called, just as she walked through the exit. She turned. Anker was struck by how naturally attractive she was in person and there was a sadness in her eyes he recognised from others. 'Can I have a word, please? My name is William Anker. I'm a journalist. I was hoping I could buy you a coffee before you leave.' He passed her a business card.

Jenny looked at the card and up to Anker. 'What possible interest can you have in me?' She stepped back and folded her arms.

'I would like to talk to you about your relationship with Peter Blackwood. You know him well, I understand? Intimately, you could say?' Anker immediately regretted his impetuous move, and it was clear that the girl was very scared. 'Listen, it's not that bad! I mean, why do you look so worried?' He tried to calm his tone, but he knew he was cocking things up. For a moment, he thought of snatching back his business card and walking away. He pushed that craziness out of his mind.

'What do you mean? What do you want?' Jenny was stepping back, glancing back to the gym doors and the safety of the reception area. 'Leave me alone!'

'For fuck's sake, I know you're pregnant and I know who the father is!' *In for a penny*, he thought.

'No, no, no!' Jenny's face crumpled into tears, and she turned, running away across the car park. Anker was about give chase. This was not good. Just then there was a tug on his shoulder, and he turned, expecting to be struck by some beefed-up gym monkey. He was relieved to see the disapproving face of Plod.

'We need to leave. What did you say to her? I came out the door and she was screaming at you!' said Brown.

Jenny Foxton's Peugeot 205 drove past them at speed, pulled out on the road, and sped away. The silence that followed felt like it lasted a year to Anker.

'Shit!' said Anker. 'Not my best first move. She'll be contacting him, so hopefully that'll give us what we need. You wanna leave the car here and we can head to the Chippy, unless you have plans?'

Tomen y Mur

The angry song of the winter's storm wailed as the heavy velvet drapes heaved in the draft, the final defence against the remanence of wind and rain that beat relentlessly outside. The two friends sat in front of the great crackling fire, which sent light dancing across the vast mosaiced floor, glinting against polished gold candle stands, sword hilts, and chainmail.

The older man leaned forward and continued to speak as a servant closed the doors to the main hall behind him, leaving the men alone once more.

'There remains only one in our realm. He is magnificent and powerful, but his enemies are many and against such odds, he is weak. He must be protected, and I am no longer able to do so on my own.' His gown hung off his shoulders, covering a slight frame. It was tied simply at the waist, bare arms showing the swirling markings of his sect. Around his neck hung many intricately carved symbols of bone and stone. 'You are the King of Men, and the King of Beasts now calls you.'

'The evening has been long, and I tire of talking. What would you have me do, Myrddin?' Uther was irritated. 'Speak your truth simply and with haste before this night freezes my balls. My warm bed beckons—you are a great friend, but on my oath, its appeal is far greater than yours.'

'We must give him sanctuary. I have created a haven 'neath a lake not far from here. It is work of which I am proud, and you shall see it soon, my lord. He will be safe for as long as he needs, but it will need keeping. My magic cannot provide husbandry of livestock, and the entrance needs to be guarded, keeping the dragon in and those that would harm him out. I know he has great sadness and fears for his future. With your patronage, his safety will be assured.' Myrddin sat back.

King Uther eyed him, pondering the request. Myrddin had always acted to show his allegiance, but Uther saw him as a cunning cat, at his side by his choice, not through devotion. It was an uneasy trust. He could no more see the limits of the man sat before him than he could predict the next storm. He had initially brought Myrddin into his council out of curiosity and suspicion with the view of keeping him close, but over time that had changed, and Uther had developed an unlikely friendship with the sorcerer, soothsayer, poet, or lunatic. What exactly Myrddin was, Uther was still unclear about.

'You know much of its thoughts; is this more of your magic?'

'I hold a *Hudcloch*.' Myrddin held out his hand. In his palm was a polished, dark stone. 'These were given to our ancestors by a great warrior with arms of gold who came to our kingdom seeking out the dragon. He gave us understanding that grew our knowledge and power. The bearer of a *Hudcloch* can approach the dragon without fear as though they are one of his kind. I have sat with him for many years, from when I was an apprentice, and we have shared our lives. We speak, but not in words. There is no conversing, but thoughts, intentions and emotions are understood. Left alone, he would give us no more consideration than we give a deer or bear. He has no interest in us. We are a nuisance to him, as a mouse is to us. Yet we have found sport in hunting dragons. The distrust has grown over years and now they strike first because they know we mean them harm. He is the source of great natural power, and he is not our enemy.'

Uther rose and stood in front of the fire warming his hands, with his back to Myrddin. 'You are as deep as the cold sea and just as full of mysteries, my friend. If it cares not for a king, why should a king care for it? It hides from sight, in fear of man, yet you say it fears not man.'

'Know this: he is a talisman, and your paths are intertwined like two great beech trees grown together. I have seen it in the sky.' Myrddin stood next to the king and placed the stone into his hand, pressing it into his fist. 'Close your eyes and open your thoughts. Feel its heartbeat. Feel how slow and mighty it beats. Feel its power in your chest. Breathe.'

Uther felt his chest pulse deeply, as though a booming drum had been struck in his very core. He saw flashes of memories. Soaring high above the earth. Flying. Looking down over mountains and lakes. Striking with claw. Columns of fire. The rush of hunting. Swimming.

He was outside of his body. Elevated. Weightless. He felt the beat of mighty wings. Air rushed through his nostrils. He could smell the scent of animals, man, trees, sea, jasmine, soil. He felt anger, fear, loneliness, joy. His senses were overloaded as wave after wave of sensory tsunamis flooded through him simultaneously.

Myrddin relaxed his grip, and at that moment Uther's knees gave slightly and he reached for the mantel to steady himself. He had broken into a sweat and his vision had tunnelled as though he was about to lose consciousness. Confused, he struck out, his subconscious prompting a warrior reaction. Myrddin had already stepped backward out of arm's reach, not through mystical perception but experience. It was not the first time he had affected the king, and he had a bent nose from a time when he was not so light of foot. Now he stepped forward, propping the king up as he came to his senses. He helped Uther to his seat, his feet still unsteady, his mind finding its orientation.

Breathing heavily, Uther looked to Myrddin.

'I should take that poker from the fire and shove it with all my might up your...' Uther's anger dissipated, and his breath returned. 'I have warned you before against such action without notice. What sorcery was that?'

'You said to speak my case with haste,' replied Myrddin flatly, trying to mask his amusement, poorly.

'Any other man...' growled Uther.

'Yes,' agreed Myrddin, cutting off the inevitable threat that would have followed and knowing he had once again tried the patience of the king, which was as dangerous as it was entertaining. 'It was better that you understood from experience. Coupling your thoughts will become easier with practice. You now see what I have known for many years: that you are brothers. If you give a king's oath to protect him as if he were your blood and keep his place and power privy to the fewest possible, he will follow you and lend you his strength. It is more than a union between kings. It is a union of realms. You will understand over time that what you do today will harness a greatness that few others can grasp.'

'Why now, Myrddin? You have held this secret close for so long—what brings you to confide in me on this night?'

'I do not withhold such things from you, my king. The future is a confusion, and it is only a short time ahead that direction becomes clear. I saw a shooting star of such brilliance; it showed me the path ahead and that it was time for your allegiance. You will be the Chief of Dragons. You have a great battle ahead, one that will need all the strength you can muster and with the dragon and Myrddin–' Myrddin made a flamboyant flourishing bow, '–you will be formidable. The dragon will not fight—he is too precious a thing to be risked—but I will teach you how you use his strength.'

'I shall give this thought tonight and tomorrow you will take me to him. Let me meet this other king and then I shall decide.'

'As you wish, my king. I shall take my leave and we shall leave when it pleases you on the morrow.' Myrddin left Uther standing in front of the fire and headed to his chambers.

Two Kings

The storm had bought fresh, crisp air to the early morning that formed vapour clouds on exhale. The now vivid green land was saturated, and vast puddles lay either side of the straight, ancient stone road they had been travelling on. It was peaceful and the only sounds were the two travellers on their horses. Uther was watching his companion ride next to him with amusement. Of all the things that Myrddin was, a horseman was certainly not one of them. To add some sport to the journey, Uther had had the stable prepare a smaller, stocky horse, usually assigned to pulling a cart, and he was enjoying the spectacle. Myrddin's tall, thin frame sat high, and his feet seemed perilously close to the ground. Uther could hear Myrddin's frustrated muttering and occasional yelp as he caught testicle between thigh and horse.

'By your God, I am grateful that our journey approaches its end. We shall head to that valley,' said Myrddin, pointing to a rocky outcrop at the foot of a steep hill that led up to the mountains above. 'We will travel on foot for the last of the journey, which will be of much relief.'

'Then there is no time to lose!' Uther slapped the rear of Myrddin's horse, kicked his heels into his and set off at speed towards their destination, glancing back to see Myrddin flailing wildly, trying to remain on his horse as it followed at pace. They dismounted and tethered their horses at the foot of the hill. Myrddin adjusted his dress, having already concluded that the last few hours were a gentle repayment for Uther's experience the night before.

'Before we advance, you must wear a *Hudcloch*.' Myrddin took off one of his necklaces of simple leather, from which hung a misshapen dark stone, and he placed this over Uther's head and around his neck. 'Be sure to keep this safe. Now we go.'

With the crude pendant around his neck, Uther could see an opening in the hillside ahead that he had not noticed before. It then occurred to him that this was Myrddin's sorcery. He followed

Myrddin through the gap, needing to enter side on to fit through the narrow entrance. Once inside, Myrddin snapped his fingers and a bright flame burned above his fist as though he was carrying a torch. The passage was wide enough for several men to stand abreast, and it spiralled down in a wide arc, at a steep incline. When the passage levelled off, light sliced through the darkness where another narrow entrance beckoned. This entrance was lower, requiring Uther to hunch down and through, and when he looked up, he was amazed.

In front of him was a vast, endlessly rolling plain. Looking up he gazed into a dark void, yet there was light all around. He stood on grass; Uther knelt and ran his hands through the moist blades and smelt the familiar aroma. Trees and vegetation were in abundance. It was as if he was above ground. He could see to either side of the great expanse where meadow met the rock that climbed up towards the infinite darkness above. They were near the edge of a great lake. Fish broke the water's skin, momentary ripples dissipating outwards, betraying their brush with the atmosphere. It was otherworldly and beautiful.

'My life's best work. So far. It took a few attempts, some tuning here and there. You will have time to explore, my king, but what say you?' Myrddin looked to Uther for approval.

Uther nodded his approval as he was lost for words.

'Here is space for him to fly, roam and hunt. He knows this place confines him, but he also understands it is for his safety. He has access to our world through the lake, and at night, when it is safe, he can soar above us as his predecessors have done for many millennia. He is an accepting prisoner of mankind—well, presently.' Myrddin took hold of a *Hudcloch* which hung from his neck and closed his eyes. 'He comes.'

An arc of fierce flame shot across the darkness above them, making Uther step back and touch the hilt of his sword. Down flew the dragon with the speed of a hawk diving towards its prey, the sound of rushing wind accompanying the spectacle until it unfurled its wings, pulling the great beast vertical and proud. It softly landed, a great gust of wind from its last wingbeat blowing against Uther and Myrddin.

'He makes a show for you.' Myrddin approached the great beast, which lowered its head towards him and tilted like a dog seeking affection. Myrddin obliged and scratched under its massive jaw. 'He has been well and is curious of your presence. He will approach you and take in your scent. Do not fear an attack, for he feels the *Hudcloch* and sees no danger.'

Uther was gauging the dragon's size. Its body was twice that of his largest horse and with tail, neck, and formidable head, he guessed the dragon's size to be at some thirty-five feet. It was magnificent and he had no fear. He could sense that the dragon had no ill intent. He too held out his hand. The dragon came forward and its great nostrils flared as it sampled the air around Uther.

'Magnificent,' Uther said absentmindedly.

'Ah, the King speaks!' Myrddin stood next to Uther. 'Before you place a hand on his flesh, you need to prepare to experience the coupling, as you did yester eve. These majestic animals carry great power for those that can receive it, and it takes time to adapt, but adapt you will.'

Enthralled, Uther walked forward and placed his hand gently on the dragon's body. Warmth surged up his limb and throughout his body. Around his hand and across the dragon's chest, its scales turned a shade of red. Myrddin watched as the two stood calmly together, each powerful, together formidable. Now it would just take time.

It was late afternoon by the time they returned to their mounts. Myrddin took a roll of fabric from his horse's pouch.

'This day has seen the bonding of two great beings, and you will carry and build upon the strength gained today. Your paths are bound.' He turned to face Uther as the material unfurled in his hands to show a Standard made of fine material, emblazoned with a rampant red dragon on a white background. 'This is yours, Uther, King of Dragons—Uther Pendragon. Let this be seen by all as a symbol of greatness and acknowledgement of the enduring bond made here on this day.'

'Uther Pendragon,' repeated the king. He considered his new moniker and nodded his approval.

Homecoming

It had been a long final term and it felt like an age since Amy had seen her parents. She arrived at Euston Station with time to grab some food and drink for the journey and she milled around WH Smith's for a book, settling on *The Secret History* by Donna Tartt. She was the last of her friends to read the bloody thing and couldn't put it off any longer—it was that or some trash written by a shamed MP. It was a five-hour journey to Bangor, so she had plenty of time to kill and wasn't sure how much charge was left in the batteries to her Walkman. The book would keep her entertained. The last time she had visited, her dad had given her a MiniDisc because he said 'the future is digital' but she hadn't got around to re-recording her mix tapes, so it was still in its box, in a drawer, in her desk, in her shared house, in Wimbledon. Remembering this, she hoped that he wouldn't notice.

The train journey through the monochrome city soon gave way to the vivid greens, blues, and yellows of England's summer countryside, which in turn yielded to the silvers and bronze of North Wales that would sing bright on the days that the sun reigned, which were few. Today was no exception.

She was a Londoner, would always be a Londoner, but as hard as she tried to deny it, she felt more settled the further away she was from metropolitan living. She was only twenty-two and planned to prove Samuel Johnson wrong before she considered giving up a London postcode.

Her parents had moved to Wales after her grandfather had died, taking residence in the family home they inherited, a farm in the outskirts of a small village in Snowdonia National Park. Her parents were definitely not farmers, and the livestock was looked after by the farm manager, whose family had also worked and lived on the farm for many generations. It was a real family affair and Amy dreaded the idea that she was going to end up inheriting the land and living out her days in chunky knit jumpers and wellies, driving a battered green Land Rover.

Her dad was waiting for her when she left Bangor Station. He greeted her with an affectionate enveloping hug and threw her rucksack into the back of the Land Rover. Conversation was easy and they talked as if they had only parted company a day ago, not the months it actually had been. Amy wasn't the most reliable of correspondents so there was plenty to catch up on—boyfriends ditched, books read, places explored, restaurants visited, and city breaks in the planning.

She felt weary from her day travelling and the Land Rover's suspension reminded Amy of just how rural the farm's location was. It was some relief when they pulled off the road and drove up the even less cared-for driveway, coming to a gravelly stop in front of the main farmhouse. In the time that had passed since her parents had moved, they had brought new life into the ancient farm buildings. The main house was a large cottage, with thick silvered stone walls, small windows and a high sloping slate roof. The front door was low, built for the days when people were shorter. However, inside it was thoroughly modern and had been sympathetically renovated, boasting under-floor heating and triple-glazing, and was furnished and decorated in 'Home Counties Chic'. There were several barns in varying degrees of renovation, from the completed workshop where her dad spent much of his time to the stooped old man of a barn at the foot of the hills at furthest end of their farm.

The car's headlights spotlighted her mum as she flung open the front door.

'Darling!' she exclaimed with arms open wide. 'Give me a *cwtsh* and come inside. I've stocked the wine cellar with Sancerre, the bathroom cupboard with Alka-Seltzer, and the fridge with meats guaranteed to give you a coronary for the morning. Now, stop your jawing, let's get to it.' Before Amy could speak, she found herself being swept straight through the stone floored hallway into the kitchen, sat in a chair and handed a long-stemmed, large crystal wine glass, generously filled with chilled wine. 'Your dad's a wimp these days, so I've been saving up my liver points to splash out tonight. No-one goes to bed and remembers it, deal? Tell me everything. If I asked your dad to update me on the gossip from the car, he'd just say, "she's tidy" and bugger off to his workshop.' Her dad looked at Amy and nodded in agreement.

***

The evening unfolded as her mum had predicted and it was late the next morning when Amy padded her way gingerly downstairs and glanced into the living room, which was evidence of the robust entertainment the night before—the floor strewn with CDs, their empty cases, and scattered Jenga blocks. The smell and sounds of sausages and bacon cooking had woken her up and she really wanted a cup of sweet tea to rid her of the taste of rancid aluminium from the many vodka shots they had ended up drinking.

Both her parents were up, dressed, and busy preparing brunch. She had no idea how both could match anyone drink for drink, be the last ones to bed and the first ones up, and never show any signs of their excesses.

'You look hanging, beautiful,' remarked her dad as he walked past, pecking Amy on the forehead and sitting down to eat. 'How are you feeling?'

'Hanging,' Amy agreed. "What's the plan for today?'

'Once you're fed and showered, we'll go out for a couple of hours—blow the city out of your lungs and the booze out of your blood.'

The path at the back of their farm led to the foothills and quickly ascended so that they were soon walking on the loose slate of the mountainside up a steep incline. The air was fresh and the pace brisk, and quite soon Amy was recovering from the excesses of the night before. Her dad was ahead, striding forward. She thought she could hear him singing. Most of the visiting outdoorsy set kept to the well-established footpaths that spidered across the countryside. However, Amy and her dad knew the mountains well and were able, aside from the very peak of the season, to avoid most of the wax jackets and ramblers. Amy smiled to herself. When she was here she felt like a local and looked on tourists as city types and intruders.

The going was challenging, made more so because of the pace set by her dad, who she had decided was part mountain goat. After a long few hours, they stopped as they had reached a peak. It was one of her favourite places. The cloud was high and thin and on days like this; Amy could see the mountains range for miles. Below them was a sapphire lake, still and calm. The silence was unlike anywhere else she had been. The wind blew on her face. She closed her eyes and took a long, slow breath.

She opened her eyes as the sound of slipping slate betrayed her dad's movement as he sat next to her.

'I wasn't sure that the move up here would be a good decision for me and your mum, but it's worked out well for us. I don't miss the city, and I think we've been at it long enough to prove the guys wrong in the office who thought we wouldn't last a month living the "good life". I still have the card they gave us, addressed to Tom and Barbara.' He picked up a small stone, absentmindedly tossed it in the palm of his hand, and then threw it down the hillside. It clattered into the distance. 'It's probably time that we gave you more of an insight into what we do up here.'

'Dad, it's hardly complicated. The Merlinis farm their sheep and pay you for the privilege. You spend your time tinkering in your workshop. Mum feeds you and knocks out paintings that tourists pay over the odds for in the village. Oh, and you mostly lose at backgammon.'

'It would be a lie to deny most of that.' Her dad was looking out, seeming distant. 'But also, this land came with responsibilities which I hadn't prepared for. It looks like we're very settled and have become used to the expectations on us and, in fact, I think we both have found our place. Our "Dunromin". We've been speaking, your mum and I, and now that you've finished your course and will be starting the next chapter of your life, we should explain our life to you fully. It's all been agreed.'

'Ooh. That sounds mysterious. Let me guess, you're under deep cover as an approaching-middle-aged couple living in the arse-end of nowhere, but in fact, you and Mum are international spies, 008 and 9? My name is Davies, Tom Davies... and this is my wife Claire... Mum says "alright or wha?"'

'Close again, but no cigar. Rain is coming, so we should get back before we get soaked.' He patted Amy's knee and stood up. 'The Merlinis are coming over for dinner and it's my turn to cook. I would say race you back, but you city types are falling off these mountains all the bloody time.' He held his hand out, offering to help Amy up.

Amy looked up at the sky, unable to see the remotest sign of rain clouds. She took her father's hand and gave him a huge shove into the mountain, and she set off, trying to make the most of the lead she had gained.

As she approached the rear of the barn, rain drops started to fall.

Sunday Dinner

The gravel drive announced the arrival of the Merlinis. Amy had grown fond of Dafydd and Kath Merlini over the years. They had been welcoming and supportive when the family moved up from London and helped her mum and dad find their feet. Nothing had been too much trouble and often Dafydd or Kath would ferry Amy to and from the station, or, when she was younger, they would look after her if her parents were out or busy. Their son, Marcus had less of her affection. He irritated her. He was a pseudo-psychic type. Though they were similar in age, they were poles apart. He had Celtic tattoos down both arms and presumably over his wiry body. He didn't work, just listened to heavy rock, occasionally helped his dad out, always dressed in black and was a follower of counterculture, just to be different. He had never been unkind to Amy—they had never argued—he was just disconnected and uninterested. And annoying.

An evening with Merlinis would follow the same format: a few quick short drinks to loosen everyone up, an enjoyable dinner with much storytelling and laughing, her dad and Dafydd would disappear when the time came to clear up, and Marcus would generally sculk around in the background, being annoying. Singing and drinking would go on until the early hours and then they would leave, driving home, over the limit, in their battered double cab defender, which probably explained the condition of the bodywork.

Tonight, another dark coloured saloon car followed on to the drive. The driver walked to the rear of the car, donned a wax-jacket over his formal suit, and retrieved a briefcase. Amy took a guess that he was a Londoner with expensive shoes; he looked awkward in his surroundings and appeared to be picking a route to the door that avoided puddles.

In the hallway, the usual melee of greeting hugs between old friends ensued. The space was further restricted by the Merlinis' two Rhodesian Ridgebacks, Zeus and Apollo, that followed Marcus everywhere. The stranger stood in the doorway, looking singularly uncomfortable.

He held out his hand. 'Mr Heaney, of Stowe and Arc Solicitors.'

'Mr Heaney, pleased to meet you. Tom Davies.' Amy's father shook Mr Heaney's hand. 'We were expecting Mr Stowe?'

'He sends his apologies. He has been called to another meeting early tomorrow and asked that I attended. It's quite a drive from London, isn't it?' Amy stifled a smirk. Londoners stood out a mile.

'We have a room set up for Mr Stowe. You're welcome to stay,' said Claire, shaking his hand and gesturing for his coat.

'Thank you, but that's not necessary. I must be back in the office tomorrow morning, so, if it's OK, we will deal with matters and then I will leave you in peace.'

The seven of them sat around the dining table. Zeus and Apollo followed Mr Heaney, sitting themselves on the floor next to him, staring at him, panting. Mr Heaney shifted uncomfortably in his seat.

'Nice dogs,' he said to them and then looked to the others. 'Are they safe for me to pet?'

'You've been around dogs then? It's always good to ask before stroking a dog. Lefty Louis didn't ask, and before that he was just plain Louis,' said Dafydd Merlini, as he held up his right arm with his sleeve pulled down to cover his hand.

Kath poked her husband. 'Ignore him, Mr Heaney, he's not funny. They're good as gold. We adopted them from a London family who couldn't look after them. See, these dogs need lots of exercise, they were bred in Africa as working dogs to run alongside the farmers as they covered their huge farms out there on horseback. They can get bored and start misbehaving if they're not out and about. So they're well suited for our lifestyle. That said, the one on the left, Zeus, can be a bit chewy.'

At that, Marcus called the dogs and they moved to him, walking around in a tight circle before laying down with an apparent disgruntled sigh.

Mr Heaney made a dry cough and adjusted in his chair once more, took an envelope from his briefcase, and set it down in front of him. He looked towards Amy.

'Miss Amy Davies?' Amy felt suddenly uncomfortable and glanced at her parents for support. 'I am here representing Her Majesty's Government. Here is a copy of my business card.' He slid a card across the round table towards her. 'I have with me an Official Secrets Act Declaration which I request that you sign. Of course, members of the public that are bound by the Official Secrets Act are not required to sign the document. Official notification is sufficient, which I am now giving you. However, protocol requires me to request that you do, indeed, sign. Under Section Five of the Official Secrets Act 1989—"if a member of the public (or any person who is not a Crown Servant or government contractor)"— that would be you, Miss Davies—"has in their possession official information in any of the six categories under the Act, being security and intelligence, defence, international relations, information which might lead to the commission of crime, foreign confidences, or the special investigation powers under the Interception of Communications Act 1985 and the Security Services Act 1989, and this information has, been disclosed to them by a Crown Servant without lawful authority; or was entrusted to them by a Crown Servant in confidence"—which will be the case after you have signed—"then it is an offence to disclose this information without lawful authority. The maximum penalty for an unauthorised disclosure under the Act is two years' imprisonment or an unlimited fine, or both."'

'Fuck off,' Amy said in bemusement. 'I'm not fourteen. This is lame. Dad, you can do better than this. God, I hope he isn't a kissogram...' She looked to her parents; her mum simply gave a shallow of a nod in approval.

'Um.' Mr Heaney fidgeted in his chair once more and removed some paperwork from the envelope. He passed Amy one copy, offered one to her parents, and retained the last.

'Fuck off,' she said incredulously as she looked down at the document that showed the Royal Coat of Arms and was headed 'OFFICIAL SECRETS ACT 1989'. 'What's the craic?'

'This is not a wind up, my love,' said her dad. 'We can explain everything once you've signed. It's OK. We've all signed it—well, I don't know about Mr Heaney, not met him before today. I'm sure he is a lovely fella, just saying, I don't know him...' He stopped as he noticed Claire's stare.

Mr Heaney now passed over a pen. 'If you would like, I can talk you through the document before you sign it.'

'God, no!'

'Please, no!'

'That won't be necessary, I'm sure,' came back responses from several of the attendees.

'Amy?' said her dad.

'What's it all about?' she asked.

repeats   'Once you've signed, we'll explain,' he said, gesturing for her to sign.

Amy took the pen, signed, and slid the document back. 'If I may have my business card back, please,' asked Mr Heaney. It seemed an odd request. Amy glanced at the card once more then acquiesced. 'Thank you. If I may have a glass of water before I go, and then I will be on my way.'

'Was that it? Can someone please explain?' Amy was confused and increasingly angry.

welsh   'Of course,' Dafydd Merlini spoke. 'Once the suit from London has left. It's a good time to get a get a drink in—we've been here twenty minutes, and I don't have a glass in hand. That's shabby hosting!'

Mr Heaney's car headlights shone through the window as he reversed and left for his drive back to London. 'I don't envy that drive back. Mind you, glad he didn't hang around. He was stiffer than a boy who's found his dad's porn stash,' commented Tom as he came in with drinks, to be hit on the arm by Claire in disapproval. 'Where to start...'

'How about the part when a solicitor, or whatever, comes in for Sunday dinner and then lays the Official Secrets Act on me. Shit. Are you really spies?' asked Amy.

Five of them were now sitting around the dining table. Marcus was sitting in the occasional chair by the fireplace.

'I'll start,' offered her mum. 'This farm has been in the family for generations. I have traced our family's ownership back around three hundred years, but before that, records are unreliable. Anyway, with the land comes additional responsibilities that aren't hereditary. Well, they come with the land, not our bloodline. Your grandparents had known that this was going to be a problem as I am an only child and the situation had been explained to me when I was younger than you are now. When I met your dad and it became clear he was "the one", he had to understand what he was signing up for. When your dad asked for his blessing to marry me, your granddad had to talk to him as we are with you today.'

'Frankly, I thought he was insane,' added Tom.

'Go on,' Amy said to her mum.

Claire continued, 'Well, when your grandfather died, and the time came, we had a stark choice: make the move here and take those responsibilities or lose the land to someone else willing to take them on. We decided that we had an obligation to carry on, like my family had done for so long before me. We weren't really sure how it would work out with your father being a city boy. So that's why we sent you to boarding school. Partly so that you could carry on with your life that you understood, with your friends and where you were settled, but also so that we could keep you isolated from this, just in case. But that all worked out, didn't it?'

Her dad carried on, 'You've finished further education, and we want you to do whatever makes you happy, but as our only child we need to explain why we are here and one path that is open to you.

Of course, it's your choice, but it's quite a leap in so many ways that you'll need time to digest it. Ok?'

'For fuck's sake, what is going on?' Amy hated not feeling involved. Her parents had always been open and honest. They were friends, not the stuffy, distant parents that many of her friends had, and she felt a little betrayed.

'The sheep. Let's start there,' decided Tom. 'The family business is sheep farming, but we don't actually sell many of the sheep. Enough so that we are seen as sheep farmers, but the rest are, well, used here, on our land.'

Claire had had enough, she could see that Amy was confused and uncertain, 'The sheep are bred to feed a dragon. We look after a dragon. There, said it.' She took a huge glug of her Sancerre. 'Wow, that feels better. Really.' She looked at Tom and the Merlinis who were quietly observing. 'I mean, really, wow. It's like a huge relief. I must have been really worried about this for years…'

'MUM!' Amy slapped the table. 'Hellooooo. I don't think this is about you, is it?'

'True enough, cariad. Sorry,' she replied.

'Just fuck right off with this dragon nonsense'.

'You say "fuck" far too often,' said Tom. 'Swearing is a sign of limited education, you know.'

'Alexander Pope said "to err is human, to curse divine,"' interrupted Kath, 'or something like that. Or maybe it was Shakespeare? I'm not helping, am I?'

Only Claire held Amy's look. Everyone else was looking down at their drinks uncomfortably. Marcus was watching with interest and raised his glass, expressionless when Amy glanced over.

'So, this invisible dragon, let's call him Elliott, lives under the bed in one of the spare rooms?'

'He's under the lake, actually,' replied Tom. 'It's a lot to take in, true enough. But this is real. Wait until we tell you about the Merlinis, that'll send you in to orbit.' Dafydd and Kath gave a little wave. 'I'll show you his home before we have dinner. It's only a short walk to the entrance and then we can talk some more after you've had a chance to take this all in.'

Amy was still certain this was all an elaborate prank, not accepting that there was any truth in the madness she had just been told. She would go along with it for now and then, at the 'ta-da' moment, feign surprise and praise everyone at their ingenuity. 'Come on then, let's go.'

Tom, Amy, and Dafydd left the house and walked in silence towards the rear of property. When they arrived at the last barn, Tom turned to his daughter and took a necklace out of his pocket. Placing it around her neck, he said, 'It's not the prettiest jewellery you'll wear, but be assured, it is the most valuable.' Amy looked down at the small dark stone that had been polished and placed in a simple silver setting and chain. It was quite unremarkable.

Welsh 'It is a *Hudcloch*,' said Dafydd. 'Today, this will protect you. Over time, it will be access to wonders that you cannot yet comprehend. As your father says, this small, grey stone is truly priceless. We hold a number of these, but we do not know if any others exist. We have some idea that there may be some in China and perhaps the Middle East, but it is only anecdotal. *Hudcloch*, loosely translated, means "magic stone" and these small pebbles are more than a millennium old. I will tell you their origin another day, when you have had a chance to take all this in. For now, wear this and keep it safe. You may find your senses become keener and you may start to feel energised. These are all part of the "coupling" which, again, we will teach you about. We are about to enter the dragon's land. He knows we are coming as sure as I know he is expecting us, because we are connected.'

Amy saw Dafydd Merlini in a different light. He seemed to be taller, more confident, authoritative. Dafydd looked to Tom. 'Shall we?'

Tom pushed the heavy doors to the decrepit barn which gave a reluctant groan as they opened. At the back of the barn, beyond the old timber and dusty, broken farming tools, was another set of doors that Amy had assumed just led outside. These were opened to reveal a large boulder formation that was as tall as the barn and appeared to have a narrow entrance visible. Dafydd walked up, turned side-on and, after glancing back to Amy and Tom, crabbed through the tight entrance. A light now shone through, inviting them to follow. It dawned on Amy that this was not prank.

They corkscrewed down the tunnel, following Dafydd who led the way with what Amy assumed to be torchlight. No-one was speaking and Amy's heart was beating faster. She was not sure if she was nervous or excited. She saw another entrance and followed her dad and Dafydd through and into the world of the dragon.

Jenny

The only sound was the car engine plinking as it cooled. She sat staring through the hedges and trees to the open space beyond. Her vision was blurred through tears and her cheeks were wet. She was too scared to go home, too ashamed to go to a friend's house, and her one safe place that stopped her thinking, the gym, had been taken from her. She had nowhere left to hide. She had driven around aimlessly, trying to think what to do, where to go, how to get out of the mess she was in, and she found herself parked up in Trent Country Park.

It was quiet this time of the evening and her car was unaccompanied in the car park. Her mum and dad used to bring her here for happy Sunday walks with their dog and other members of their church. They would feed the ducks and their dog would jump into the lake. Her dad would get cross that the back seats would get smelly and muddy.

That was all so long ago, when everything was simple. When her mum found out, she would kick her out of their home. She would be left on her own with a baby she didn't want. An absent and disinterested father. She'd be a single mum. Council flat. No career. No life. She had worked hard, been a straight 'A' student at school, earned her First-Class degree in politics. She had been making waves in her local party, it was all going so well and then it all crashed down. Her stomach was aching with stress.

How did a journalist find out? Why did he care? What would happen if her parents found out from reading it in the paper? Or if a friend from church told them? Her head was spinning with questions. She felt sick.

She rang once more but didn't leave a message and dropped the phone on the passenger seat next to the bottles. He wouldn't come. If he came, he could sort everything—mum and dad, the baby. The baby. She wept. She didn't want a baby. Ever. He wouldn't come.

She couldn't see any other option. There were no other options. She untwisted the cap to the bottle of vodka she had bought the day of the test result. This time would be the last time. She gulped down a mouthful of the rancid-tasting spirit and immediately coughed violently. She heaved to be sick, eyes watering, her throat was burning. It wasn't like that in the movies.

She unscrewed the bottle of her mum's prescription Prozac and paused. She looked at the handful of pills and then palmed them into her mouth. She drank more, this time with commitment. She repeated until the pill bottle was empty.

Jenny relaxed back into her car seat and turned the radio on. *Ordinary World* by Duran Duran was playing.

She was unconscious before the song ended.

She vomited.

She choked.

She convulsed.

She soiled herself.

Jenny died alone in a public car park.

The Meeting

Amy was trying to process what was happening. She felt numb to it all, wide-eyed, like a young child mesmerised watching someone play peek-a-boo with them for the first time.

Before her was a plush meadow with a thick forest beyond. There was a lake, next to which stood a white-washed, stone cottage with a wooden jetty and a small rowing boat. There was light but no sky, and the cave seemed to reach high up into the darkness. The scale of the cave seemed limitless. The air smelt mountain-fresh, like a spring day.

'Fuck. Off,' she muttered to herself.

Just as she looked to her companions, the centre of the lake erupted, sending a huge column of water high into the air, from the middle of which jettisoned the dragon. It flew around in a graceful arc and landed gently close to the party of visitors. Amy staggered and fell backward, landing with a bump on her bottom. She sat on the ground, mouth open in awe.

'He does like an entrance,' said Dafydd as he walked towards the beast that stood on all four legs and seemed to be two or three times his height. He held out his hand and the huge spear-shaped head of the beast came down and appeared to gently nuzzle his hand. It made a guttural sound that seemed to be affectionate. Its nostrils flared. She could hear it sniffing and exhaling, like a dog smelling the scent around it.

Tom walked forward and was greeted in the same manner; he returned to Amy and offered his hand to help her up.

'Don't worry. You're safe,' he spoke softly, reassuringly.

Amy reached up and was helped to her feet, she hadn't stopped staring at the magnificent animal before her. Its wings were now folded, swan-like. She could see its huge trunk expand and contract as it breathed. It was now sitting on its haunches, resting on its huge thigh muscles. Its tail was thick and motionless, aside from the last six feet or so that gently moved, almost in a wag. It was an unremarkable colour for a remarkable animal—it was elephant grey, but covered in scales rather than hide.

Tom walked forward holding Amy's hand until she was in proximity of the dragon. It lowered its head and took in the air around Amy. As it smelt her, she smelt sulphur, reminiscent of burnt matches and oranges. Or was it more a Christmas smell? None of it was unpleasant. It was reassuringly familiar.

'Before you hold out your hand, you must be prepared. Don't be scared. He is curious about you. When you touch you are likely to feel a rush of emotion. It doesn't hurt. You are safe. It is hard to explain, but don't worry. Embrace it,' said Tom. He was still holding her hand and as he lifted it, the dragon's huge snout slowly lowered. Amy wanted to move it away, but she wanted to stay. It was all so much, so she only had trust to guide her.

As they touched, the dragon's scales over its sternum slowly changed colour to pale red. Suddenly, Amy felt like she was flying high above the ground, her wings beating against the air, her powerful heart beating. Cold air was rushing into her nostrils and pressing against and drying her eyes. She could see the coast in the distance. It looked like Anglesey, but the land was totally covered by plush green tree foliage. There were a few faint trails of smoke meandering up through the canopy, fading as they ascended. The mountain range beneath her was familiar, mossy greens, silver slate and sapphire lakes. There were no roads of asphalt, no towns she recognised. The sky was clear and pale blue. She felt incredible, powerful, free.

She looked down and headed into a dive, the air rushed past her, the faster she flew. She felt her wings fold into a stoop. The sound of the air roared around her ears as her speed increased, air flooded her nose and lungs, and the lake grew ever larger as she dived down, faster, faster. She roared into the cold mountain water, sound dulling suddenly. Almost immediately she burst through the surface of the water, unfurling her huge wings and seeing she was in the cave circling the stone cottage. She looked down, seeing three figures and recognising herself.

At that moment, the dragon raised its snout and Amy came back to her senses. She was standing as before, in front of the dragon.

'What happened to me?' Her knees felt weak, and she was unstable.

'What did you see?' asked Dafydd.

'I was flying. I saw us.' Her heart was beating hard in her chest. 'It was familiar, but it was like it was ages ago, before all the towns were built up. I need to sit.'

'Come,' said her dad, putting his arm around his daughter and leading Amy to the door of the cottage. Dafydd winked at her dad and said, 'You go first,' and waved Amy to towards the door. She turned the old iron doorknob and the ancient plain wood panelled door opened inward.

She stepped through into a large square reception room, made of stone, with a flagstone floor. The scale was impossible to compare to the dimensions outside. The two men entered behind her, and Dafydd walked past her and through the door straight ahead that led into what looked like another large room. Amy followed. Too much was happening for Amy to be able to pause and make sense of any of it.

The next room was formally set out. A low table was set in front of the large fireplace with three wooden-framed, sofa-style seats arranged in a 'U' around it. On one of the seats was Amy's rucksack. A large window looked out to where the dragon was now resting, beyond which was the jetty and lake. They sat, on one sofa each. Amy noticed the fine embroidery of the seat furnishings. There were highly decorated wool blankets that were thrown over the sofas and it all sat on a large, square, patterned rug. It was, well, snug. She ran her hands over the embroidery, feeling the textured material. The room smelt faintly of cinnamon and cloves. She looked around. The whitewashed walls were covered by many paintings of various sizes and framing.

'This is the Keep. Through the other doors in the hall are the Great Library and the other leads to the kitchen and stairs to the bedrooms, etc. They are rudimentary, but they work. You'll soon know your way around.' Dafydd passed Amy a glass of fresh, cool water, which she drank without pause.

'Go on,' she said finally.

'There has been a building here for as far as our written records go, although I think this current building is around five hundred years old, judging by the build techniques. I will take you into the library a little later. We have records that go back the beginning. Why don't I start there? At the beginning,' said Dafydd. 'Myrddin created this place to protect the last of the dragons—'

'Myrddin?' interrupted Amy.

'Myrddin Emrys, Merzhin Ambroaz, Merlinus Ambrosius, or nowadays simply Merlin,' explained Dafydd.

'Merlin? King Arthur, sword in the stone, lady in the lake? OK, why not. There's a dragon napping on a lawn outside. I am in a cave, deep underground, where there is daylight. And a cottage that's like the TARDIS. Of course, there's going to be Merlin.'

'Yes. Good. It was a little before King Arthur, in the reign of his father, King Uther. Myrddin used his magic to create this cave. And he bought the dragon here in secret because he thought it was the last of his kind. We had hunted and killed them over hundreds of years, and he could see that without dragons, nature would lack balance and imbalance would create chaos. The beliefs that Myrddin followed, which I follow, mean that we can converse with all living things and Myrddin grew a deep understanding of these magnificent animals, made possible because of the *Hudcloch*—one of which are you wearing around your neck.' Amy felt the pendant. 'I will explain more about that another time. This place has great power. There are few spells that have this durability. It is truly a great piece of wizardry and held as an example to all that have followed since. This place is constant, plentiful, and impenetrable. Among many of its wonders is that time passes more slowly here. You can be here for three or four days and when you return it can be later the same day you came in. It's not very accurate—time wasn't really too much of a consideration fifteen hundred years ago. I was once researching and spent a week here, and when I returned home, I had only missed dinner on the day I came in. Hence your bag. If you are minded to, we can stay here for a few days so that you can become accustomed to the new truth you face. It is all arranged and when we return, it will only seem like we have been gone for a few hours, probably. You don't have to decide now. Let us show you around and answer some of your questions.'

'I really don't know what to say, so I'll keep saying that for now. Do you have anything stronger than water?' she asked.

'What would you like? I am afraid the glass will be the same, but how about a chilled glass of the wine you were having before we left the house?' Dafydd gestured to the glass she had just emptied, and it was now full of wine. Fine condensation covered the outside as though its contents had been freshly poured.

Dafydd continued, 'We have spent much time here, learning old knowledge, experimenting with new ideas, and recording all we do, as well as caring for our dragon, of course. Your father has learned much since your family came here. Likewise, I have been studying all my life and I am still a student. There is more for me to learn in the Great Library than I could absorb in several lifetimes. Come, let me show you the Great Library.' Dafydd stood and the three of them made their way to the library.

The room was long and narrow. Along one side were great windows that ran from the ceiling to the floor, filling the hall-like room with light, illuminating the rows and rows of books. Amy looked up and guessed it must have been two storeys tall, with gangways running seven or eight feet apart and sliding ladders to climb between. There were piles of scrolls in pigeonholes, volumes and volumes of bound books. 'We have written records from around 300AD in a variety of languages; Latin, Gaelic, middle Welsh, English, some Cornish, Arabic, French and few others. This collection is quite priceless. This is why we all remain apprentices. As I have said, I have been studying all my life, but I still only know a fraction of what there is to learn.'

'I am trying to piece this together. So, what are you?'

'You could use "wizard,"' said Dafydd.

'Fuck off,' said Amy.

'Ah, there we are,' said her dad, 'normal service resumed.'

Dafydd smiled. 'It's not something that one publicises. I leave it to the crackpots and pseudo-psychics to claim their divinity. "Wizard," "seer," and "prophet" are simplistic terms for the followers of our faith.'

'How many others are there?' asked Amy, who was walking along the book wall, running her hands over the leather-bound book spines.

Her dad spoke, 'We are part of the Order of St George. It was once called the Order of Draic, but that wasn't considered "Christian enough".'

Dafydd interrupted, 'It will always be the Order of Draic to us.'

'Draic, George. To-ma-to, tomato. It's not that important. As the Old Bard said, "What's in a name?"' Tom looked back to Amy as Dafydd scoffed. 'Anyway, the Order was established over fifteen hundred years ago and has been supported by the Crown ever since. That's why you had to sign the Official Secrets Act paperwork. We're just a small part of the Order. We don't know how many there are. All the official involvement is fronted by the law firm that sent Mr Stiff earlier. We receive payments through various sources—part farming subsidies, part from trust funds—and the solicitors handle everything for us. Our role is to act as keepers for the dragon.'

Dafydd stepped in. 'As for us, others like me, I am not sure. I was raised with the knowledge in the same way that you were taught Christianity, only we kept our faith secret. There are "druids" who meet up at Stonehenge every year, new-age hippies driving beaten-up transits from one festival to another and the like, and, well, they are some way from our beliefs. I am sure they get the support they seek from the belief system they follow, but we are the real deal. Marcus is learning his way, as I did mine. Outside of our family there are probably others, but for obvious reasons they will be well hidden.'

'You've gotta understand that it will take me some time to accept everything you've told me in the past few hours. I mean, dragons, spells, wizards,' Amy gestured around. 'Part of me still thinks this is some elaborate practical joke.'

'Is not what you have seen so far proof enough?' asked Dafydd. He didn't wait for an answer, 'OK, unlike your Jesus, I am willing to perform on request.' With that, he raised his right hand and clicked his fingers. A bright white flame appeared and burned in the air a few inches above his fingertips. He blew gently and the flame moved slowly, levitating through the air, towards Amy. He clapped and it disappeared. 'Some more?' he asked rhetorically. He pointed past Amy. She turned and saw a lectern at the other end of the library. It shuddered briefly, then started to grind along the floor towards them.

'Dafydd, that's enough. You might be frightening Amy. Besides, you'll scratch the floor,' said her dad. He looked to Amy, 'I know I keep saying it, but it is a lot to take in. Let's go outside and sit with the dragon. You can have some time to think over what you've seen, and we can talk some more. How's that?'

'Yes,' said Amy, 'Let's go outside and sit with a mythical animal outside a magic cottage in an enchanted cave and talk more with my dad who is in a secret society with a wizard. I think I might need that.'

Marcus

He had deliberately sat apart from everyone else gathered that Sunday evening. He didn't want to be part of the circus. Marcus had known of the plans for the night, and he did not agree with them—not that any of them gave a toss for his views. He didn't see why Amy had to be told anything. Her parents weren't long at their job, and she had no interest in any of it. She would go back to London, get a job, and remain the infrequent visitor that she was. Anyway, Amy was stuck up. She always ignored him, walking around like she owned the place, but none of them really belonged here. His family had been part of it for generations. His dad, his grandfather, and so on—it went back as far as Marcus could be bothered to learn.

This evening made him remember when he first began to understand his abilities. He had started to realise that his parents weren't like his friends' families. Outwardly they did all things that his friends' families did: church on Sundays, day trips, and play-dates at friends' houses (but never at his). But at home, life was different. They hardly ever watched television, or listened to the radio. Instead his dad would tell him stories of their ancestors, or they would go for walks where his dad would teach him about all the plants and animals. He was told stories of how the stars and earth were formed from a great consciousness, fables of animals which explained their purpose in the great order, how plants could be worked together to make lotions and ointments, and his dad would show him tricks that he didn't yet understand.

***

He was eight years old. The sun was rising, and the grass was damp from the early morning dew. He had woken as his father had left to work the sheep with the dogs and his mum was around in the house. His dad had been teaching him an incantation and he wanted to practice. It was quiet and he was going to give it one more try before he had to get ready to go to school. He gripped his

Hudcloch, which had been cut to the shape of a cross and he focused on the earth in front of him. '*Dod*' was all he thought. He waited. He closed his eyes and searched the darkness. He started to feel as though his skin was pushing rhythmically against soil around him. He could feel the soil loosen and the sensation of breaking free. He opened his eyes and looked down. An earth worm was labouring its way out of the ground in front of him.

Marcus jumped up, punching the air and gave out a huge whoop of joy. Finally, some progress. His father made this look easy, and it was the first significant step forward Marcus had made. He had started to think that perhaps he couldn't find the strength within himself. Today a worm, tomorrow a beetle, perhaps. It would take patience, but he felt so relieved that he had started. It would just be practice.

He ran in the house. 'Mam! I did it! I did it! I made the worm come to me!'

He had been given new lenses to see the world. His mind's sight was blurred and confused to start with, but as the time passed, he began to find his focus. As his skills and abilities improved, he became less interested in conforming with his peers. He started to realise how little people saw and understood of the world of which they were a small part, their ignorance annoying him greatly as he become older.

***

Marcus had his father's willowy build and that, along with his increasingly reserved nature, made him an easy target for the wrong type of attention at school. He was fourteen years old and walking home from the bus stop when a couple of his classmates singled him out. They started to push him, call him names. He didn't remember what they called him. It was irrelevant. What they said was less important than the way they said it. They took his bag from him and threw it over the dry wall into the muddy field behind. Marcus climbed over the wall to collect it and they followed him, intent on harming him for their amusement. Marcus's ability had improved significantly by this time and in that moment of fear and anger he forgot himself. He called out for help, but not audibly. He was strong enough that his call was answered. Some of the nearby herd of sheep came running over.

The boys initially thought it was amusing until the rams started butting them relentlessly. One boy fell over. He was the larger of the two and had instigated the bullying, and a lucky or well-timed headbutt from a particularly well-set ram caught him above the eye, splitting his skin.

Marcus smirked as he remembered how the boy had started to cry and they had both scrambled, now muddy and dishevelled, back over the wall and off to their homes. Marcus had stood in the field, surrounded by a small flock of sheep, laughing at the boys and shouting that they were running away from sheep. He had been really proud of his achievement, but his dad had shouted at him when he retold the story that evening. His dad had been furious and said that whilst the boys didn't have any clue that he had in fact bullied them, he couldn't risk ever showing anyone what he was capable of.

One of the dogs nudged Marcus's shin, bringing his attention back to the room, where Claire and Kath were chatting.

'I think I will head home,'he said and he stood to leave.

'You've not had dinner yet. The others will be back soon, just be patient. Come, sit with us,' said <u>Kath,</u> tapping the seat cushion next to hers.

'You're OK. I will get something when I get home. It's a clear night and the dogs will enjoy the exercise. We'll go over the hill rather than round. See you later.' He nodded to Claire and set off, with the dogs, Zeus and Apollo, lumbering alongside.

As he left the house, Marcus was angry that they had taken Amy to meet HIM. She wasn't the one that looked after him and she didn't contribute in the way that his dad did. Marcus had only met him once, on his tenth birthday. He had been taught about dragons by his dad and perhaps his dad had sensed that Marcus was getting to an age when children started to work out that Father Christmas wasn't real. Marcus found it fascinating that children trusted anything their parents told them because they were raised on lies like Father Christmas, tooth fairies, the bogeyman, and Jesus, son of Christ. Childhood was based on non-truths.

On the morning of that birthday, his dad gave him a handmade card that had a dragon shaking hands with a boy. It was a terrible drawing - it looked like a winged cow with a pointy tail - so bad in fact that he had to ask his dad what it was. When he opened the card, it simply said 'Today is the day. Penblwydd hapus!' He was beyond excited and wanted to go then and there in his Thomas the Tank Engine pyjamas, but he had to wait until after breakfast. He ate in double-quick time, taking some bacon and wrapping it in kitchen tissue to give to the dragon as a treat. His parents had bought him a Sinclair ZX Spectrum, which he had yearned for and hounded them to buy him for ages, but it sat unopened as he impatiently waited for his dad to be ready to go. He remembered standing on the jetty in the cave as his dad called the dragon to come. He was holding his dad's hand, butterflies in his stomach. His dad pointed up and he saw it come out the darkness from above. It glided towards them and landed gently by the Keep and waiting for Marcus and his dad to approach. To Marcus, it was huge, and it smelt bad. He was getting more and more scared as they approached. The dragon reached down and took a deep, long sniff of Marcus. It snorted, turned and then with a huge beat of its wings that blasted wind into Marcus's face, it left, flew high and dived into the lake, not to return.

That was that. He was so disappointed as they returned home. His dad explained that the dragon took years to get to know and trust someone and that the dragon could be unpredictable. Marcus should never, ever go and visit it alone. Not that he listened.

Of course, his dad had lied again, the dragon wasn't unpredictable at all. He had initially sneaked into the cave and tried to make his way unseen to the Keep, but as soon as he came on to the meadow he could feel the dragon was near. It would always approach, but it never landed. It would just circle above him and then disappear up into the darkness or dive down into the lake. The cave was a sanctuary for Marcus, where he could sit and be alone. He had found the Great Library in one of his early surreptitious visits and he read and studied hard. He enjoyed learning and the more he read, the more the world made sense to him—and the more disillusioned he became with the life around him. His teachers knew nothing. Well, they knew a version of something, but with all their knowledge they lacked understanding. There was wisdom in the literature in the library. All the kids his age were into drinking cider, playing rugby, listening to chart music, and trying to be popular. They were facile, ignorant, annoying, like Amy.

He spent more and more time in the cave and by the time he was in his late teens he would stay for weeks at a time. When he returned home, he would have only been gone for hours. The longest was a whole day; he had entered early in the morning as the sun rose and came back to the sun setting. He arrived home to find his mum worried about his absence. After that, he always said that he would be going to meet a friend in town. The bus journey was long and unreliable, so they didn't worry if he was away for a while. They never asked which friend. They didn't seem interested. That seemed to be their attitude towards him in general.

He was learning so much more on his own than his father was showing him, but there was so much more to learn. He was impatient and from the very beginning of his apprenticeship it seemed like his father had held him back. He yearned to learn the meaty stuff. If he had learned at the pace his father wanted to teach him, he would be, at best, a clever circus conjurer who wasn't allowed to perform in public.

He began to practise what he had learned from the books and scrolls. There was no order to the books. There wasn't a Ralph McDell's *One Hundred Easy Spells and Incantations*. Learning which magicking he was capable of and the satisfaction of nailing a new one was the most rewarding experience Marcus had. Much of the literature was withholding its knowledge through the secret of language and he could just about decipher old English and was gradually learning Latin, but the other scripts were defeating him.

His skills were so much more developed than his dad knew and that secretly excited him. When his dad would show him something he believed to be new to Marcus, he would pretend to struggle to master it and then, after he felt he had delayed long enough, he would execute it perfectly. His dad would be impressed and would always say that he was a natural. What a fool.

Whilst his dad was in the cave he did not know what Marcus was up to, so, when he was certain his dad was down there he could practice without fear of being caught. Tonight, the sky was clear, the moonlight cast shadows across the hills, making his and the dogs' progress brisk. He had been working on coupling and no longer needed to focus all his efforts on that one task, meaning he could be aware of his own body as well as the animal whose mind he was entering. He still needed to concentrate to make the initial connection though, and when they reached the ridge of the first hill, he called his dogs to come to him. Zeus and Apollo sat before him, and he placed his hands on their heads. Instantly, he was coupled. His sense of smell and hearing magnified. It was always over-powering to start with. His dogs' heart beats were raised from the climb, and they were thirsty and excited. There was the faint scent of other people coming from the valley ahead. Marcus decided he would sit a while and explore the strangers with his dogs.

He sent the dogs off, leaving Marcus crossed legged, eyes closed, silhouetted against the night sky. They moved fast, he felt their chests pumping, muscles working. It felt primeval. The sound of panting and loose slate slipping under paw filled his mind as the scent of the strangers increased. Both dogs stopped and crouched. From the vantage point higher on the hill, they looked down and saw the two caterpillar-like tents below. Two figures sat around a single stove. They smelt like a man and woman. They were cooking, the scent of the food was strange, metallic, salty. He felt the dogs' saliva glands start to pump. It was appealing to the dogs. He recognised the smell as a Vesta dehydrated meal, probably beef curry—he didn't want to taste it if they ate it. Time for some fun. He muttered an incantation below his breath and pushed both hands away from his chest, shoving outwards. At that moment a gust of wind blew down the hill and tipped the unstable gas stove over, billy tin toppling, spewing the hot contents over the ground between the couple.

'Dan! I told you that wasn't a good place for it!' said the female as she stood up and brushed down her trousers. 'I'm going to stink of nasty curry for the next two days, you idiot!'

He was also up, trying to rescue what was left of their meal from the toppled pan. 'For fuck's sake, Priya! That was the last of the water. If you get another meal out, I'll go back to the lake and get some more. I needed to go anyway so we had some for the morning. Are you OK?'

'Yeah, just hungry. I would have preferred my dinner in me, not on me. Never mind. See you in ten,' she replied.

Priya crawled into one of the small tents as Dan picked up a collapsible water container, turned on his torch, and started off down the hill. The dogs parted company. Zeus headed off to track Dan while Apollo stalked downward towards Priya in the camp.

As Priya rummaged in her rucksack for another food pack, Apollo quietly padded to the spilt contents by the now-righted stove. Marcus grimaced as he tasted wet soil and part-cooked rice. He could smell faint deodorant, sweat, the sweeter scent of a female. She was ovulating. One of them had a cat, though the scent was vague. Apollo moved back into the darkness, away from the small battery lamp that illuminated the improvised seating area and returned to a crouch.

Dan wished he had put his boots back on. The hillside was getting damp under the moonlight, which made the grass slippery and where there was bedrock, the slate was either shingly or covered in moist moss. He had twisted his ankle a few times and his legs were tired from the long walk they had completed during the day. It was not the environment to be in flip-flops, but they were a welcomed relief for his feet once they set up camp, he should have thought about it before setting off. He stopped as he heard a sound behind him. He looked back and panned along the hillside with his torch. Nothing. He carried on. The lake was calm and its surface mimicked the moon above. It was only a few more minutes away.

Zeus had slunk down as Dan had turned, its keen eyesight watching the torch light beam a line above where it lay, motionless. Zeus watched as the man carried onward, carefully checking his footing before each step until he reached the edge of the lake. Dan knelt and held the container under the water. *Jeez, the water was freezing up here*, he thought.

Priya sat down on the fold-away stool. Wrapping her arms around herself for warmth, she looked up and gazed at the stars. It was mesmerising. There were so many more stars than they could see from the back garden of the small, Manchester terrace house she shared with Dan and his cat. Hopefully, their friendship would advance over this trip. She had responded to his flat-share ad in *Loot* six months ago and didn't expect to fall for her roomy. They had so much in common, especially 'the great outdoors', and they just hit it off from day one.

With his eyes closed, sat on the hill high above them, Marcus muttered, '*Yn awr.*'

Apollo came forward out of the shadows growling. Priya snapped out of her gaze, and, alarmed, looked at the powerful, large dog snarling at her.

'Good doggy,' she said. What was she saying? Idiot. She edged back towards her tent, heart pounding. The dog didn't move. It could smell adrenaline.

At the same time, Zeus leaped forward, landing within a snout's distance of Dan, who was still crouching, barking loudly. That was enough to surprise Dan causing him to flinch and lose his balance and fall. forward into the cold lake, taking his breath away and losing his bearings momentarily.

Priya was close enough now to spin and dive into her little tent, and, scrambling, she turned and zipped down the door.

Up on the hilltop, Marcus was laughing hard as he told the dogs to come back. He could have done anything at that moment, but it was enough to scare the shit of out of the townies. The control and power had aroused him, and he felt himself engorged. When the dogs returned, he petted them briefly before starting on their journey home.

When he reached their home, the house was in darkness and the kitchen door was unlocked, as was normal. Aside from the dogs, he was alone in the house, and he didn't bother to turn the light on as he moved around the kitchen, making himself a cheese and salad cream sandwich and pouring a glass of water. The sense of arousal was still running through him, and he felt like masturbating, but, first he thought he'd play Wolfenstein 3D for an hour or so. He kicked his shoes off and headed to his bedroom.

Blackwood

He closed the dossier, looked across the green leather of his desktop, and sat back.

'So the World Wide Web is considered a threat to the State?' He rubbed the bridge of his nose wearily and replaced his glasses.

'Yes, Home Secretary. No, Home Secretary. Not a direct threat but a security risk. Now that the source code is royalty free, we anticipate an exponential growth in the internet's usage. All the information that sits out there in the ether will be far more easily tracked, documented, shared and therefore accessed without a decerning eye making sure it is credible.'

'Credible?' Blackwood smiled. He had learned in his time in politics that credible meant controlled. He liked Graham Southall, who was an experienced secretary, but he was very old-school, reminiscent of a character from a Le Carre espionage novel. He lacked vision and an eye for a suit in any colour other than brown.

'There is some conversation around regulation, Home Secretary. However, no-one considers it an issue and I think that is short-termism and will prove to be a mistake. The internet removes barriers: it has no head office, no publisher-in-chief, no board, no shareholders, no appointed or elected leaders or controllers. It knows no territories. It is simply not accountable. It is the Wild West. The new frontier. It will attract all those that see its unlimited potential, legitimate and otherwise. It will become the back-alleys of Soho, Manchester, Glasgow. Every city around the world accessible in all its grubby darkness in one's front room. CERN has gifted a pandora's box to the modern world and I fear only a few of us see it for it really is.'

'Well, it is a new media. Personally, I think it exciting; just imagine all the information that could be tapped into, entire libraries online, accessible to all. Imagine all that information locked up and hidden in the British Library, or the Natural History Museum, available to someone in Rome, or New York, at a touch of a button.

Think of the knowledge that will be able to be shared quickly, international collaboration without days of flights and fax machines. Simple uses like sharing family photographs with far-distant relatives. Its application is boundless—it certainly goes far beyond sending and receiving email. I am surprised by your unusually enthusiastic opinion Graham, and I am not sure I agree. I do give you that it could be the home of pornography, gambling, crackpots, and conspiracists, for sure. Beyond that, well, let's just wait and see.'

Southall nodded. 'Gower Street is extending its interests to include internet activity and will be providing regular updates in their report. They are forecasting huge growth in new registrations of websites and are monitoring as they grow. Currently there are just under five hundred web sites registered globally. They are predicting that we could see over two and half thousand by the end of next year. There is one estimate that forecasts over two million websites in the next five years. It is an information plague, Minister. They are planning to set up a Cyber Centre in GCHQ to get ahead of the wave. The idea is to focus on recruiting Oxbridge maths grads who can create algorithms to read website content and highlight anything of interest. It is apparently proving to be very labour intensive at present and they will no doubt be looking for additional funding,'

'No doubt,' agreed Blackwood. 'I am under pressure to cut spending and MI5 and MI6 are always holding out their cup, asking for funding for counter-terrorism. The internet will be another excuse for more cash under the guise of National Security. They will be moving into their new HQ next year, which, of course, has run well over budget, and they are just spending and spending. When will I have the expenditure report? They have had *carte blanche* for far too long and I am going to get a grip on these departments as a priority.'

'The Director General's office is aware their report is overdue. They are not used to being under this amount of scrutiny, Home Secretary, and, well, they are the secret services.'

'Who report to me,' interrupted Blackwood. 'Please chase that up Graham. I am very much in the spotlight and need to show some decisive actions to keep the PM and press happy. What else do we have today?'

Southall 'The Met Commissioner has called and requested an urgent meeting so I have moved a few of your scheduled appointments and he should be in around noon.'

'No doubt he will be looking to press home HIS need for adequate funding. My departments are like nestlings; perpetually chirping, open mouthed, for more money. Can you see if we can move that meeting to lunch? Last night's function ended late, and I only had a few mouthfuls of my dinner before I spoke, then left. It must have been gone one by the time my head hit the pillow and I was up at 5 AM.'

Blackwood stretched his legs under the table. Home Secretary was a grade-A appointment and he had deserved the promotion. He was the first ever black member of a British Cabinet and he had to fight his way up through the ranks, not just beating but smashing his opponents along the way, and he was still only in his mid-thirties. Nothing had prepared him for the workload and his opposition was not just limited to those sitting on the other side of Parliament. There were many in his party and around the Cabinet that resented his views, age, and ambitions or simply didn't think someone 'like him' should have landed a role this significant. Southall was not, from what Blackwood could tell, one of those. It was apparent to Blackwood that Southall took great pride in his role and genuinely believed he was acting out his civic duty. A rare attribute in the corridors and offices of Whitehall.

Southall 'I shall call his secretary. Commissioner Jenks is never knowingly under-lunched, so I suspect that will be fine, especially if you host him at the Club, Home Secretary,' Southall made a note in his Filofax.

'Yes, very good, I could do with a couple of hours out of the office today. What else do I have on?'

'Now that we are changing your schedule, you will be in meetings until around 7 p.m. and you have a long-standing dinner appointment with the PM.'

Blackwood groaned internally. Rachel had known of his ambitions when they married and had always supported his career, sacrificing her own promising prospects as a barrister to be the mother of their kids. However, she was tiring of his absence from home. There wasn't a guide to parenting and they went from being a power-couple to clueless and exhausted parents of twins at what seemed interstellar speed. They had help, but Blackwood was very aware that he wasn't being the father or husband that he wanted to be. That night was meant to be date-night—nothing extravagant: dinner in Pimlico, a few drinks away from the house, and then back to watch *Cinema Paradiso* on VHS. It had been their favourite movie when they were at university.

'Can you please call Rachel and let her know my new schedule? I will give her a call after lunch.'

Southall pause his writing, 'If you don't mind a word from the wise, Home Secretary, a call from you would take a brief moment and would be well received.'

Blackwood had forgotten himself and appreciated the prompt. 'Quite right, Graham. Tonight was meant to be date night; a rare treat these days. If there is nothing else, we'll end the meeting here and I will call Rachel.' Blackwood looked to the door, indicating the meeting was over.

Southall 'One more thing, Home Secretary. A Mr William Anker, who works for our friends in Wapping, has been trying to arrange some time with you. He has my direct number—I am not sure how he came by it, but, he is quite, erm, let's say persistent.'

'I know that name, which isn't a good sign. W Anker. Did you know that part of my studies included psychology? There was a German psychologist called Stekel who spoke about compulsive behaviour and choice of occupation being driven by ones given name, nominative determinism if you will. It would appear this gentleman is a living example. Is he broadsheet or tabloid?'

Southall smiled, 'Nominative determinism. Very good sir. I could almost fit the bill, Southall working in Whitehall. Maybe that is a stretch. But I see it. He works for one of the redtop tabloids, Home Secretary.'

'OK, I would suggest that you arrange for his number to be blocked and leave the press office to deal with it. They are parasites—the journalists, that is, not our press office. They claim the importance of the freedom of the press and what do they do with that freedom? They pursue their own agendas, making personal grudges national news. They exploit disasters, scandalise mistakes, vilify innocents, and promote the vacuous to maintain their circulation and generate cash, which is what it is all about in the end.' Blackwood had suffered at the hands of the tabloids for years. His open support of gay rights, his active voice against racism, and his belief that to prevent crime you need to deal with society, not just the lawbreakers, were all deeply unpopular opinions with the redtops. He was the wrong colour and came from the wrong background to easily gain the support of most of the broadsheets, but at least with the latter he could use reason. The redtops only knew vitriol and prejudice. 'Apologies for ranting. Now, if we are done, I had better call Rachel and face the music.'

'Shall I send flowers?' asked Southall as he closed his Filofax and stood to leave.

'After your perceptive advice a moment ago, you disappoint. If I did that, she'd beat me with them when I got home. She will be disappointed, but I am sure she will understand, and I will have to make it up, I am sure.' Blackwood watched Southall leave the room and close the oak-panelled door behind him as he picked up the handset and dialled their home number.

Hours to Days

Dafydd was carrying a number of books in his arms when he came to sit with Tom and Amy. As he sat, the books spilled onto ground. 'I thought I would bring some reading for you.'

The dragon was lying near, eyes shut. It seemed to be sleeping. Amy stretched out her legs. She was starting to relax and accept the bizarre situation. It was as fascinating as it was confusing. She collected the books up, glancing at the spines and placing them in a pile.

'There's quite some reading here.'

'Yes, and I am afraid that you cannot take them with you. They can't leave—if you took one it would not pass through the rock, so you need to read here. There is no rush. These are a good starting point. I assume you don't understand Latin?'

'*Veni, vidi, vici. Alea iacta est.* Erm...' She searched her mind. '*Cogito, ergo sum. Carpe diem.* And of course, my favourite, *in vino veritas,*' she replied, recounting any Latin that she could think of.

'Dulce est interdum ineptire!' he replied.

'Ok, you got me.' Amy had learned basic Latin for two years in her secondary school, but had dropped it as soon as she could, preferring a living language. 'Parles-tu Français?'

'Mon Dieu! Mais bien sur. Je peux parler plusieurs langues. Comment ça va ton gallois?'

She laughed, and guessing at what he had said, replied, 'No, and that's pretty much the limit of my GCSE French too. Let's stick with English.'

'Those books will give you some history, from the start with Merlin and some of the key events since. This secret and the power this place holds have been fought over for centuries. The dark times, through the battles of Arfderydd, of Edward the Confessor, of William the Conqueror, the War of the Roses, the Civil War, and the "War To End All Wars"—both of them—have all have played their part in our history. Often the secrets of this place can reveal the true source of many conflicts.'

Dafydd passed Amy one of the thinner, leather-bound books, which she thumbed through. 'This is why you asked if you asked about my Latin?' she asked as she could tell from the script the language was ancient.

'Before you start, let me give you a gift.' Dafydd held both of Amy's hands in his and closed his eyes. She could see his lips moving, but whatever he was saying was inaudible. 'There,' he said, 'You will find your grip of languages much improved.' He winked. 'Have another look.'

Amy looked again at the open page and handwritten script. It was in Latin, but she could read it. She looked up at Dafydd.

'You are now multilingual. You will understand all the languages in our library. A useful by-product is you will find most European languages a breeze, though you may not be conversationally eloquent at first, but it will come with ease. We have several volumes in Arabic, which I would recommend. I find the language quite beautiful. This gift cannot be taken away from you by anyone else but me, so use it wisely as I believe you will. You see, already you have benefits! Try not to show off too much!

'The book you hold is one of the first. That is, in fact, written in Merlin's own hand. We were once druids, many, many years ago. Our beliefs were passed on by oral lore and over time, as we became literate, we started to record our knowledge, and the Great Library was born. We are students of our nature, and we learn how to harness it. It's what we call *Mamddaear*, and it's the Earth's power. It is everywhere: in the air, soil, water, you, me, that rock there. It is everything. *Mamddaear* needs balance and each living thing on the Earth is connected to *Mamddaear*, from the smallest of creatures to the greatest. An ant, for example, donates and draws a tiny-winey part of this power, but there are billions of ants around the world so collectively they have much greater power. A blue whale is probably the most powerful single being and it has a strong influence on *Mamddaear*, but there are far fewer, so, you see, balance. This

connection with
Earth's power

?

connection is called *Grym*. Back in the days of Merlin, dragons were the greatest of known animals and they were "*Grym Pwerus*", basically, a hugely powerful conduit for *Mamddaear*. Dragons are revered by us because of their connection, and this is where the *Hudcloch* comes in. We were given the *Hudcloch* by what we believe to have been Saint George. We think that Saint George used these stones to defeat the dragons, but we simply don't know the history as it was before we kept written records and has been lost to time. Either way, the *Hudcloch* magnifies our own *Grym* and those of us with strong enough *Grym* can couple with a dragon. You see, as with the ants, individually our *Grym*, our antenna if you like, is comparatively weak, but like ants we are social animals. So even before we could speak languages, we were able to communicate together using our *Grym* and share a common goal. That unity of purpose makes us collectively extremely powerful and is what has enabled us as a species to dominate the planet over time.'

'That and opposing thumbs,' interrupted Amy.

Dafydd laughed. 'True. Today we all see dolphins as intelligent animals and they do possess strong *Grym* and a pod becomes *Grym Pwerus*. The same with humans: we have multiplied and thrived on this planet and because of our size and number we are now unknowingly *Grym Pwerus*, which means we have the greatest influence on *Mamddaear*. And, as you say, we have thumbs. However, as we have become more sophisticated and have started to understand our world through science, our ability, our conscious connection to our *Grym*, has weakened and this will, I am afraid, start to impact our planet as *Mamddaear* becomes more and more imbalanced as our influence grows.

'I am not dismissing modern science. Scientific advancement is essential. The wheel, combustion engine, antibiotics, nuclear power, microchip, these are all incredible. We no longer try to treat cancer by sticking leaches on a patient's leg, or say someone with dementia is a lunatic. Sadly, humankind is evolving away from *Mamddaear*. However, those like me can understand *Mamddaear* with more clarity as we understand more of the mechanisms of the world.

'Science and our belief work in union not opposition. We are not stuck with a belief system decided upon by our predecessors thousands of years ago and rewritten, misinterpreted and abused. We understand that when humanity was in its infancy, we looked at our surroundings simplistically, as child would, and as humankind has gained sophistication so we have also continued to evolve and gain our deeper knowledge. Our beliefs are not rigidly stuck to the stories of our lore. If Merlin were alive today, he would have a home computer, drive a car, eat MacDonalds. It's just that in Ancient Britain these things weren't around. As an aside, there is an interesting essay suggesting that Leonardo Da Vinci was one of us. I will dig it out for you if you remind me.

'When you touched the dragon, what you felt was your *Grym*. The dragon spoke with you. A dragon doesn't speak a language as you know it. But you will learn to understand what he says to you. That vision you had, that was a strongly positive experience for the dragon and that means he accepted you. As you spend time with him you will develop the ability to speak with him without words and eventually without touch. We can do this with all sentient beings. At one time all people could to varying degrees and many could do again, we have just lost the knowledge. An apprentice starts with a worm, then ant and builds from there, coupling with more sophisticated minds as they learn. It's like learning languages.

'Merlin saw that Uther was open to his *Grym* and he nurtured the bond between Uther and the dragon. Using this, Uther won the battle at Paschent, defeating the son of the man who murdered his father. The King vowed to be the protectorate of dragons and it was Merlin that gave Uther the title Pendragon. Since then, the Crown has provided refuge for the dragon and kept its presence in utmost secrecy. We, our sect, have sworn to serve and protect The Crown and the dragon ever since.'

'But with all this knowledge and power, you disguise yourselves as sheep farmers and hide in a cave? Couldn't you get out there and make a difference?' Amy replied.

'To what end? The dragon would be caged, like an animal in a zoo, paraded like a bearded lady in front of scientists, perhaps dissected. We would be ridiculed. Our beliefs would be dismissed as science fails to understand, as it has for centuries. The final threads that bind us to *Mamddaear* would be lost and then we would all be lost.

'We must also respect balance. Let's say I walked the world curing every person with an ailment I met, I would be acting against balance. It's like Newton's Third Law, do you know that?'

'For every action there has to be a reaction?' said Amy.

'Correct. As I say, we humans are constantly creating an imbalance, we are interfering with the natural order that is *Mamddaear* and if I cast a spell ridding the world of, say, AIDS, the scales would tip further against equilibrium and an equal and opposite adjustment would be necessary. That could be a plague, famine, war. You see, if we "solve" one "problem" we often create another. Even though the weight of humanity's footprint is heavy we must tread lightly. We are like travellers walking on a pristine beach—there will be evidence of our journey. But *Mamddaear* will wash it away over time.'

'To have that power and not use it for yourself… You must be tempted, right?' questioned Amy.

'I could build a life of opulence for me or you, or your family, or anyone I chose, but that is not our way. There have been those, like Cornelius, who have abused their understanding for their own gain, and it would be a lie if I said I haven't influenced some events to my favour, but that is the greatest lesson we learn and the first. Merlin didn't act against *Mamddaear* when he helped Uther and Arthur and we have acted for *Mamddaear*'s advantage ever since. There will be a time for us to step into the light, but it is not now.

'The Order has helped keep our faith alive. Initially the role was passed down, father to son, then we had the Cornelius incident. Since then the apprentice has been chosen by the incumbent wizard. We, the Order, are not just custodians of the dragon. We are custodians of a knowledge and at some point in the future, it will be time to re-educate the rest of mankind, but for now, yes, we hide. I will pass on this responsibility and learning to my apprentice.'

'So Marcus is your apprentice?' asked Amy. 'That would explain a lot,' she mused.

'That is his expectation. I am afraid that his connection is weak, and he will find his path hard to navigate, but it is still early.' Dafydd stood. 'Now, what say you that I make us something to eat and you start having a read?'

Amy sat and read. She and Dafydd talked, and time passed unnoticed. Hours seemed to become days as she lost herself in books and experiences; they ventured into the woodland and she was introduced to foraging, collecting mushrooms, wild garlic, nettles, blackberries, and sweet chestnuts. She was beginning to be taught the rudiments of the Merlinis' faith and wizardry.

The dragon was always nearby, flying overhead or sleeping. They stayed in the cave, reading, talking, sleeping, and walking through the expansive meadowland that seemed to reach for miles.

***

Amy had lost all track of time when Dafydd said it was time to leave. The experience had been completely absorbing and Amy could have stayed for longer. They left the cave and returned to evening darkness, walking back to the farmhouse. She was tired and disorientated from her time away and was pleased to walk into the familiar, warm comfort of home.

'Ah, there you are!' said her mum as they walked into the kitchen, through the boot room. 'Oh my, you've been in there for a while, judging by your scent. Sat by a fire, did we?'

Her dad called out from the other room, 'I'd say dinner is in the dog if we had one. Dafydd, I poured and had your drink. Your boy has sulked off already.'

Dafydd replied with 'Thanks, Butt!' and, taking a bowl, started to serve himself some food. 'If you don't mind, we'll head off once I have eaten. I could use a shower and my bed.'

The kitchen clock told Amy that they had been away for three hours, but she had slept soundly twice in the cave. To her she seemed to have been away for three days. She took the glass of wine her mum passed her and drank it in one.

'I'm off to bed, it's been quite a ride this, er, however long it's been. I'd like to go back tomorrow, if that's OK?'

'That would be fine,' said Dafydd, smiling. Amy headed off upstairs to bed. As she lay, she could hear the faint murmur and occasional laughter of convivial conversation until sleep washed over her.

Lunch

Blackwood's club was a five-storey building in St James' with a Portland stone Palladian façade and plush marble interiors, softened by heavy, richly coloured, and patterned textiles. It was Victorian architecture at is most grandiose. It was as discreet as it was exclusive, being anonymous amongst the other substantial and imposing properties that lined the streets in that area of London. In the rooms of this club, and a small number of others like it, in this small area of London, the real power was held. Membership was never discussed and was strictly invitation only.

Peter Blackwood had had to carefully navigate through his contacts and use all his political skill, attending countless lunches, imbibing vast quantities of spirits, to prise a reluctant invitation for membership. It had taken two years of tactful effort for Peter, but he was in and would be in for life. Of course, now he was Home Secretary, the substantial membership fees would be a claimable expense. He felt that this was entirely appropriate as he could conduct business in a confidence not afforded in Whitehall and the surroundings were fitting for a person of his position. Peter had been discerning with his privileges—he truly believed that a person's integrity was measured by how they acted when no-one was looking and there had been several points in his career where his propriety could have been questioned if he had not exercised careful judgement. There were rumours that other Members of Parliament were claiming property costs for their extended families, or lovers, and he had heard one Member had claimed for a replacement swan house on the ornamental island in his large pond in his back garden. He detested such abuse, which had become endemic in Westminster. It was a subject in his sights.

The club's atmosphere carried a constant murmur of hushed conversation and the scent of expensive fresh cigar smoke and alcohol. There was an abundance of middle-aged, white men in varying stages of obesity or probable pre-diabetes and Blackwood's tall, slim stature and dark complexion made him conspicuous in his attendance. Not that he was unfamiliar to that, as he grew up in South London. His parents were first generation immigrants who had come to the UK from Jamaica as qualified medical doctors. The family spent Peter's early years in Streatham in a modest terraced house and it was there that he realised how much harder he was going to need to work, just because of the colour of his skin. In his local school, bullying was indiscriminate. If you were overweight, you were picked on, if you were Irish, you were picked on, and if you wore glasses, you were picked on.

There was a boy in his class who was picked on because his name was Leslie and that, apparently, made him a girl. Any opportunity to poke fun, or actually physically poke was generally taken. He was black, so even the most unimaginative saw an easy distinction to identify him as a target. During school, it was a level playing field and Peter could verbally joust with the best of them. You had to stand up for yourself, even against the odds, to survive, and Peter believed those early lessons helped shape him. Outside of school, in the shops, walking home, when he was out for dinner with his family, he could feel the difference. There was malice in the attention. If they went into the sweet shop on the way home, the shop assistant would watch him over the white kids he was with. He had been spat at in the street, refused service in some cafes and shops, and countless times told to 'go back from where you came from'. Some of his community chose to challenge ignorance, many opted to tolerate it, nearly all were angered by it, but he used it as motivation.

His parents were hard working and quickly established themselves in practice. His mother was particularly entrepreneurial, and by the time Peter was ready for secondary school, they owned several surgeries, enabling them to move to the space and greenery of Virginia Water, Surrey. Peter was admitted to an international public school. He loved learning and the environment was supportive and diverse. His quick witted-humour and open demeanour meant that he was popular, and the multi-cultural environment enabled him to flourish.

His early days in London had embedded themselves within his DNA. It hooked him and he would spend much of his free time in the West End, the lights, noise, bustle, size, smells, and sounds of it feeding his addiction. However, it was not a place of equality; he was a young black male and was frequently stopped and searched under the sus law. If he drove his BMW, that his parents had bought him, in central or suburban London, he would be stopped almost without exception. It became a way of life. Casual racism was cultural.

By the time Peter was accepted into university, he had made strong friends in a circle of affluence and influence. His dad had said to him when he was quite young that 'you are who you run with' and Peter had taken this to heart. By the mid-eighties, whilst his career in politics was starting, his parents had built up a portfolio of health-related businesses and were becoming very wealthy, although it was never discussed as a family.

Peter didn't fit in the old money environment he worked hard to be a part of, but because he never really found acceptance, he no longer looked for it. He would walk his own path but wear the clothes and speak the words that would make him blend in. He always won people over. That was what made him a formidable politician.

Southall had booked a table in a discreet corner of one of the smaller dining rooms and Blackwood positioned himself so that he was looking out over the other diners and the entrance to the room, which was quietly busy. He recognised a few faces and exchanged subtle nods of acknowledgement. He was early, of course. His mother had taught him that if you are not early to an appointment, you are late. He reviewed the menu whilst he waited for the Met Commissioner. The variety of British game was superb. The cheffery was always exquisite, and it was no surprise to Blackwood why so many of the members looked waxy and overweight. He looked up as movement caught his eye and lumbering towards him was Commissioner Jenks. He suited the surroundings.

Jenks was over six feet tall, in his late fifties at a guess, greying and overweight. He wasn't wearing his uniform today, instead a navy-blue blazer with brass buttons that appeared too small to be buttoned over his potbelly, white shirt, held at the collar by what looked like a school or club tie, rotary badge in his lapel, brown chinos, and highly polished black shoes. Blackwood sighed to himself. This was going to be a long hour and a half. He stood and offered his hand.

'Commissioner,' he greeted.

'Home Secretary,' came the reply as Jenks shook his hand briefly and they both sat. 'Thank you for agreeing to meet at such short notice and for extending this hospitality.' He picked up the menu and started to review. 'I needed to talk to you about a delicate matter that couldn't wait for our usual review. I see grouse is in season. It would be a shame to pass that by.'

'Indeed it would. I am sorry, but this meeting was at short notice, and I am pressed for time today. I have around 45 minutes,' he lied.

'Well, we had better order sharpish, then!' Jenks looked around and, waving, caught the attention of a member staff who approached. 'Veal sweetbreads with black pudding and walnut crumb and spiced carrot purée and then the roast grouse with game chips.' He held up the menu without looking at the waiter.

'For you, Mr Blackwood?' asked the waiter.

'I have a dinner appointment this evening, so salad niçoise please. Would you bring my dish with my guest's starter. My guest will have the 1988 Burgundy, and would you see if you have the '91 Domaine Vacheron Sancerre?' He offered his menu to the waiter with a smile. Jenks had chosen to ignore the timing mentioned, so, Peter took that as acceptance and was pleased that he could now excuse himself earlier than planned. He would leave Jenks to eat his main course alone, free of guilt.

'Of course, sir.' The waiter left to attend to the order.

'How are things at the Yard?' asked Blackwood, opening the conversation.

'We have been working closely with City of London since the Bishopsgate bombing. They are busy constructing the Ring of Steel, which is causing us some headaches. We've a lot on with counter terrorism ops generally, the Provisional IRA are keeping us busy. We've seen a rise in MDMA, or Ecstasy, hitting the streets. It's been spreading out from rave culture and seeping into licenced night-clubs through the West End. We and Essex Police seem to be facing some real issues. Cocaine seems to be gaining traction so we're planning a no-tolerance approach to unlicenced dance events, and we've upped our stop and search policy around parts of London to try and keep it under control. It's changing. The old guard of family firms are making way for more organised, foreign gangs who seem to be much more violent. I'll explain more next time we meet.'

Blackwood 'You know my views on stop and search. It is not a sustainable policy. It is not managed with prudence and ethnic minorities are shown to be disproportionately stopped.'

'I will not change the policies of the Metropolitan Police Force on a whim for the purposes of political correctness, no matter how strongly you, or another Home Secretary, feels about it. Ethnic minorities are disproportionately found to be in possession of controlled substances.'

'Based upon the data collected, which is based upon skewed statistics because black youths are more likely to be selectively targeted…'

'I realise that this a matter close to your heart, Home Secretary…' Jenks' face had started to flush.

Blackwood paused and took a breath. The man opposite him represented the ingrained prejudices that were a root cause of so many of the issues he saw around him. Jenks wasn't a racist in the goose-stepping, black-shirt-wearing sense that was commonly understood. His prejudices were more subtle. He had been raised on the stories of the 'glorious British Empire', and 'cowboys and Indians' movies, where good guys wore white hats, and the bad guys were brown-skinned. No doubt, if pushed, Jenks would have problems with 'queers' and 'the Germans' and every other stereotype that the lazy tabloids and mass media sustained. He chose not to question why Jenks made the last statement. Nothing positive would come from it.

'As Home Secretary, the governance of our police forces is very much close to my heart. Times are changing, Commissioner, and we need to be on the bow, leading the way, otherwise we will be lost in the wake.' Their drinks had arrived, and the waiter had set their places for their lunch.

'Your health, Commissioner.' Peter raised a toast.

'And yours.' Jenks raised his glass and took some wine, which he enjoyed, so took some more. 'How is life at home? Twins are a baptism of fire. We had our three much younger than you and they have all fled the roost, which is a relief.'

'It is a challenge, but one that Rachel is taking on and has stepped up to. Our roles, yours and mine, are demanding and I get little time to be at home and the father I would wish to be. But there is time, and I will make it up.'

'Good. Good. Family is important. The pressures of our roles are demanding, as you say, Home Secretary. Can I call you Peter?' He didn't wait for consent. 'Peter, I need to ask you about Jenny Foxton. She was an intern in your office, I understand.' Their meal had been served and Jenks forked a mouthful of his first course. 'This is outstanding.'

'Jenny was bright and pleasure to have around. I accepted her internship as a favour. Her parents are friends of my family, and I was pleased to help. What of it?' Peter sensed there was more to this.

'Would you say you had a close relationship with her?' Jenks had finished his food.

'Yes, I would.' He decided on brevity, sensing there was more coming.

'Did that close relationship become physical, Peter?' A slight curl to the edge of his mouth gave Blackwood the tell that the Commissioner was enjoying this. 'You wouldn't be the first one.'

Blackwood wiped his mouth with the stiff white linen napkin and set it down. 'No, it didn't.'

'I am afraid that Jenny was found dead a few days ago. Cause of death is still being investigated but is most probably suicide. As part of the investigation, her mobile phone has been reviewed and there are multiple calls logged to a mobile phone number associated with you, Peter. Also in her possession was a business card for a William Anker, a journalist. We are just trying to gain some understanding. Her parents did say that Jenny had worked for you and that you seemed quite close. You understand, we are just looking to avoid any embarrassment for you, Home Secretary. It is all quite run of the mill. Assuming, of course...' He tailed off as to invite an expected response.

Peter's stomach knotted in shock. He had experienced much in life to date, but never before the sudden loss of someone he knew. She was so young. He thought of her first day in his office; she had sheepishly greeted him with a limp handshake. She was wearing a red Jaegar trouser suit, which looked shop-pressed. Her hair was scraped back and it had reminded him of Rachel when they went to a friend's wedding in Bath years earlier.

'Suicide? I don't know what to say, Commissioner. It is quite unexpected news. She was a lovely girl. Very promising. She was a delicate soul.' He took a sip of wine, his mouth dry.

'Delicate?' asked Jenks. The waiter came forward to refill the Commissioner's glass just as he reached forward for a condiment, catching the waiter's arm and forcing red wine to be spilt. 'God damn you, you idiot!' shouted Jenks. 'Fucking moron! I have a meeting this afternoon and now I have a stain on my shirt. My tie is going to be ruined.'

The waiter looked mortified and immediately apologised, 'I am very sorry, sir,' he said. The maître d' was tableside almost immediately, shoeing away the waiter and fussing around Jenks.

Jenks was fully flushed and now in full flow with 'do you know who I am' statements.

Peter wasn't really paying attention and he started to regain his poise. 'Commissioner, really, it's a drop or two of wine. Please remember you are my guest, and I am sure the club will make amends.'

Jenks looked indignant, but he stopped protesting and after a little more fussing around, the staff left them again to their lunch.

'You said delicate. About Jenny, you said she was a delicate soul?' reminded Jenks.

'Yes. I've known Jenny since she was a child. She was always quite withdrawn and nervous. Really very bright, academically successful, but she was morbidly shy and withdrawn. She struggled with anorexia in her mid-teens, but she seemed to get over that. The internship was a favour to her parents. We took her under our wing, my office, and we tried to help her out of her shell whilst she was with us. She was really very popular. I was very fond of her, but it was only a fondness, Commissioner. Poor girl. How's the family?'

'I am not personally involved in the ongoing investigations, but considering your position and connection with the deceased it was deemed prudent to speak with you. And what of the calls to you? There were all multiple calls on the day of her death.'

'I really don't know what to say to that. I am not sure when we last spoke. I had spoken to her a few times since she finished her internship. I had been trying to help her, like a mentor. I am afraid I can't remember the last time we spoke, but my office can check my records.'

'This wasn't your government number, Peter. The calls were made to your line ending 0756.'

'Ah, OK. I took that number a while ago, I had planned to switch over—you know we are advised to regularly change our mobiles. I used it for a while, but, moving contacts, et cetera, is such a faff and I never use my personal number for work, so it seemed an over-precaution. It's been switched off and in a drawer somewhere at home, I think. I will try and find it.'

'If you would, Peter, that would most useful. Standard procedures, you know.'

'You said she had a hack's card with her?' asked Peter.

'Yes. It was thought to be unusual by the investigating officer. He has spoken with the gentleman and apparently, he had no recollection, says he gives them out all the time. It was only the card that prompted a close look at her phone and review the call history.' Jenks didn't acknowledge the different waiter who arrived and placed his main course down.

'I must leave for my next appointment. I will reach out to Mr and Mrs Foxton. They must be devastated. Rachel will be saddened by the news; she's met Jenny a few times. It's such a tragedy. Enjoy your meal, it smells amazing. There is no rush, and the bill is covered.' Blackwood left Commissioner Jenks, who nodded and focused his attention back on his plate.

Leaving the main doors of club, and waving down a taxi, Blackwood did not pay any attention to the man standing on the corner of Bennett Street, discreetly taking photographs.

Peter called Southall from the taxi and asked that he cleared his meetings for the afternoon and headed to their home in Belsize Park. The taxi rattled to a stop outside their white-fronted, four storey home and Peter made his way up the steps to the front door, picking up a soft toy that must have fallen out of the stroller earlier in the morning. They had bought the house as a project property when he was promoted. It was close to Parliament; the area was up and coming and his parents had helped with the purchase so that they had the money for renovations. The lower and ground floors had been finished; the children's nursery and bedrooms being downstairs, and the ground floor was now the kitchen and main living area, open plan as was becoming chic. Dark hardwood floors, a French style kitchen, and chandeliers all gave an opulent and airy feel. Peter put down his briefcase, undid his tie, and kicked off his shoes. Only then did his stockinged foot find the one piece of Lego that hadn't been cleared up. He picked it up, rubbed his foot, called out his arrival, and headed to the kitchen, where poured a soft drink and sat at the island, looking out over the back garden.

'Hi, darling,' greeted Rachel. She gave him a kiss on his cheek. 'You call me and say you're blowing out our date night and then you come home early. Surprise planned? Rosa is with the boys downstairs. Shall I go and put on something black and simple for an early dinner?'

Peter looked at Rachel. Even in her baggy sweatshirt and joggers she looked attractive. Her dark hair was tied up and if she had makeup on, it wasn't obvious, she just looked fresh.

'Afraid not. We've had some terrible news and I needed to come home to deal with it.'

Rachel's playful express changed, and she came round the island and sat next to him. 'What's happened?' she asked with a concerned voice.

'Jenny Foxton has died. It was suicide.'

'Oh, that's terrible.' Rachel held his hand, 'She was so young. How did you find out? Why would she feel the need to do that?' she asked as she gave him a hug.

'Commissioner Jenks came to see me about it. He suggested that I had an affair with her, which I thought was pretty low. She apparently called me on my new number that I haven't switched to yet, so I need to find the phone and shut that down before anyone else draws similar conclusions. We also need to call the Foxtons, they will be devastated. Perhaps we can go and see them tomorrow?'

'I think I know where the phone is. It's up in the drawer in your desk.' Rachel left and headed upstairs to one of the rooms yet to be renovated which was a makeshift office for Peter when he was at home.

She returned with the Nokia 1011 and handed it to Peter. He switched it on. The monochrome screen lit up and after a few moments the phone pinged, and the voicemail message symbol appeared. The couple exchanged glances and Peter dialled in to retrieve the messages. He listened, and without saying anything, he passed the phone to Rachel, who replayed them. They sat in silence for a moment. Rachel's eyes welled up with tears of grief. She hadn't been close to Jenny, but Jenny's distress and despair was clear in her voice. Peter's stomach had knotted again. There was nothing he could do. Had she spoken with him, perhaps she would have been alive today. He hadn't felt this helpless since being a child. He looked to Rachel and felt compelled to say, 'It wasn't my child, you do know that?'

Rachel put her arms around his neck and pressed her forehead against his. 'Of course I do. You didn't need to say that. She told me you were old and ugly anyway.' She gave a little smile as a single tear broke free and rolled down her cheek. 'The poor Foxtons. It wasn't enough that she died so young, but at her own hands too. Pregnant outside of marriage, and they are very Catholic. If the loss alone wasn't enough for them that will devastate them. Let me get you something a little stiffer. You should call them and your parents, she was close to them too. I don't expect you will be able to get out of dinner with the PM, this evening?' she asked.

'Probably not. In any event, I think I should brief him. The optics of this could cause some issues and we should be ahead of them if they do arise. I had better call the Commissioner also and tell him about the pregnancy, although he probably already knows. Thinking it through now, that's probably why he came to see me.'

1648

The fizz-crack of the flintlocks sent a plume of blue smoke into the air, momentarily obscuring his field of vision. He heard the returning volley of shots and the *viip* of the lead balls as they flew past unseen. He dropped his side arms. They were emptied and of no further use. Drawing his broadsword, he ran forward, through the dissipating gun smoke. One of his shots had found its mark, piercing a man's metal breastplate high to the left, the ball exiting through his neck. The man was kneeling, clutching his throat as bubbling blood flowed freely from the wound; he would die quickly. John Astley could remove him as a threat.

Of the three remaining men, one had taken his discharged matchlock musket by the barrel with the intention of using it as a club. He was coming forward to engage Astley. He swung wildly downward, and it was easily parried by Astley's sword. Astley had drawn his dagger from his waist with his other hand and he thrust the blade deep into the chest of his assailant as he continued to advance, knocking the mortally wounded man to the floor. The dagger was caught, probably snared on the man's heavy tunic, so Astley released his grip on the weapon.

He looked to his right and saw one man was frantically trying to re-prime his musket. The other man held a pike. He was hesitant and looked nervous. Astley let out the loudest roar he could muster and sprinted forward. The pikeman was inexperienced and startled by the sound. He raised the pike weakly and said 'please' as Astley grabbed at the pike with one hand and pulled. The pikeman was unbalanced and stumbled into the downward strike of the sword. It cut through flesh and collar bone, slicing muscle, rib, and lung. He was done for. The blade slid free, and Astley's focus turned to the remaining man.

The musketeer had moved backward whilst he hastily recharged his weapon and was raising to take aim. Astley kept moving. The weapon's accuracy was poor, and it was long and heavy, making it unwieldy and slow. He knew the musketeer had to shoot quickly and they both knew he had one chance. He lowered the musket and shot from his hip, dropping the weapon to seize his sword. The musket ball buried itself into the soil safely some distance from its target. Before the musketeer had unsheathed his sword Astley was upon him. He kicked him in his torso, stepping through the kick, knocking the man off his feet and backward. He landed with a thud, winded and vision blurred. Astley thrust his sabre down, twisted, withdrew, and repeated twice more, until the man lay limp on the mossy ground.

The engagement had lasted a few intense minutes at most. No words had been exchanged other than the one plea. The sounds of battle had gone, replaced by an eerie silence. The smell of sulphurous burnt gunpower hung in the still air. The region was a Royalist stronghold and the men that Astley had encountered were not, judging by their military prowess, the small skirmishing unit that he had initially suspected. Most likely they were lost stragglers who had unluckily crossed his path.

Astley's heart rate was slowing, and he felt the perspiration that had flowed for the last few minutes on his brow. Taking a kerchief from his pocket he wiped his forehead, cleaned his blade on the tunic of the last-slain soldier, sheathed his sword, and retraced his movements, collecting and cleaning his discarded weaponry.

As the adrenaline faded, he started to feel the pain in his shoulder. There was a deep, new dent in his gorget, made by a musket ball that must have hit him in the initial volley. To its right, his red coat was wet with blood where a large part of the shrapnel from the shattered musket ball had ricocheted, penetrating deep into his shoulder.

He sat at their small campfire, the embers of which were still glowing and heating a pot of meat stew. He attempted to remove the shrapnel, but, with only his left hand he lacked the dexterity, and the pain was intolerable. He used his kerchief to stem the flow of blood as best he could by plugging the jagged and painful injury with its material. Pushing the cloth into the wound made him feel faint. He knew this needed attending to—many combatants died not on the battlefield, but days after (if they were lucky, in their homes) from fever and delirium from an infected and foul injury.

He ate his fill of the stew and filled his canteen. Sated, he returned to the task at hand. He didn't have the means or time to bury the vanquished. He checked their pockets for orders or other papers that could be of use, took their shot and powder. Their blades were inferior to his, so he piled them together next to the four bodies which lay in a neat row, like four morbid siblings tucked together for a night's sleep.

His orders were clear: he had to make his way surreptitiously to his destination. The missive he carried was by the hand of the King himself and it been smuggled at great risk by a network of spies and sympathisers from his captivity in Carisbrooke Castle. Astley was responsible for the last leg of its journey. He checked his breast pocket and was reassured that the letter was still on his person and undamaged. He returned to his horse and recommenced his journey north-west towards the mountains.

It was still a full day's ride to the valley marked on his map and the sun was low, casting long, dark shadows down the hillside when he arrived. He felt weak and thirsty. As he approached the stone cottage and its single barn, a figure came from within. He was dressed simply in the robe of a monk, but he didn't look like a man of God. He was tall and gaunt. His hair was unkempt, and he wore beads around his neck. Astley slowed as he approached, he glanced down at his pistols to ensure they were primed and rested one hand on the pummel of his sword.

'Good morrow. How now?' called Astley once he was within distance.

'Well, and you?' replied the monk. 'I would say you are John Astley. Word was sent of your arrival. We share many friends.' He bowed slightly and gestured for Astley to approach. 'I am Master Wyllyam, and you must be gut-foundered from your long ride. Come inside, food has been prepared.'

Astley felt relief and let the fatigue and pain he had been fighting wash over him. He slumped forward and then slowly fell off the horse, landing limply and unconscious.

Wyllyam dragged Astley into the cottage and, removing his weaponry and tunic, rolled him onto the straw filled bed. Astley's white shirt had been reddened through loss of blood, his face was pale, his skin was covered with light perspiration, and his breathing was shallow. He was near the end of his life. Wyllyam inspected the wound and pushed his finger deep. He found the projectile and, hooking his fingertip underneath, pulled it back. As he did so, more blood flowed as though the remnants of the shot had stemmed the blood flow.

He had a simple binary decision; he could repair the injured man and in doing so reveal his darkest secret, likely instigating his own torture and death by drowning, hanging, or fire, or he could step back and let this stranger drift into history.

He took the blooded letter from the tunic and read it. The King's orders were calling for a daring rescue by dragon: a foolhardy, reckless command driven probably by desperation. He walked to the fire and threw the letter into its heart and watched it catch and burn to ashes. He turned to Astley, who lay still, life having ebbed away.

Phoenix

DAFFYD

'25th February

The dragon has been lethargic for some weeks and appears to be unwell. I have not ventured from the cave for some time. There is much unrest across the country and the New Model Army appear to be gaining the upper hand, feeding off the weakness of the crown which I can only explain to the weaker Grym being afforded the King and his troops. I am fearful that if the dragon does not regain its strength our King will be lost.

'I been reading through our literature, and I have tried to use the incantations of Gwydion, Atlantes, Alatar, and the great Merlin, but none seem to have a prolonged effect. Some of my efforts have caused minor mayhem; through my poor translation I conjured a Shirime which came to me late evening as I rested by the lake. I was unsure of its intentions as it approached, and it was dressed in a fashion that was not familiar to me. As it came within proximity it dropped its robes, bent over, and spread its ample buttocks to reveal a giant, shining eye. The sight was most off-putting, but once it had completed its task, its origin as well as its rectal peeper had been revealed to me. Shirimes are simple beings, innocuous of nature. I felt it unnecessary to rescind my magic and allowed the creature to recover its clothes and retreat at pace into the forest. If the Chorts that reside there do not feed on it, I am sure it will be back with the view of entertaining itself with the joy of scaring me, which I will feign for its benefit. I shall welcome the light relief.

28th February

'I have burned three candles since I last wrote in my journal. The dragon grows weaker and now refuses to fly. Although it greets me with affection, I can see that it is unhappy. I have found its scales are becoming dull and loose to the touch. I did attempt to extract one, but the dragon did twitch and gave me a look that warned me not to proceed. I have mixed many ingredients into a broth of health, and I am having some success at encouraging the beast to imbibe small amounts at a time. I have sought answers from the bones and from meditation but there is nothing that suggests the beast is to die. Mamddaear is in equilibrium, so perhaps my fears are unfounded.

'I had word that a member of the Order would arrive, and he was present today. He was weak from an injury that proved to be mortal. He carried a message from the King, calling to be rescued from imprisonment on the Isle of Wight. The beast does not have the strength to fight, nor even to fly. I cannot leave it whilst it suffers this illness, and I cannot get word back to the King. I am torn between my oath to serve our King and my oath to protect this noble beast.

'I have hatched many plans that would directly change events, but I must not go through with any for fear of betraying the Order. I have listened to Mamddaear, and it will unfold as it should, and it will be clear to me when it is time. It would seem to me that the only course of action is to remain here and focus my efforts on the treatment of the dragon, bringing him to health so that his Grym Pwerus can aid our King.

3rd March

'I was woken from my slumber by a sound which was unfamiliar. I ventured from the Keep discovering the dragon in a state of much distress. It was pacing and moving with great agitation. I approached and touched its head. The heat was intense, and I withdrew my hand in fear that I may damage myself. The dragon was breathing with difficulty, and I could feel heat coming from its skin. I withdrew some distance, and as I did so, the dragon started to change its colour to become a bright red. The heat was intense, and I was forced to move further back. The dragon sat upright on its haunches and lifted its head high and in doing so extended it wings. It was a glorious sight to see the rampant dragon. From its mouth flew a jet of white flame high into the air above. Immediately following, the dragon was engulfed in a pyre that made the very land on which it stood burn. The heat beat me into retreat as I watched the inferno. The flame was so bright and intense that I could no longer watch and had to look away. In a short while I felt the air start to lose its heat and I looked back. Where the dragon had laid was dark ash and smouldering soil. As the smoke cleared there appeared a new creature, born of the flame; a phoenix. It took to the sky and flew away into the darkness.'

Dafydd stopped reading and closed the book. 'That was the first full account of a dragon's lifecycle, written by the Master Wyllyam in 1648. The previous report wasn't so detailed, but you can read it another day. He was slightly mistaken: the phoenix was an infant dragon. All phoenixes are newborn dragons. Through his observation we learned that dragons reincarnate. Their life cycle is not fully clear—we think they live for around five to six hundred years, as the previous dragon reincarnation was around 1060.'

'That's insane,' said Amy. 'The dates. They tie in with William the Conqueror and this writing is from the English Civil War?'

'Yes, the dragons *Grym Pwerus* supports the Crown. When it is weak so is the Crown. This is why its presence is so precious and such a secret. Although a new dragon is born with each cycle, it is the same dragon, of sorts. It retains memories. You recall your experience when you first touched and coupled with the dragon? The scenery that was shared with you, that must be a previous life. Anglesey's woodland was cleared long ago for arable land. So it carries with it an epoch of memories and experience, which is a sign of its *Grym Pwerus*. I keep saying memories, but it's more of an access to a stream of consciousness that is *Mamddaear*, which we can all plug into. Left to complete its cycle, a dragon is reborn from its own flame, and nothing remains of the previous incarnation. They must have reproduced at one time. We simply don't know, and the dragon cannot tell us; it has no memories during the process.'

'That would explain why we aren't finding dragon fossils and bones?' asked Amy.

'We think so, although the remains of the ones that were killed through hunting seem to have been used at the time. Perhaps we have objects around in museums that are of dragon bone but attributed to large game or whale bone. There is no need to press the point as it is convenient for us; we can keep dragons and wizards a part of modern fantasy for as long as possible,' replied Dafydd. 'The dragon likes you and I have found him to be an impeccable judge of character.'

'You always refer to the dragon as "he"?'

'Yes, force of habit. If you want to call it "her" or anything you want, you fill your boots. I don't think he cares particularly.' Dafydd took up another book and passed it to Amy. 'I think you are highly receptive to *Mamddaear*, do you want to want to see what you can do?'

'What do you mean? Magic? Me, really? Fu–' She stopped herself. A rush of excitement ran through her. 'Is the Pope Catholic? Of course I do. Yes, please!'

'We will start with something simple and see how you go. To help you tune in, you should hold your *Hudcloch* tight and close your eyes. I want you to try and clear your mind. It's like meditation and it can take time so don't be disappointed if it doesn't come immediately. I will whisper the *Englyn* into your ear; we never speak our magic out loud and eventually you will only need to think of them. The gift of language I gave you will help you remember the words, so don't panic.' Dafydd lent forward and muttered in her ear and then sat back. 'I am going to take some stones from the ground and hold them in my hand. When you are ready, clear your mind, grip your *Hudcloch*, feel the stones as though they are in your hand and tell me how many I am holding. Okay? Ready when you are.'

Amy did as instructed. She tried to clear her mind. *I've done it*, she thought. Then she swore to herself—she was thinking. Again. She concentrated on nothing. *I wonder what's for dinner*, she thought. She swore in her head again. *Right. Focus. Think of nothing. Blank. Space. How far away is the moon?* She opened her eyes. 'I can't do it.'

'Yes, you can. Just close your eyes. Breathe. It's like going to sleep: that moment just before you lose consciousness, when you feel you are weightless and empty. It will come, try again,' said Dafydd patiently.

Amy tried again and after a few moments opened her eyes and with a smile said, 'Three!'

Dafydd opened his palm to show a single stone. 'You are rushing. We have time. Just slow down.'

'Again.' Amy didn't like to fail at anything. What other people said was stubbornness, she preferred to think of as tenacity. 'Let's go again.'

Dafydd readjusted his seating, making himself as comfortable as he could. He realised that they might at this for some time. 'No cheating. Go.'

Two Pints

Plod was standing at the bar laughing with the landlord when Anker walked in. It had been raining. His hair was matted down his forehead, and as he walked over, he turned his collar down and wiped rain from his face. The cold air outside had caused condensation to form on the windows of the Chippy and the atmosphere felt damp. It was unusually busy and there were no booths available as he walked up to Brown.

'What's so funny?' Anker asked.

'I didn't know the story of his crooked nose. It's great. Can I tell it?' Brown looked to the landlord who nodded his approval. 'Two pints, please,' he asked, then he turned back to Anker. 'So, back in the day, he was at a superheroes fancy-dress party, and he was busting for pee. It was a house party and he had to queue for the toilet, but eventually it was his turn and by this time he REALLY needed to piss. You know, when you're jigging on the spot and thinking of anything other than needing a piss. He was fumbling around trying to undo the fly on his pants and was so desperate that he gave up and just pulled them down and started to go. The door to the bathroom slammed open and this drunk girl, dressed as Wonder Woman, came in.

'She was staggering around and saw that he was using the toilet, so, she pulled down her bottoms, sat on the side of the bath, and started to pee. She was hammered, right, so she lost her balance and fell backward into the bath and banged her head on the other side. She screamed and there was blood in her hair, everywhere. This all happened quick, right? So, he turns around and stands in front of her to pull her out. At this point, her boyfriend – the Hulk – came in the bathroom and saw him standing between his girlfriend's legs, her in the bath with legs spread-eagled, both their pants down around their ankles, blood and tears. Well, he couldn't speak fast enough and because his pants were around his ankles, he couldn't move fast enough either. Boom! Broken nose. Apparently, the Hulk, who played Prop for the local rugby club, was apologetic when his girlfriend had explained what had happened. Fucking love it!'

Anker laughed and nodded to the landlord, who simply stared back at him straight faced and said, '£5.40.'

'Jenny Foxton has committed suicide,' said Anker before he drank from his glass, 'I had a call from the police because they found my business card in her things in the car. I said that I give out my cards all the time, especially to girls in clubs, so I had no idea who she was. She must have been a fucking mess, I said so to you after I met her; she looked like she was on the edge. Seen it before.'

Brown shook his head. 'You have no empathy at all, do you? She was someone's daughter, and she was pregnant. It's no wonder you live alone in some damp bedsit in South London. You're lucky that you pay me to talk to you—otherwise, you'd be standing here on your Jack.'

'It's a new build flat. With a gym and coffee shop on the ground floor. Everything that *Rising Damp* isn't. You rang me, what've you got for me?' asked Anker.

'I wish it was a soul, but they asked who it was for and when I told them, they said they were out of stock. So, it's work related. I have friends all over the place. Forty years in a job sees a lot of people come and go and unlike you, I am personable. One of those old colleagues contacted me to let me know that that Blackwood had a last-minute meeting with Commissioner Jenks at Blackwood's club. I was there before they arrived, and I have photographs of both of them going in and leaving separately.

'I managed to speak with someone who works at the club, one of the waiters and he has gone on record to confirm that Jenny Foxton's name came up in conversation. Apparently, Jenks managed to rub the waiter up the wrong way. He almost lost his job, he's been demoted, and he has an axe to grind. He didn't seem too worried about discretion after I offered to pay him. The money they are on is shit for the hours they work, and they have to put up with pompous wankers like Jenks. He was working his way up in the force whilst I was there. Real self-abuser. He did as little day-to-day policing as he could. Probably too scary for him. He moved into management and started to climb the greasy pole, probably one of those funny-handshaking mob.

'I've incurred expenses gathering both pieces of information. Here is the statement, the photographs and my bill to date.' Brown handed Anker an envelope.

'Fucking excellent!' said Anker, 'How do you do it? You have excelled! With these and the recorded messages, I've got enough to publish. I have tried to call to get a comment from Blackwood—spoke to his office and got the usual referral to the press office. This might even make front page if it's a slow news day tomorrow.' Anker was motioning a headline as he spoke. '"Minister quizzed over suicide," that's not snappy enough. "Black's Wood", that might be too cryptic. I'll get the next round in. A couple of pints will help my creativity.'

'I'm not the journalist here, but are you sure you want to push this? Jenny was only a bit older than my daughter and she obviously had some troubles. Why is this in the public's interest?' Brown was used to digging out those things people didn't want found, but this was uncomfortable. Usually the targets were fame-hunters, would-bes, has-beens, nasty, or nutters. This was different and he quite liked what Blackwood stood for.

'Of course it's public interest. This is about the man's integrity. He holds one of the highest Offices of State, he is responsible for law enforcement and national security. If he can't keep his hands off his junior staff, who's to say he can be trusted with state security? It's dynamite. I'm going to shoot off, write this up, and get it filed.' He emptied his glass, wiped his mouth and then patted Brown on his shoulder with the same hand. 'I'll call you tomorrow and we can look into following this up.'

Back at his flat, Anker settled on his sofa. Before he put the ThinkPad on his lap and his feet on the coffee table, he took out the small, wrapped-up piece of paper from his wallet, tipped some of the white crystal content onto his knuckle, and snorted hard. Just a little assistance to keep him focused, he thought. He was on fire. He loved this part of the job. Partly satisfied with the knowledge that he was the first to break a story, partly satisfied that it was his work and contacts that found the story to break, and partly because he always loved the email from his editor congratulating him because that last part was the money. It didn't take him long:

HOME SEC QUESTIONED OVER PREGNANT GIRL'S DEATH

William Anker

The Home Secretary, Peter Blackwood, has been assisting police with enquiries into the death of a young woman, whose body was discovered at Trent Country Park early on Thursday.

The body of Jenny Foxton, 23, of Cockfosters, Hertfordshire, was found in her car in the early hours. Miss Foxton was pregnant at the time of her death and up until recently was working in the Home Secretary's office as part of his personal staff.

Blackwood, married with twin sons, has been a controversial appointment as Home Secretary and has been outspoken on many issues around immigration and law and order. It is understood that Blackwood was questioned by the Commission of the Met Police two days ago in the swanky private members' club, Smithson's in London's St James's.

The cause of death is yet to be determined. Neither Blackwood nor the Foxton family were available for comment.

ENDS

That should do it, Anker thought as he clicked 'send'. The piece was short, and he wouldn't have submitted it if the story wasn't so strong. He predicted there would be a strong reaction, with enough interviews, comment, and opinion to would keep him busy with copy for the next few days, provided the editor agreed to run it. Anker was confident that this was gold, so they would go to print. He opened another bottle of San Miguel, picked up his Walkman, and went to lay in bed, waiting for the cocaine to relax its grip on his senses and permit some sleep.

Beetle

'Just watch.' Dafydd shook his cupped hands and then threw the contents on the kitchen table. The collection of small animal bones rattled to a stop. He glanced at Kath who was seated at the table, watching. Dafydd scooped them up and repeated. The bones fell exactly as they had before. 'One more time,' he said, looking to Kath. Again, the bones rattled over the worn, uneven wooden surface and came to rest in an identical formation. He looked to Kath once more.

He scooped the bones up, tied them up in a small pouch, and put it to one side. 'I have tried this, too.' He took a coin and, muttering, flipped it on to the table. Heads. No-one spoke as he repeated this ten times and on each occasion the coin rested heads up. 'Enough of that?'

'OK,' agreed Kath.

'Last one,' he said. He placed the salt and pepper pots some distance apart on the table, took out a match box, and opened it, tipping a small beetle onto the table. He closed his eyes and muttered once more, and the beetle scuttled to the pepper mill. He gently picked up the beetle and repeated, placing it with a different starting point. Again, the beetle headed immediately to the pepper mill. 'I have tried many variations, and I am getting the same response. I have been asking for guidance as to who my apprentice should be. This is a difficult position, but I have no doubts the answer is clear. I have seen enough. You have seen them together, Amy and the dragon. The bond is undeniable—it was from the very first time she touched him. The memory shared was his most precious, his happiest. I had gone back through our texts and there hasn't been a connection recorded to be this strong since Uther. Her *Grym* is strong, and she has a natural affinity to *Mamddaear*. She can't see it, of course, but she draws power to her like I have not seen. I have taught her some rudimental enchantments and she took to them instantly, correctly, and they lasted.' He flicked the beetle off the table and watched as it righted itself on the floor and started to head to the back door. 'Every question I asked about the path ahead tells me that Amy should be my apprentice, not Marcus. The dragon met Marcus, what, twelve years ago? It wouldn't go near him. I should have seen it.'

'I've been watching the two of you, and it's obvious that you see more in her. I know that I make light of everything and the Davies do the same, I think. That is how we handle this, all this. It's madness if you look from the outside. We're just a group of nutters that believe in dragons and magic and nonsense, living in the middle of nowhere. No-one could believe the truth and you've bombarded Amy with the whole thing in next to no time. It is a testament to the cleverness, or open mindedness, of that girl that she hasn't run off and sent in the whitecoat and net brigade to take us all to a secure unit.

'You're now saying that you want to take that university educated girl from Southern England, who's been raised on traditional religion and science, and ask her to throw aside all she has been taught, throw away all her opportunities, and live here with us to learn from you?'

'She will not throw aside anything. She will be thinking differently, yes, but it is not what I want. It is what *Mamddaear* will see happen. As you can see, the path is unavoidable, she will be drawn to it. Even if she headed in a different direction she would end up here.'

'The decision is Amy's to make. You'll need to speak to Tom and Claire first. God only knows what they are going to think. I understood before I married you that I wasn't just becoming your wife. We had also known each other for ages and your, erm, eccentricities were endearing, over time. Then when it was all explained, I was almost relieved. As much as we joke and you play the fool, I see you for what you really are and how important you are to this place.' She reached over and placed her hand over his. 'You'll need to steer this with caution. Marcus will not react well to this news; it will break his heart,' said Kath.

Dafydd nodded. 'It will unfold as it should. None of this was apparent before now and it is unavoidable. It will be difficult for Marcus and us, I have no doubt, but this is the path forward and the journey will become clear as we travel it. You know in your heart from what you have seen and what has passed, that Marcus is not right. All the signs were there. Perhaps I was blinded by hope that he would change. He is my son, but he is not the apprentice.

'I cannot un-teach him what he has learned, but I cannot have more than one apprentice. With his current knowledge he can carve a meaningful place for himself and contribute in ways that will not be seen by others. That will give him the satisfaction he needs, over time.' Dafydd sighed. He knew his words were hollow and that Kath could probably see through them. 'I have some work to do in preparation and I will go and see the Davies this evening. Amy has been in London and is due back soon. When she returns, that's when I will to talk to her and Marcus.'

Marcus had been standing against the hall wall, just outside the kitchen door, eavesdropping. Burning embers of anger and jealousy ignited and intensified as he heard every word. His fists clenched so hard that his knuckles turned white. He turned and silently walked upstairs to his room, gently closing the door behind himself. His head was spinning, and emotions were rushing through him: betrayal, envy, sadness, anger. He wanted to break everything, wanted to call a lightning storm, but he was still in control enough not to betray his hidden skills. He could make a train derail and crash, cause a landslide, invoke a tsunami, start a fire. He was so close to starting the incantation, but had just enough will power to hold back. He could do any of it, or all of if he wanted to. *Fuck them all. Fuck dad. Fuck mum. Fuck it all.* He took his rucksack from the top of his wardrobe and quickly filled it with his waterproofs and personal stereo, and headed out of the house. He didn't know where he was going, but he knew for sure he couldn't stay there any longer.

Dafydd set off to the cave. He had to make sure that everything would be in place.

Wimbledon

Amy had only planned to visit her parents for a long weekend, and she had stayed for many weeks. Although she hadn't, she felt she had outstayed her welcome and that it was time to head back to her home and digest everything she had experienced. She felt that she was returning to London a different person to the one who had left.

The Victorian terrace house she shared with two friends from university was a short walk from Southfields tube station. They had become tight-knit and socialised together often, but now university was over and the tenancy agreement was due to end, they would probably go their separate ways as they found jobs, moved back to their hometowns, or travelled. They took care of the property they shared. They had all agreed when they decided to lease together that it was their home and would be their 'safe place'. They rarely held parties, no-one had locks on their doors, and partners were seldom bought back. That all meant that the property was well kept and clean, and when she swung open the door and dropped her rucksack on the floor, she smelt the scent of home. She called out, but no-one answered. There was a small bunch of daffodils on the kitchen table with a welcome home note from her flatmates. 'Glad you are back from the wilderness, we are in the Felix. X.'

Amy showered, dried her bobbed hair, jumped into her favourite baggy cargos, Kangol t-shirt, denim jacket and headed out to meet her friends. The Felix had become their second home. It was a fresh, new bar owned and run by a couple of women who she thought were only a few years older than she was. It was unusual for owners to be of their age, almost unique that they were female. She had overheard people ask them for an introduction to the owners and it was entertaining to see their reaction of incredulity or embarrassment when they released their faux pas. They were always great hosts but behind their *bon viveur*, they were clearly ambitious and driven; the rumour was they were close to closing a deal that would mean more sites, even a national franchise. Their attitude fed into the venue, and it attracted people of a similar age, and it was always lively. Blackboards with carefully calligraphed white chalk menus and large mirrors were on the walls. It had an open-plan layout with a bar running the full length of one wall and bench-style seating. At weekends there would be a queue to enter, but as Amy and her friends were regulars, they were always waved through.

It was 'Thirsty Thursday'; Thursday evening was the new Friday night and it had become popular to go out, adding an extra evening to the weekend. Lucy and Ann had arrived and laid claim to their place early, guaranteeing a seat and table space before it filled up. They spotted Amy as soon as she walked in, and both came and greeted her with hugs.

'So good to see you,' said Ann. 'Kieran's been pining for you. Every time he comes in, he asks when you'll be back. No doubt he and his knobby mates will be in later. What have you been up to?' she asked.

'You wouldn't believe me if I told you,' said Amy as they sat and filled glasses. 'So, what's been going on while I've been away?'

'I've been offered an analyst job in the City,' said Lucy proudly. 'It's in Canary Wharf and I've found a flat share in Limehouse. I can't wait! My dad said it's not the proper City, but you should see the cranes that are going up and the Jubilee Line will be opening in the next year or so. Once you are out of the main square it's a bit of ghost town at the moment, a bit rough actually. The offices are cool, though. It's a big American bank, so if I play my cards right, I'll be off over the "pond".'

'Here's to that,' said Ann raising her glass. 'It's been quiet without you kicking around, Amy. How's the family?'

Before she answered, Ann spotted Kieran accompanied by his usual friends. They acknowledged each other and whilst Kieran came over, his friends greeted others and headed to the bar. As much as Amy tried to hide it, she was attracted to him. The attraction was mutual, and they had flirted on and off since they met in the Felix a while ago. She didn't like short men as she was tall at five feet eight—Kieran was a few inches over six feet and was still slim. He had been quite sporty in his teens and kept active, so he was holding off any early signs of adult spread around his waist. He was funny and engaging, but not cocky. In fact, he was a bit of dork. He shared her love of films, but he crossed the nerd line with comic books and seemed have an encyclopaedic knowledge of music from the 70s and 80s. He was twenty-five and worked in a local company in some sort of support role, but they hadn't really talked about work as Amy had been at university, so it wasn't common ground. She thought that he would get on with her dad and it was that sort of thought that had kept him at arm's length. She wasn't really looking for a partner, but was enjoying life as she was.

'Ah, she's back!' Kieran said as he gave her a brief hug and kiss on the cheek as he had done with Ann and Lucy, although this lingered slightly longer. 'They'll be pleased here to see you back. Takings have been down while you were away. So, how was the trip?'

'Good, turns out that my parents are secret government agents, our tenant is a wizard, and we have a dragon that lives under a lake. So, same old,' she replied.

'Run of the mill stuff, then. As we're sharing secrets you need to know that I am Batman and Steve over there is Robin.' He pointed to his friend at the bar who was the shortest member of the group and overweight. 'The sight of him in his leotard is enough to bring any uber-criminal to his knees.'

'Twatman and Throbbing,' she quipped.

'Oww, great porn film name, wanna star?' He held up his hands and looked through them like film lenses, 'Humm, perhaps a role off camera would be better. You could be my fluffer.' He smiled.

Amy punched his arm, 'You keep dreaming, Twatman'.

They all sat, talked, laughed, and drank together, and as the evening progressed, Steve suggested they started to play Spoof for shots. Each of the group held out a hand with up to three coins in their closed palm and took a turn guessing the total number held, but they were not able to call the same number as another. The person who guessed correctly would be out of the next round and so it would go on until one person was left, and they would have to drink the random cocktail, in one go, that the previous loser purchased. The activity expediated their alcoholic intake and after several rounds Amy and Kieran were left in the final head-to-head.

Kieran stared at the closed fists before him and then into Amy's eyes, looking for a clue. 'Three,' he guessed.

Amy didn't want to lose and wanted to see Kieran drink the Aunt Roberta cocktail that sat in between them. Steve had lost the last round, and this drink was a mix of gin, vodka, absinthe, brandy, and blackberry liquor, a combination she didn't relish having to knock back. She had an idea. Although quite drunk, she tried to centre her thoughts and she recanted a brief chant in her mind. She then knew Kieran had two coins, as did she. *OK*, she thought, *that's the easy part, let's see how much you learned.* She changed chant.

'Hurry up!' called Steve, slapping the table.

'He's right, isn't he!' said Ann. Lucy oohed. Kieran and Joseph were leaning forward, waiting.

'Five,' said Amy. Kieran opened his hand to show two coins. Amy did likewise and in her palm were three coins. Not only had she felt his cash, she had also conjured another coin. *I DID IT,* she thought to herself and smiled broadly. 'Come on then, fella, knock it back like a good boy, Twatman!' She slid the glass towards Kieran as everyone cheered.

Lucy stood. 'I will raise a toast, to my flatmates and new-found soulmates.' Her companions drummed the table with their hands. 'The last few years have been a blast, and I will always remember these days. Although we will soon close a door on our shared home, let's not let these friendships end. Amy, you are a neat freak and annoyingly clever. Ann, you make so much noise during sex, my ears still bleed, but you make a mean curry. You lot,' she said as she waved at the men at their table, 'You're boys and everything that comes with that, but you buy the drinks. I love you all.' They all cheered.

'Right, back to ours!' announced Ann. 'We'll stop and get some provisions from Kystals on the way home.'

The six made their way back to the house carrying several plastic bags with freshly bought alcohol. The evening was taking on a chill and the streets were quiet. The trees had lost most of their leaves and the streetlights cast long spindly shadows down the road. Amy and Kieran were walking at the back of the group.

'Tarantino will be one of the greatest directors in Hollywood history. *Reservoir Dogs* was almost Shakespearean in accomplishment. Stripped back locations, character development, slick script. It's got to be up there as one of the all-time great gangster movies,' argued Kieran.

'It's not a gangster movie, it's a heist movie. *The Getaway* with Steve McQueen and Ali MacGraw knocks *Reservoir Dogs*. What about *The Sting* or *The Italian Job*? If you are talking about gangster movies, then Tarantino has tough competition: *Goodfellas, Once Upon a Time in America, Scarface, The Long Good Friday*. If you want something a little more British, and the true godfathers of the genre, there are no others than the *Godfather* movies,' said Amy.

'Unusually for franchises, the sequel was better than the original. *Godfather II* was better than *The Godfather*,' added Kieran.

'Controversial,' said Amy. 'Not sure I agree, although *The Empire Strikes Back* was the strongest of the *Star Wars* trilogy.'

'Ok. So what is your all-time favourite movie? I bet it's some cliché like *It's a Wonderful Life*, or *Breakfast at Tiffany's*,' asked Kieran.

'Tough question. I used to sit with my dad on rainy Sundays when we lived in Chingford and watch all the Ealing comedies, which he loves. So, I would say it's a toss-up between *The Ladykillers, School for Scoundrels* or maybe *The Man in the White Suit*. That's a sentimental selection, I know, before you shoot me down. What about you?'

'*Scarface*, all the way. Well, maybe *Jaws*. We should have a movie night, bring our favourite film on video. We'll get a take-away, have a few drinks…' asked Kieran.

There was Kieran's move. 'I'd like that, but don't be turning up with a *Carry On* movie.' As they walked into her house, Amy noticed the red light on the answer machine was winking, and out of habit, she pressed play.

'Amy, it's dad. Give me a call when you get this. I have news we need to tell you.' The message beeped its end. It was unusually curt for her dad, but Amy didn't think too much of it.

'I'll call him in the morning—who's up for a game of Shot Jenga?'

Her question was met with rousing approval. Drinks were distributed and the table cleared, and it was set to be a long and noisy night.

Mad Dogs

Marcus was sitting alone at a corner table in the Black Lion. The pub was quiet as it was late afternoon, not that it was ever busy during the day. It was the only pub in the village, which meant if you were local, everyone knew who you were. It only served hot food at lunchtime at the weekend, and it was closed on Mondays and Tuesdays. The carpet was busily patterned crimson, and its exposed timber beams were painted black with white-washed walls. The few pictures that hung were monochrome photos of local rugby legends from bygone days. At the bar, there was a row of brass beer pumps with several turned around, indicating that barrels of local bitter were out, and a RNLI collection box in the shape of an old lifeboat sat next to a grey payphone at the far end.

He had been in there for an hour and had only seen two other customers come in; the old boys were sitting in another corner of the pub in companionable silence nursing their pints of beer. He didn't see the point of old people. They shuffled around looking for things to fill their days, hoping for visits from their long-fled offspring and waiting for death. The television on the wall was playing Sky Sports to an absent audience and the bar was devoid of staff. He thought that they should rename it the Mary Celeste.

Marcus didn't need many people to be around. In fact, only one witness would do. He took a sip from his drink. It tasted foul. Many things in life confused him and why people pretended to take pleasure from drinking this shite was beyond him. It wasn't the taste but the effect they craved, and if they only opened their minds they could experience so much more without having to consume nasty-tasting liquid. He was only partly paying attention to the room as he was coupled with his dogs, who were in the kitchen at home. He was biding his time. His anger had passed, but he was resolute in both emotion and action.

Back at their house, Dafydd came home through the front door, pulled off his rubber boots and called out, 'I'm back. All done.'

Kath was in the living room, reading and she looked up. 'Get me a cuppa, would you, hun?'

He opened the kitchen door and quietly cursed whoever it was that had left the back door open to swing in the wind and let the warm air escape.

Through his dogs' eyes, Marcus could see his dad walk into the kitchen and make his way to close the back door. '*Yn awr*,' he said quietly. Zeus started to growl, the hairs down its back standing up to form a low ridge. Dafydd looked over to the dog and started to lean towards him, extending his arm as if he was about to stroke the family pet. At that moment, Zeus lunged up and forward. It bit down hard, catching the soft tissue around Dafydd's cheek, nose and jaw. Marcus could hear the crunch as his dad's jaw succumbed to the pressure and Marcus's mouth filled with the warm, wet sensation of blood. Marcus knew he could not disengage from the coupling, even as he felt sick, which forced a gag, tears welling in his eyes. He fought them back and took a sip of beer to counter the phantom taste.

Dafydd fell back against the stove under the force of the dog's weight and power, unable to call out as Zeus had his face held in its vice jaw. He tried to push the dog back as they tumbled to the floor. He flailed around, reaching for something, anything to help him. The dog released its bite momentarily and came back in, this time finding his neck and tearing into Dafydd's muscle, piercing his windpipe and jugular. He tried to call out, but he could make no sound. He could only hear growling. Marcus sensed his dad was gripping on the dog's ears, trying to pull its head back as it shook vigorously, tearing more flesh.

Dafydd was kicking against the floor, trying to gain purchase. The only noises were the growling of the dogs, the scratch of their claws, and Dafydd's heels hitting the stone floor. Apollo, who had been hesitant, now took a bite into Dafydd's calf, pulling and tearing his jeans, shredding his calf muscle. Life was rapidly draining from Dafydd. All Marcus could see was a mass of flesh and blood, his nose filled with the smell of meat and his mouth with the taste of iron from the blood. He could hear the burbling gasps from his dad's final breaths as his heart stopped beating. Marcus didn't want to see anymore, but he could not uncouple just yet. He was pale and sweating. The old men noticed his appearance.

Kath heard a tremendous crash from the kitchen and then more noise that she couldn't place. 'Hun?!' she called out. 'Everything okay out there?' There was no answer but the sounds were continuing. She tutted and stood up. Kath opened the door to the kitchen and at first glance wasn't able to decipher the scene in front of her. She gasped in horror as she realised, and at that moment, both blood-covered dogs attacked, slamming Kath to the floor in the hall. She had instinctively shielded her face and neck with her arms as they jumped but both dogs had latched on to an arm each and were now pulling against one another, like two dogs playing with rope. She was screaming out for help. Apollo released its grip and bit down on her side, crushing ribs, its teeth and her bone puncturing her lungs. Kath's tendons in her arms were severed, so she was defenceless as Zeus gripped her neck and tore into her throat. Blood fountained up the wall to the ceiling. Kath became limp as the dogs continued to ferociously bite and tear at flesh and sinew.

Marcus slumped forward, his head shattering his beer glass, bringing him to his senses in the pub. Both older drinkers had come over and were already at his side, helping him to sit back.

'I think you've had enough, butty,' said one. 'You're the Merlinis' lad, aren't you? I'll give them a call and get them to come and get you.' The other man had walked behind the bar and raised the landlord who was now coming to offer assistance.

'No, thank you. I am a diabetic. I just need some sugar—a Coke or some chocolate would help, please,' he lied. He was free of the dogs' senses, but all he could see was look in his parents' eyes, the fear, the blood. 'If you can call me a cab, I'll get home and use my insulin pen. Thank you, I don't know what I would have done if you hadn't come to help me.'

The elderly men sat with Marcus, again in silence, as they waited for the taxi. They saw him into the car and Marcus sat in the back, maintaining his silence as it wound its way up the valley towards his house. It was almost done and then he could relax. *Just a few more minutes*, he thought.

The car pulled up outside their home and, getting out, Marcus said, 'I need to go and get some cash, back in a minute.'

He walked through the front door and closing it behind himself he leaned against the wall. He felt dizzy. It wasn't necessary to go further into the house. He glanced down the hall briefly. He could see a mass lying motionless on the floor, the walls and much of the flooring still wet with blood. The smell hit him, making him nauseous, and he retched dryly. He focused and found the dogs were nearby, calm, and not aware he was in the house. He opened the front door and retched once more, this time bringing up the contents of his stomach. 'Call an ambulance!' he shouted. 'Stay in the car!' He ran back to car and jumped in, closing the door behind him. 'The dogs! My God! My mum and dad—the dogs have killed them!'

Two Funerals

The sky was an uninterrupted pale blue and the autumnal sun's rays illuminated the remaining translucent bronze leaves that were pinned sparsely to the branches of the yew trees which lined the avenue. Peter and Rachel walked in silence, the cold air clinging to their breath, accompanied by the gentle sound of their crunching feet on the carpet of mottled brown and yellow leaves. The avenue ran straight and long towards the symmetrical red-brick Victorian crematorium ahead of them, poetically marking the journey's end. Both Rachel and Peter wore black and were protected from the November chill by long woollen coats. They held hands as they approached the main doors and the respectfully murmuring throng of mourners.

'This is not our era for funerals; this is the time we should be attending christenings and first birthday parties,' Peter whispered to Rachel. 'Are you ready?'

'Never for this,' she replied. Rachel's parents had both died relatively young and her best friend was killed in a car accident just after her eighteenth birthday. She had had her fill of funerals for a lifetime and the day was already bringing back memories and emotions she thought she had dealt with. She hadn't known Jenny well, but her age and circumstances seemed particularly tragic to Rachel.

The father of Jenny's unborn child had come forward. They had met each other through voluntary work for the church, they had been on a few dates and then went to a party where they drunkenly consummated their relationship in the host's loft room amidst cardboard boxes and forgotten possessions. Neither of them had expected the pregnancy and both were unprepared. He had panicked and had stopped taking her calls and had been avoiding her, scared of the situation and not knowing what to do. Both families had conservative, some would say old-fashioned, values and the young couple felt crippled by their circumstances and how their families would react.

Peter had spoken with the coroner, who had agreed to record misadventure as the cause of death. It was the first time that Rachel had seen Peter use his position to influence another for personal reasons, and she admired him even more for his act of empathy. His involvement had reduced the shame that the Foxtons were feeling, although that was little compensation for the loss of their only daughter. Rachel struggled with such out-of-date thinking and was resolute that her twins would be raised to feel safe and able to talk through any issues with their parents. It seemed such an avoidable tragedy.

They approached the Foxtons. Mrs Foxton's eyes were puffy and red from tears. Mr Foxton stood tall and stiff, trying to maintain an air of control. Rachel hugged Mrs Foxton while Peter shook Mr Foxton's hand.

'I am so sorry for the attention that my association caused. I was flattered that you asked me to speak—are you sure you are happy with my words?'

'Yes, we are very grateful that you are here and willing to speak. Jenny looked up to you and we know how you helped her. The coverage was distressing for Barbara, but we knew that it was misplaced. We just wanted everyone to leave us alone. I may consider some action when we have had some time.' Mr Foxton's voice cracked slightly, and he moved on to greet another mourner.

The Blackwoods took their seat. They hadn't attended the prior religious service; they had made polite excuses but in truth Peter's attendance had been frowned on by the PM and the press office. The days that followed the speculative story run by Anker's paper had caused a minor scandal. The government had been doing well in the polls and their policies were being well received, so an opportunity to disrupt their good run was jumped upon by all opposition. There had been questions in the House, questions raised over Blackwood's integrity and over the stability of his marriage. The tabloids had increased their already attentive eye on Peter and his family. Paparazzi buzzed and flashed with increased intensity, following Rachel on walks in the park, shopping, or the various playgroups she attended with the twins. Reporters had been contacting their network of friends looking for any crack that could be prised wide open. The Blackwoods were not unfamiliar with the attention and the story had subsided, but it had caused unwanted attention, both professionally and personally. Rachel tried to take it in her stride, however the constant pressure was tiring and increasingly emotionally challenging.

After the initial greeting and prayers, Peter was called forward. He took his place at the lectern and looked out over the packed room. He was taken aback by how young the mourners were. Aside from the immediate family, he guessed most of the congregation were younger than twenty-five. Jenny was clearly far more popular than she had perceived.

He cleared his throat with a shallow cough. 'I was asked by Dennis and Barbara to say a few words. I have known Jenny since she was a young child. She was a gentle spirit, one who would help another without condition. Whilst Jenny struggled with her own challenges, she was the first to selflessly help others and her charitable work was much valued by the Church and those that benefited. She worked hard at school and was a student of distinction. My office was delighted to have had her join us for a period and she bought a vibrance to our working day that we have missed since. In her quiet, understated way, Jenny impacted many of us in the brief time she was with us. She was a light in the darkness, and we should not measure how long, but how brightly she shone. She was frail, as is all mankind, and that frailty was, ultimately, the cause of her end, her body unable to cope with the accidental stresses put upon it. Let your lasting memories of this young life be the many joys she bought each one of you.'

He read *She is Gone* by David Harkins. When he finished, as he stepped down to retake his seat, he saw the faces of Jenny's young friends: so many, so young, so full of grief. He hadn't been satisfied with the conclusions of the police investigation; when they saw her medical records they were quick to conclude suicide and closed the file. He knew there was more, it can't have been a coincidence that the business card of the journalist that broke the story was found on the passenger seat of Jenny's car. How did he even know she was pregnant? That detail was only confirmed after the autopsy, which was some time after the story broke. As he sat down he began to think over the details. He wasn't prepared to let this end here. /

Under the same sky, several hundreds of miles away in Bangor, the Defender rattled to a holt and Amy and her parents climbed out, straightened their formal clothes, and headed down the steps towards to entrance of the crematorium. The blue sky of the morning had been blanketed by grey clouds and a light saturating drizzle clung to the air. The group from the previous service were dispersing. Amy noticed a shorter, pot-bellied man carrying a floral 'Mum' to his car. It looked too large to fit into the boot of the Fiat Panda he was approaching.

A younger couple walked past her and acknowledged Amy with a brief smile and the male said, 'Nice day for it,' as they carried on by.

This was the first funeral she had been to and was already nothing like the ones she had seen in TV programmes. The black Ford Granada hearse was already parked under the car port and Tom had gone to greet the funeral director standing by its rear doors. At first glance he was smartly dressed, then she noticed his trousers were too long and were creased over what looked like the comfortable shoes advertised in the glossy mail-order inserts in Sunday papers. Claire took Amy's arm and together they walked into the crematorium hall.

The room was empty aside from Marcus, who was sitting on the front row. He turned as they entered and stood to greet them. He was dressed in a long black robe, tied around his waist with a black leather belt. Unusually for Marcus, he had tied back his dark long hair into a ponytail, he was unshaven, and his facial hair was growing unevenly with a hint of ginger around his chin. He had

MARCUS like RatMan

always been thin, but Amy thought he looked gaunt, tired, and ridiculous in his robes.

Claire and Amy gave Marcus a hug, which he didn't return.

'How are you doing?' asked Amy.

It was the first time she had seen him since he moved back to the cottage. After the 999 call was made by the taxi driver, the Armed Response Unit arrived and dispatched the dogs. The days that followed saw the property closed off so that the police could complete their investigation and the deep cleaning contractors had time to remove signs of the carnage that had unfolded. During those few days Marcus had stayed with them. Amy's parents did attempt to convince Marcus to stay longer as they were concerned by his reaction to the violent loss of his parents, but he was insistent to move back to the cottage as soon as he was able. Amy was relieved that he wanted to return to his home. Their few conversations were strained, and she felt uncomfortable in his presence.

'I am good,' was all that he said, and he sat back down and stared forward at the two coffins.

'Bless him.' whispered Claire to Amy, 'He must be devastated.' She looked to Marcus, 'You know if there is anything we can do you for you, you only need to ask. Tom will carry on working the sheep for as long as you need.' They sat on the other side of the aisle and waited for Tom to join them.

Amy was picturing the chaos that had ensued the day before when her father had attempted to round the sheep up and bring them in. He had only helped Dafydd a few times over the years, and in truth, that meant he sat on his quad bike and watched as Dafydd just called them to him and they followed. After four hours of he and Amy riding around the countryside they had emptied their petrol tanks, covered themselves in mud, worried the sheep and ended up leaving them to fend for themselves. Tom said if the dragon was hungry he'd fly out for a takeaway. If Marcus wasn't going to be able to take the reins in the next day or two they would need to hire in some help.

Tom joined his family and sat down, taking those present to five, including the celebrant. [priest in charge]

Marcus stood and looked at the Davies. 'I can't do this, any of this. It's all bollocks,' he said and he walked out.

Tom went to follow Marcus, but Claire held him by the arm. 'Leave him, he needs to deal with it his way.' He retook his seat and then indicated to the nervous looking celebrant that he could start.

The celebrant delivered a brief perfunctory service and Amy watched as the curtain closed around the two plain wooden coffins, drawing a close to the lives of two people that Amy realised, at that moment, she had become fond of. It was so sparse. She had expected more people, but there were no other family, no friends, no flowers. The sterile end of two vibrant and interesting lives saddened Amy and she started to cry.

She was not only crying for the loss of friends, but also at the loss of the final thread of youthful innocence, the stark reality that life is finite. No matter what we achieve, whether we are good or bad, rich or poor, young or old, when we die it ends. There is no fanfare, or grand procession. In that moment she understood the comfort that others took from religion; the belief that it was all part of a master plan, or that your life's endeavours would be rewarded eternally, and she wished that, perhaps, it could be so for the friends that lay before her. She felt a resolve to make sure she lived a full life and that when she died, she hoped that there would be standing room only at her funeral. She remembered her conversation with Dafydd where she spoke what Latin she knew. *Carpe diem* had a clarity to it that she had not previously appreciated.

The three of them sat in silence for a short while until the doors to the chapel opened and the funeral director apologetically asked if they would leave so that the next mourners could take their seats. The Merlinis' tatty Defender had already gone when Tom, Claire, and Amy returned to the car park, which was filling with cars for the next funeral. They drove home with few words being exchanged.

Termination

The open plan office in Wapping was in a glass-sided building, giving views out over the London skyline that prickled with cranes and development activity. Each floor was filled with banks of desks, separated by low screens to provide some degree of privacy. The sound of phones ringing and people chatting filled the air. Anker's desk was on a small cluster for four. He tried his best to be at his desk for as little time as possible and it was disorganised and untidy, covered with old newspapers, magazines, draft copy with editor's comments, and expenses receipts to be claimed. He slid some papers to one side to make room for his laptop, breakfast and take-out coffee cup and sat down. The light on his desk phone was flashing so he started to retrieve his messages, making notes of who to call on the first piece of paper that came to hand. He had been working on a few new stories and there were the usual messages from agents, spokespeople, and Plod.

The last message was from his editor. 'Anker. Calvin. We have a meeting at 11:00 AM in my office. Don't be late'.

Anker checked his watch and groaned as he realised that he wasn't going to be able to eat his hot bacon roll in the two minutes before his meeting was due to start.

Calvin McHenessey's office sat squarely in the middle of the floor. It was called the Fishbowl because all the walls were glass, enforcing the editor's omnipresence over his staff. McHenessey had a fearsome reputation as a hard-line journalist and employer. He rode the line between revelation and litigation like a rodeo professional, supported by his publisher's deep pockets and sharp and aggressive legal team. He had turned the fortunes of the newspaper around, making it the unrivalled daily read, a fact that he would remind his staff of regularly. He had been a supporter of Anker and had seen off many potential lawsuits and encouraged him to be tenacious and dogged, because 'there is always a story if you push long enough'. McHenessey rarely sat at his desk, preferring the two worn, red Chesterfields that were positioned in front of it and stood in juxtaposition to the ultra-modern decor of the rest of the premises. Behind the desk stood a glass case with rows of industry awards showcasing the newspaper's and McHenessey's achievements. He was always impeccably dressed—tailored suits flattered his slim build, and although he was slightly shorter than average, he commanded attention. Only a slight reddening to his cheeks gave an indication of the habitual heavy drinking, late nights, and early mornings that were his professional background and the culture that he fostered in his workplace.

'Will, we have a problem. Take a seat.' McHenessey indicated to the sofa. 'It appears that your reporting on Jenny Foxton ruffled some feathers. Our owner has been on the phone.'

'Flash in the pan that story. Still, we got to break it,' Anker replied.

'There have been some questions raised over the source of your story and how you knew that Foxton was pregnant before the medical report was released.' He held up his hand before Anker could speak. 'I am not going to ask you for your source and I do not wish to know how you came across the information, but we cannot be pressed on it. You know that the government is discussing press self-regulation at the moment, and we do not want to rock the boat any more than is necessary to satisfy our readership.' McHenessey knew that he had to always maintain plausible deniability and being able to swear on oath that he was unaware of some practices had been a get-out-of-jail card more than once. He had seen other editors fall foul of contempt of court when other attempts at litigation had failed. McHenessey was too seasoned for that. 'I am aware that you "interviewed" Foxton in the car park of her gym the day that she died. This is known to the police, but as they concluded it was suicide and have a complete file, it is inconvenient to explore that further.'

'So what if they did? No crime has been committed in my having a conversation with her, if I did, which I don't recollect. She died of "misadventure", not suicide, if I may be pedantic,' snapped Anker.

'That was the coroner's conclusion and I have it on reliable sources that this was at the request of Blackwood. He is a powerful man, Will, and whilst he has many detractors, he is gaining support. It looks like he is a man of some integrity which is worrying for someone of such ranking, as they have a habit of doing what they consider to be right, rather than what is practical. It seems that he has a bite as well as a bark. He has made it clear to our boss that he will champion against our best interests unless we take some action.'

Anker's heart rate raised as he realised the direction their conversation was taking. 'OK,' he said slowly, inviting McHenessey to continue.

'We are going to let you go, Will. But, I have said that I am only willing to remove you from staff. We will still want to work with you on a freelance basis. You should think of it as a positive. It is really for optics. I know you don't like coming into the office and now you don't have to. You can work on researching full stories without filing deadlines and we pay more. It will help your reputation as journalist of standing. I will see that you are well rewarded for your quality work, of course.'

McHenessey was still talking but Anker was no longer listening. The loss of his business card was huge. He knew that it was the power of the brand, not his own dynamic personality, that opened many doors, and legs, for him. He would just be another jobbing journalist. He would lose his expense account that had been unchecked for several years, the paper happy not to question his sizable monthly expenditure on entertainment, which had paid largely for his social activities because of his circulation-grabbing headlines. 'This is a massive over-reaction, boss. We've run countless other stories that were speculative or skinny on source. I don't get it?'

'It's not down to me, it's from above, and I have done what I can. I'll get you back in once the dust has settled and this judicial review is completed. Twelve months, maybe eighteen. It's just the game, Will, you have been playing it long enough to know it can all change on spin of a dice.'

'But, it's not...' started Anker.

McHenessey interrupted, 'Don't say fair. You sound like a spoilt kid who's lost a game of marbles. Grow some cahunas and fuck off before I lose my temper. I'll give you until lunch time to clear your desk, your key card and system access has already been blocked by HR. Don't be an idiot and spoil the goodwill I have for you.' McHenessey stood and started to walk around to his desk chair, this was the cue that the meeting was at an end. 'Close the door on your way out. Don't slam it. You know I treat everyone the same, Will, so if you are not out by noon, security will escort you out of the building. Let's avoid that embarrassment for us both, shall we?'

Anker stood. He knew what was about to happen as he had taken part in the ritual many times before. As he closed the door to the office he turned. Many of his co-workers had formed a line back to his desk and he had to walk the gauntlet, some patted him on his back, others clapped (some slowly), he heard comments 'dead man walking', 'unemployment line that way', 'best of luck', 'too bad, too sad, never mind'. It was common practice; he hadn't taken it seriously before, but as the recipient it didn't have the same level of enjoyment as being a spectator. He picked his coat up from the back of his chair, left the building, and headed to the Chippy.

He was on his fourth pint of lager by the time Colin arrived. Unusually for him, Colin was in polo shirt and jeans under his winter coat.

'I had the day off today to do some work around the house that Carol's been asking me for ages to do. Your phone call saved me. I hate DIY, that's why I am a private investigator, not a sparky.'

The landlord looked up from his Sporting Life. 'I was interim manager of the White Oak in Moss Side, back in the 80s, and decided that I would fix a dodgy socket. Caused a power cut in streets around the pub, started a riot. I stick to the Yellow Pages now.' He returned to his newspaper and Will and Colin took their drinks and moved to a booth.

'What happened, then?' asked Colin.

'Blackwood had me sacked. What a fucker! I am sure he's been through worse. It wasn't even a big story that revolved around him.' Anker took another long drink.

'Are you sure it was him? Isn't that abuse of his position or something?'

'McHenessey called me in and basically said that the story pissed Blackwood off enough that he made it known he would cause trouble for the paper. Spineless bastards. We've had some serious court time over other stories, gone the distance and won, or settled. I don't understand why they would throw me under the bus so easily. He said it was to do with the government review on press self-regulation. Massive overreaction or quick cave-in. Either way, not sure what I am going to do now.' Anker finished his drink.

'You'll get plenty of work. You've had loads of stories run. Think of your connections, the ears you have access to, the numbers in your phonebook. That's worth money, Will. You'll get calls. Why not go freelance for a while? Being self-employed is the best career move I have made. I wish I'd done it sooner. If I was still in the force, I wouldn't have been able to walk out the office and come and meet you today.'

'But I didn't want to be here—you made your decision. I've had this put upon me because of Blackwood. He's not a saint, he can't be. Call me old school, but I believe in an eye for an eye. I am going to find out all the dirt I can; he's a politician, they all have skeletons in their closet, and I now have the time to find them,' Anker said with determination.

'Vendettas aren't good for business, Will. I can tell you many stories that end badly because of a grudge.' Brown reached for his coat and pulled out a hand-sized, orange device with a large screen on its face. 'Don't dwell on it. Here, have a look at this. This is a consumer GPS unit—that's Global Position System. I read that Mercedes are going to bring out car with a version on the dash, but this is designed for mountaineering. Apparently, they are built with some degree of inaccuracy as governments are worried about subversive applications. However, I know a man, and he has tweaked it so it should be really accurate. So now, if I pop one of these,' Colin took out another small disc and put it on the table, 'in a bag, pocket or tucked under the seat of car, I can track someone's movements while I sit at home watching golf and drinking tea. Pretty cool, huh?'

'Great, I'll go and shove that button up Blackwood's arse.' They both laughed.

'Please don't. Its new and clean,' said Brown. 'I think that he is still using that mobile number. I will check later and keep an ear out if anything comes up, as a favour. I can also arrange for email accounts to be accessed now, but that is through a third party, so if you want that you will need to pay upfront.' Brown finished his drink. 'Another?'

'Do bears shit in the woods?' said Anker. 'I will just go for piss. Back in a mo.' He was feeling quite drunk. He hadn't eaten, and it was only his acclimatisation to alcohol from several years of heavy, regular drinking that was preventing him from slurring. He was beginning to lose a little of his balance as he stumbled down the narrow stairs through the gents' toilet door and into the single cubicle.

He took the wrap from his pocket and tipped the crystals on to the back of his hand. 'Cheeky knuckle to keep me going,' he said aloud. The effects of the cocaine were almost immediate. He felt energised as he licked the back of his hand, sniffed and wiped his nose, removing any remaining evidence of white powder. He rinsed his face in the Victorian-style sink and looked into the faded and dirty mirror above; his pupils had already dilated. Plod would see it immediately, but they were both 'off duty' and tonight he didn't give a shit. As he returned to the table, the GPS unit had been returned to Brown's coat pocket. Anker swept up the device, which was the size of a casino chip, flipped it, and absent-mindedly put it in his pocket as Plod returned and placed the new drinks on the table.

'Really, Will?' he said. 'Can't you have one night off? Your pupils look like shark's eyes. I'll hang around for this one, but it looks like you have plans that I don't have the energy for these days. Do you want to call your mate, Andy, see if he's up for babysitting you from here? If you do, you can call him from my phone and meet up.' Brown took out his Ericsson mobile and slid across the table.

'I should get one of these,' said Anker. He typed in Andy's phone and was answered. He made arrangements, handed the phone back to Plod and then drank his pint of lager in one. 'You're alright, you know. I'll give you a call in a day or so.'

Plod nodded. 'Wanker'.

Anker headed off, through Soho. Whatever was going to happen tonight, he was determined not to remember it in the morning, an objective that he was already well on his way to achieving.

Home Truths

Marcus made his way to the Keep and sat down in front of the fire. His parents' funeral service was facile and a waste of his time. His parents were dead, they didn't give a shit, and the only people there/were probably there to report to the Order. None of that was important. It was his now. Where his father had been disinterested and disengaged from his faith and the truth, he would be the opposite. He was free to pursue the path which he knew had to be followed, and he would no longer be held back by his father. No more restrictions on how much he practiced and what he learned.

He had surprised himself with how well he had adjusted after his parents had died—he had expected more emotion. If he allowed himself to dwell on it, he would feel sad, but he was strong enough to push that aside. It was a sign that it was the right thing to have done. The house was quieter without the dogs, but he had enjoyed being on his own. He was free to stay up all night and play first person shoot 'em ups on his PC. He was starting to explore the internet and the boundless opportunities he saw it offered. The fact that pornography was freely and quickly available was a serendipitous bonus. Pretty much whatever he could imagine he could find images for, and it was becoming a challenge to search for a kink the internet could not fulfil.

'Hello, son,' came a voice, pulling Marcus back from his thoughts with a jump. He stood and turned and Dafydd Merlini was standing in the doorway. 'New look?' he enquired as he looked over Marcus, dressed in a dark robe. 'That doesn't look practical or comfortable.'

Marcus was assessing the situation in silence.

'Yes, I am dead. You and your dogs killed me. And your mum. Why your mum? I can see some twisted logic in taking my life so that you can step in the role that you have coveted for so long. But your mum? And why use the dogs? You have clearly developed ahead of my training so you must have been able to conjure a thousand less violent ways to take the life of the person that gave life to you?' His voice was raised. He looked complete, unharmed. He was dressed as usual in working trousers, jumper and shirt, like he had just walked out the kitchen as if nothing had happened all those days ago.

'This is your magic. I watched you die.' Marcus was still processing what was happening and he was walking towards Dafydd. He wasn't scared, he was curious.

'You know nothing of the skills you seek. You are still level one, a novice. If you take the life of another seer, their consciousness cannot return to *Mamddaear* until your consciousness returns. So here I shall remain for now. Ironic, if you think about it; you murder me to be rid of me, only to guarantee my presence.'

'Have you come to collect me, to kill me?' Marcus felt the spark of anger in his stomach, and he searched his memory for a spell.

'Not yet. I am here to understand, although I had known your true soul for years. I saw enough many years ago. On your tenth birthday when you came here for the first time, do you remember?'

'I do,' replied Marcus, in a monotone.

'The dragon saw you for what you are. I didn't accept it immediately. You were my son, but I heeded the warning and watched. I have seen everything. The first time you hit back against those bullies. Your "experiments"; remember when we had chickens and you told them to fight until they had all killed each other? You lied, of course, and told us that a fox had broken into the coop. I was present when you made that horse bolt with its rider, and it was me that calmed the animal down as I saw your intention to make it gallop into the path of the van. I was with you when you scared that young couple, that were wild camping. I told you that being in here limited our access to above ground, but that was a lie I fed you so that I could observe your real self.'

Marcus guessed he was close enough to strike at his father. He made a move, a sudden dash, towards Dafydd, to tackle him. Dafydd pointed at Marcus and with that, Marcus was lifted and thrown across the stone floor with force. He landed and rolled, like a discarded cloth being blown down a road. The force winded Marcus. He looked up. Dafydd remained where he was, his expression unchanged.

Marcus was angry. He knelt and started to recount an untested *Englyn*. It would send a fireball towards his father. Nothing happened. He stood. At that moment he felt a huge force hit his chest, taking him off his feet again and slamming him backwards some five feet against the wall. His head hammered into the whitewash, smashing the glass of the pictures on the wall, sending frames and canvas to the floor. His skin split under the pressure, and he fell to the floor, slumped against the wall, momentarily unconscious.

He came to with his head throbbing. There were no broken fragments around him—the wall was as it was before he hit it. His head wound had bled, and his neck and collar were wet from blood. As his vision came into focus, he saw his father standing in front of him.

'You are powerless in here. I saw to that on the afternoon you killed me, and you ripped your mum's throat and abdomen open. You tasted her blood, tissue, and shit as your dogs tore into her. Didn't that pain you? The resolve it took to do that is strong, or you simply have no feelings. We need to talk. Be warned, your attempts at violence are futile and I will meet them measure for measure.'

'Are you going to kill me?' Marcus asked again. His anger had subsided, and he was now feeling vulnerable and a little scared.

'You are my son. I won't kill you, even after what you have done. I am at a loss as to how we can be so different. I wish to protect life and you wish to take it.'

'You don't understand,' snapped Marcus. 'You have misinterpreted our purpose, been blind to *Mamddaear's* wishes and all our learning. You are wrong and you were wrong in stopping my progression. You are wrong to think that bitch can take my place.'

'You know nothing.' Dafydd turned to walk to the seating.

Marcus seized the opportunity once more and clambered to his feet, rushing to knock down his father. As he moved forward another punching impact thudded into his side, pitched him through the air, and landed him against a chest of draws. He fell like a rag doll on to the floor. There was a clatter as candlesticks that had been on the table were sent to the ground. He was again winded, and his sight was distorted by the pain as he fought to catch breath.

'I said I won't kill you, not that I couldn't kill you. My patience is running thin, and let's face it, I don't need to afford you any more consideration than you gave my wife, your mother. If you come at me again, so help me, the pain and suffering you will feel as I prolong your death with seem like an eternity.' The very ground was stirring under the power being emitted by Dafydd.

As the tremors subsided, Marcus's vision and breath returned, and he felt searing pain in his side as the force that hit him had cracked two ribs. The candlesticks were back in their place on the table as though they had never been disturbed. He coughed and slowly stood, tripping slightly as his robes were caught under a foot.

Dafydd seemed to scoff. 'As I said, very practical.'

'Fuck you,' said Marcus. 'So why are you here, in whatever magic this is?'

'I needed to understand why, and you need to understand what happens next./Was it just jealousy?'

Marcus had sat down opposite his father. His body was hurting everywhere and it felt like he had twisted an ankle. 'I am the heir; it is my right. You have never treated your abilities and knowledge with the gravity they deserve. You are a poor imitation of those that preceded you and you will be lost in time like dust in the wind. I have been reading and learning in secret for years and it was apparent to me long ago that you were only acting as caretaker, preserving the responsibilities until I was of an age to take over. Then you decide that that London bitch is better than me! Me! Years of study and practice, but you think she is better than me. Fuck you, you deserved it. If Mum was still alive, I would have had to carry on the farce that I was just a "nice young man". She was necessary collateral damage.'

'Collateral damage!' shouted Dafydd. The fire flared in the hearth, spewing sparks and tinder. 'You can be safe in the knowledge that few think of you as a nice young man.' He paused and took his son's stare. 'All those books, all that reading, all that knowledge, yet no wisdom. From the day you met the dragon I had been cautious. At first I thought that perhaps your connection was weak, that we could work on it, build it up. Over time it became apparent that the problem ran deeper. To know that your child has the capacity for such acts as you are is cancerous. It ate away at our very core. As a seer, the future that we are allowed to perceive is often only a likely outcome, like a trajectory of current travel, or it can be an interpretation of events. Often its clarity is only possible some short time ahead, but it was clear back then that this was not your path.

'I cannot trust you with the power that is gifted to me. That's why I tutored you in the only the basics as I knew there would be another direction to follow. I saw that my death was coming, although I could not see the means, and I was able to make plans. From this day forth, you are banished from this place. Your name will be removed from all reference in our journals. You shall be erased. What knowledge you have I cannot take from you without wiping your memory and I want you to walk the rest of your life knowing what you have lost for the sake of your greed…'

'NO!' cried out Marcus. He stood up in rage, ignoring the pain that shot from the many and various injuries he carried.

'You shall resign your position in the Order and leave this place forever. To ensure that this will be so, your *Hudcloch* is mine.' With that, Dafydd reached forward and the necklace was ripped from Marcus's neck and flew into Dafydd's open hand. Marcus felt his now naked neck. 'I will leave you with two more gifts.'

Dafydd stood and faced the fireplace. Kath appeared next to him, their backs to Marcus. They turned in unison to show their bodies in the condition left after the dogs had completed their frenzied attacks. Marcus tried to look away, but he was paralysed. He tried to close his eyes, but they were held open. He could see his mum's abdominal cavity, innards chewed and hanging. Her neck was torn to the bone, bite marks were down both arms, and she was stained red in her own blood. His dad had no face, just a mass of raw tissue, his jaw missing. His neck was also gouged and torn, his right leg taken to only bone between knee and ankle.

'You will see this, your work, each time you become absorbed in happiness. I will strip that emotion from you and replace it with disgust for the rest of your days.

'I cast a spell on that day so that I will remain here for all time to provide my apprentice with tutorage. I am now the Guardian of this place and if you return, I will inflict upon you such vengeance that you cannot imagine. Your act of patricide and matricide will never be mentioned, that is the mercy I will show you. If you do not do as I ask, I will send Chort after Chort to destroy all that you own and anything you cherish. If you do not heed this warning I will torment you until death's release. Believe me that it will be relentless, but I will never take your life and spare you the punishments levied this day. Do you understand?' Kath had disappeared and Dafydd was now back to his initial form.

'I do.' Marcus was overwhelmed. He felt nauseous at the sight that had been presented to him, and he felt true grief for the first time since his parents died, but it was grief for the loss of his future, not his parents.

'You will leave now. Be gone,' Dafydd said, and then there was darkness.

***

Marcus woke. He was in his bed. The sun was rising, and bird song came through the open bedroom window. He ached everywhere. He went to roll to his side and pain shot from his fractured ribs. He groaned, forcing himself to sit up on the side of the bed. He felt his bare neck again to be certain. He had hoped it was just a weird dream, like the others he had been having since his parents died. He padded his way downstairs into the kitchen to get a beer to quench his thirst and there he would plan.

The Guardian

Amy hadn't slept well the night of the funeral, and it was the first time she had visited the dragon since Dafydd and Kath's deaths. It felt strange to be in the place without Dafydd, but that was now her reality. She stopped by the lake and waited. The dragon would come shortly, as he aways did. Sure enough, she heard the beating of its wings as it approached, landed, and settled next to her. She had become in tune with the dragon and no longer needed to physically touch it to understand it. She could tell that the dragon knew of Dafydd's death and was saddened by it, but there wasn't a sense of loss. Amy understood that Dafydd hadn't died, rather he had left his physical body and returned to *Mamddaear*, to rejoin the greater conscious. She looked at the dragon.

'I hope you are right. I'm still not completely sold on the whole "the earth is one organism thing", but we'll see,' she said aloud.

HaveFaithi   nYourmento   rYoungOneT   heT
ruthWillComeToY ouInTime

Amy looked up in amazement at the dragon, which stared back at her, its expression unchanged. The words were not clear, but, she understood after a few moments. 'Did you just speak to me?' she asked. 'Damn, I'm talking with dragons now. I must need more sleep,' she said to herself.

The dragon nudged Amy. It was gentle for an animal of its size, but it was with enough weight to almost knock Amy off her feet.

'Hey! What'd you do that for?' Amy asked.

GoIntoT heKeepThereIsSo meoneWaitingFo rYou

She heard the voice again. It was deep yet gentle. She looked at the dragon quizzically. It stared back and then nudged her once more. Amy looked towards the Keep and then back to the dragon. Its tail tip flickered slightly as if it was pleased it had been understood.

'OK,' she said and walked over to the Keep and into the main room. She felt someone behind her and turned to see Dafydd Merlini. 'What the…?'

'How many times do I have to remind you about swearing?' he said. Amy came forward to give him a hug, but she squeezed only space. 'I am an apparition. We can do many things, but bringing ourselves back from death is not one of them.'

Amy stepped back and looked at him. She was becoming less and less amazed as more bizarre events unfolded. She was learning to accept what was happening and question later. Dafydd was dressed in a long simple gown of black and his hair was longer— shoulder length—but he looked well. She could see Marcus in his physical appearance. 'What is it with you and your family wearing gowns? We are in the twentieth century, you know. It kind of suits you, though,' she said.

'Thanks. I thought that a cotton shirt, jeans ,and boots probably wasn't the look I should be going for.' He held out his arms and gave a twirl. 'It does look wizardy, doesn't it? Anyway, sit. We need to talk.'

They sat. 'On the day that I, erm, left, I had planned to speak with you. You have a great ability, and I would wish that you became my apprentice. I believe that you have made this decision independently of me?' Dafydd asked.

'Yes,' replied Amy, 'With what I have seen and what I have learned so far, I can't see anything more I would wish to do. I haven't spoken with my parents, but they will be delighted to have me at home. I haven't really thought any further ahead than that.'

'To further and assist your learning I am now here, for you. I am now the Guardian of this place. I cannot leave the cave, but I shall protect it and its secrets. I have all the knowledge that exists in our Great Library, and I will tutor you. You have much to learn as the apprenticeship usually starts in infancy. I have no doubt that you have it in you to learn quickly and be true to our teachings. Marcus shall resign his place—we have spoken. His path leads him away in a different direction.

'In the immediacy, you need to help your father, otherwise our sheep will be walking to Cardiff. He is a hopeless shepherd and additional help will not be permitted by the Order. You have the skill to connect with the sheep, as you did with the earth worm. They are just larger and take more effort, but we will practice here. You will be able to ask them to come to you and they will follow. Come, I have called a flock, which waits outside.'

'Before we go. The dragon. I think it spoke to me,' Amy said Confused.

'Ah, indeed. Your progress is already excellent. You will find this exercise to be easy. You have learned to turn the dragon's thoughts into our words. It will become easier with practice. Do not underestimate this gift: the dragon choses those that it will couple with. This is all good indeed. Now, let us go and teach you shepherding.'

Dear John

The letter from the insurance company was delivered that morning and it lay opened on the kitchen table. Two cheques were attached, and the letter confirmed that as sole beneficiary of the Trust, Marcus received a hundred percent of his parents sums assured. Once the estates were wrapped up, he would receive their savings as well. They had lived frugally for years, and their savings alone were a low six-figure sum.

He knew he had to work with speed. He didn't trust his father's word. Why should he keep to it? Anyway, it wasn't really his father. He was now ash, tipped over the Garden of Remembrance, not that anyone would remember him. Marcus didn't need to go back to the cave, or the Keep. Other wizards had made the spells written in those ancient papers. There was no reason why he couldn't make his own. He knew enough. It was his time to break free.

He picked up his day sack and muttered an *Englyn*, *Rhiannon's Bag*, creating a sack that could never be filled, and he went around his room, packing his belongings. He rummaged through his parents' bedroom to find his father's oracle bones and any items that might have value that he could sell. There wasn't much in the house that belonged to them; the cottage was fully furnished and was a grace and favour as part of their retainer. He knew his mother had some old jewellery stashed in one of her drawers and he carefully went through all their dressers and wardrobes until he found the small silver box. It was ornately decorated in an Edwardian style, though it was dull and dark with tarnish, showing its neglect. Inside it was lined with rich, red velvet that was vivid compared to the exterior. The box contained a mixture of rings and necklaces, carelessly discarded so that they were a mass of knotted silver and gold chain. He was about to close the lid when a leather cord caught his eye. He pulled and on the end was a bland, rough, dark stone. He smiled. It was a forgotten

Hudcloch. He put it in his pocket, the box in his bag, and continued his sweep of the house.

He had been careful not to disturb the property too much, he wanted it to look as though he had left, only taking a few of his belongings. He gave each room a final review from each doorway and was satisfied that he had collected anything of any monetary value. He had no intention of returning and they could sell or burn everything else for as much as he cared.

Moving around the house had aggravated his injuries. They were superficial in the main and his ribs would repair over time, but he was still sore from head to ankle and felt weary from the pain. He took a sheet of paper and, making a cup of tea, sat down at the kitchen table to rest for a while and write his farewell letter.

Dear Tom and Claire,

It has been a very difficult time for me, and this house and area is full of memories of Mum and Dad, and I cannot bear it. They left me some money, enough for me to set up somewhere else, and that is what I intend to do. I am sure that you will be able to cope without me, and the Order will support you with anything you need. I am not sure where I will go, but I will drop you a line when I am settled. I left the spare car keys on the table and the car is at the station and I will pay for parking for the day.

Yours,

M

This was nothing like the letter he wanted to leave. He had written and rewritten countless drafts of the letter in his mind over the course of the day, but there was no point in saying what he really felt. There would be time for that in the future. This would do. It would tie everything up nice and tidily, and he would be free to move forward. He had some business to attend to in London and then he would head up to Scotland, where properties' prices were lower and there was plenty of space where he could remain out of sight whilst he practiced and prepared.

He changed back into his black t-shirt and jeans which he felt would attract less attention. He would keep his gowns for a time when he had more confidence. It was more important that he blended in and disappeared for now. He locked the back door, washed up his cup and set it on the draining board, replaced the milk into the fridge, picked up the insurance letter and cheques, threw his daysack over one shoulder, and double locked the front door. As he stepped into the Defender, he looked back at their family home. It was just a cold, old building, lifeless and abandoned. It was time to go, he thought.

The train journey to London was uneventful and he enjoyed the deepest sleep he had had for many days, uninterrupted by nightmares. He arrived in Euston Station as rush hour was starting and he made his way across the concourse, through the ant-like throng of commuters that were opposing his progress in all directions. He had booked a hotel room on Euston Road and as he approached, it wasn't what he had expected; the hotel was a tired Edwardian town house, with a flickering neon 'vacancies' sign in one of the bay windows. As he entered, the old floorboards creaked beneath his feet and the air smelt musty. The Ambassador Hotel was unlikely to live up to its name, he thought, pinging the brass bell on the reception desk. After a few moments the receptionist came from the doorway behind the desk. She was a short, round, middle-aged woman with a stern, unimpressed expression. 'Hourly or overnight?' she asked.

'Hourly? No, I have a reservation. Merlini, Marcus Merlini,' he said, pondering why he would book a room for an hour.

The lady flipped the pages to a tatty A4 notebook, she found the scrawled note and tapped it with her index finger. 'Ok, love. It's £70 a night, plus £70 key deposit. Leave the bathroom as you found it. Keep the noise down, no visitors after 11:00 PM. You can't take the key out the building, so hand it in each time you go out. It's payment in advance. How many nights you staying?" she asked.

As few as possible, thought Marcus. 'Five,' he said.

The number was arbitrary, and he would look for somewhere else in a few days. He paid in cash, took the key, which was tied to an overly large red key fob, and headed up to the top floor where his was one of only two rooms. The shared bathroom was on the floor below. He didn't feel inclined to visit until it was necessary. The top floor of the hotel was uncomfortably warm and as he swung open the door it hit the wardrobe behind it. He stepped in and there was just enough space to move around the bed to prise open the sash window that juddered up three or four inches before jamming. Marcus sat on the bed. The tired mattress gave little resistance. He sighed to himself. He had not spent much time preparing this part of his journey and he was already regretting parting with five nights worth of money as he was now certain he would move on tomorrow and there would be a no refunds policy.

He opened his bag and pulled out his father's only suit and formal shirt. He had tried it on recently and it was a good enough fit. Marcus looked at himself in the wardrobe mirror approvingly. He put on the necktie, tidied his hair into a ponytail, wiped his lace-up leather shoes against the back of his trouser legs, pulled down the sleeves of jacket, and admired himself once more. *That'll do*, he thought. He had a couple of hours to kill before the casino opened and he was hungry, so he decided he would walk to Kensington, take in the sights, and have something to eat along the way.

It was cold and he didn't have a coat; he thought that his life in the hills of Wales would keep him warm, but it was almost as cold in the city as it was in the valleys. He considered casting a little spell to keep him warm, but he didn't want to draw attention to himself, so he pulled up his jacket collar and hunched up to try to preserve some warmth. The road was busy with juddering traffic moving slowly like a segmented mechanical millipede. The winter air mixed with the exhaust fumes, tingling in his nostrils. The streets were lit by the cacophony of lights coming from streetlamps, traffic signals, vehicles, restaurants, billboards, cyclists. It had a unique beauty that Marcus had never seen before. There were so many people, marching or meandering in all directions. He decided to stop at a Southern Fried Chicken Shack restaurant that had a large glass window. There, he could rest, warm up, eat, and people-watch in relative comfort.

Without the abundance of wildlife, he lacked the natural guidance system he had learned to access. Each creature was connected to *Mamddaear*, and he could use all those small connections to build locational awareness. It was how birds migrated to and from Africa and salmon found their way back from the deep seas, up the rivers and streams, to the places of their birth. In the mass of concrete, steel, and tarmac, he was not able to make a connection and he was quite lost. He was so accustomed to the connection it felt like he was without a sense, and it was unnerving.

He flagged down a black cab and it took twenty minutes to cover the remaining distance. The casino was on the lower ground floor of a substantial hotel. He had to become a member before he could enter, and he had brought his passport with him as proof of identity. Whilst filling out the forms, he made a mental note that he needed to plan this more carefully. If he was going to be successful, he needed to have multiple identities. He paid his minimal membership fee and then was allowed to enter the casino floor.

It was early evening, which probably explained why it was relatively quiet. It was a large room, probably once a ballroom, and the walls were covered with mirrors, swags of material, and a splash of gold wallpaper. It was opulent bordering on chintzy. There was an array of green baize tables around the floor with stools awaiting guests. Not all the tables had croupiers in attendance. There was a large crowd around the roulette table and, judging by the noise, they were already quite drunk. It looked like a party of people together. He headed to a blackjack table that had two open seats, sat down, and placed five hundred pounds on the baize in front of him. The other players nodded in acknowledgement and when the hand was finished the croupier efficiently counted the money, confirmed the value aloud, and then slid Marcus a pile of multi-coloured chips. *Game on*, he thought.

He had read up on how to play, but for the first few hands he took his cues from the other players. He had plenty of time and it was of no consequence if he lost some money initially. After quickly losing a hundred pounds it was time for him to concentrate. He muttered an *Englyn* and looked at the cards in the dealing shoe. His next two cards were dealt. He lifted the corner sufficiently to see the values and they totalled fourteen. The dealer had the ten of hearts face up. Two players before him took their turns, the first sticking on eighteen, the second busting. Marcus looked at the dealer's card that faced down and knew it was the seven of clubs. He looked at shoe and sensed that the next card was the four of diamonds. That would do for him.

'Twist,' he said.

As the evening progressed, he was careful to fold or bust himself enough times that his winning was not conspicuous, but he was started to fatigue from the concentration and was beginning to get bored. The croupier had paused the game to shuffle the decks and reload the shoe and so Marcus decided to up his own game and now changed his *Englyn*. This time, it didn't matter what the order of the cards were—he would just call for the cards he wanted.

The risk was that he might call a card that had recently been dealt, but he was only going to try this a few times and the deck was newly shuffled, so it was a low chance. He simply focused on low value cards for the players before him and made sure that he had a picture and an ace, whilst ensuring the dealer didn't. He won the next four rounds of blackjack, making ever-increasing bets with each hand until his hundreds were worth thousands. His table companions had begun to applaud his success and he felt someone take the empty seat next to him. He looked over and had his stare met by a young, attractive woman. Her blonde hair fell over her bare shoulders, and she was wearing a black, figure-hugging dress that accentuated her breasts. He flet himself blush a little as she put her finger under his chin, lifting his face slightly, bringing his eyes back to hers.

'Hello, lucky. Do you mind if I play with you a while?' She had an accent he couldn't place.

'Of course not,' he said.

The croupier coughed, attracting Marcus's attention and making him realise the table was waiting on his call. 'Twist,' he said. The card dealt was flipped and he busted out with a total of twenty-four. The table groaned in unison for his loss.

The woman placed her hand on his thigh and said, 'Perhaps I bring you bad luck? Should I leave?'

'No. Please stay,' he replied.

The croupier exchanged glances and a slight smile with another of the players around the table. Marcus saw, and it annoyed him. He looked good enough to have her interested in him.

'What would you like to drink?' he asked. He held up his arm and a waiter came and took his order; she had a vodka and tonic and he just plain tonic.

They sat at the table. After a few more hands, Marcus gave his companion some chips. He didn't know the value, and he was not concerned. He had plenty. Her name was Veronika (with a k) and she was from Eastern Europe. She smelled of sweet vanilla and the skin on her arms was silky smooth.

He lost track of the time but he had managed to keep his attention on his winning cycles. The croupier had changed, and the floor manager had joined the table, standing discreetly at a distance. Veronika was now sitting with one arm resting on Marcus' thigh, her gentle touch arousing him. He had initial embarrassment, but she seemed to know, and he cared less the longer they sat together. He was not used to attention; it had been obvious to everyone at the table other than Marcus that she was flirting with him. The crowd around the roulette table had dispersed, but the room was filling.

'Come,' he said. 'Let's try our luck at roulette while the table is quiet.'

He exchanged his pile of chips into larger denomination so that he could carry them and was given rectangular black chips with gold lettering, but there were still too many to carry in one hand. He offered one to the croupier who politely declined. Marcus stood and watched Veronika walk ahead. She walked like a supermodel and he was totally absorbed. He still had some smaller chips in his pocket, and he started slowly with simple red and even bets, losing both. Veronika was dotting chips randomly around the table, smiling and clearly enjoying herself.

Marcus was feeling very tired. It was only the dopamine in his blood produced by the company of Veronika that was keeping him going. The adrenaline had subsided as his confidence in his trickery had increased. There was no anticipation, no jeopardy. He wasn't feeling the thrill of winning because he wasn't, and it was a foregone conclusion, as was the next win as he placed two of his higher value chips on the double zero. The table had filled as the wheel was spun and the little white ball was sent on its trajectory until it danced and jumped coming to rest in zero.

Veronika grabbed Marcus by the cheeks and kissed him with excitement. They played a few more rounds, Marcus allowing the ball to land without intervention, and he lost some winnings to the house.

'Veronika, it has been long a day for me, and I'm tired. I think that my luck is starting to run out, so I think it is time to leave.' He handed her some chips, 'Here. You can carry on,' he said.

'No, baby! Why?' she protested. 'Let's go on somewhere. I have friends in a club nearby, or perhaps we can stay here?' She stroked his chest and titled her head slightly.

'Stay here?' The suggestion excited Marcus.

'Of course,' she said. 'There are always rooms in these hotels. You go and have a drink at the bar, and I will sort it, baby.' She kissed him on the lips and pushed her body up against his. As she walked away, she looked back and sent a smile that seemed so white and perfect to Marcus.

He didn't want a drink, but he could do with a pee and to wash his face to revive himself, so he headed to the bathroom. *What a difference a day makes*, he thought. Yesterday he was at home in the countryside of Wales in a cold, empty house, and here he was in a swanky London casino and the chances seemed to be growing that he was going to have sex with someone whose beauty he had only seen in the media. He zipped up his fly and walked to the sinks. He was alone in the bathroom, which was decorated in dark, red wood and polished marble. There were no electric hand driers, just wooden boxes by the wash basins that held white, pressed small towels. He wanted more of this and he felt very happy.

He turned the shiny chromed tap on, cupped his hands, doused his face and looked up. In the mirror he saw his face and hands covered in blood. He wiped his eyes and face and looked again. Standing next to him on either side were his mum and dad, their distorted and mangled bodies still glistening with wet blood. They said nothing, just raised one arm and pointed at him in the mirror. His mother's mouth opened and she started to scream, a long, high-pitched, monotone keening.

Marcus screwed his eyes tight and clenched the sides of the wash basin. His heart was pounding, and he felt sickness in his stomach. He opened his eyes, and they were gone. His face was wet with water and pale. He took a towel and wiped his face, disorientated. He headed back to the casino floor.

'Mr Merlini?' came a call. He looked over towards the origin of the call and saw the floor manager, winged by two large men who were squeezed into dark suits a size or two smaller than they needed. They walked to him, 'Mr Merlini, I am Daniel, the casino manager. I wanted to introduce myself to our newest and most successful member.' He held out a hand which Marcus took, and they briefly shook.

'Your, erm, companion has sent a message to say that you are staying in room 720. I am pleased that you are staying tonight. I will see that you are our guest this evening if we can agree that you will return tomorrow evening to allow us chance to win back our money?' He was smiling, but Marcus could see the real intent in his eyes.

'Thank you,' he replied. He had lost interest in anything other than leaving.

'From your accent, I would guess you are a long way from your home, Mr Merlini. Are you here on business or pleasure?'

'Both,' he replied, 'Please forgive me, but I am not feeling very well and need to go to my room.'

'Of course, Mr Merlini. Enjoy Veronika and we will look forward to seeing you tomorrow.' Daniel gestured towards the exit. 'Until then.'

Marcus took his chips to the cashier's desk, and they gave him bundles of cash, all fifty-pound notes, bound in bill straps marked '£5,000'. The cashier slid a large brown envelope through the gap in the security glass. He filled it with the cash and made his way, with intent, to the exit. The doorman waved forward a waiting black cab and he headed back to his hotel in Euston. Once in his room, Marcus tipped out the cash onto his bed and counted the piles. He had made seventy thousand pounds in one night. He kicked off his shoes, threw his jacket down, pulled off his tie and laid on the bed, exhausted. He wasn't going to sleep naked in these sheets. He rolled to his side and sharp pain reminded him of his injuries for the first time since he arrived in London. He rolled gingerly to his other side and then quickly drifted into a deep sleep.

Meanwhile, in room 720, Veronika was impatiently smoking a cigarette, tapping her knee nervously and drinking the combined contents of the miniature vodka bottles from the mini-bar. Her two male companions sat waiting for Marcus. No-one was speaking. It had been a week since she hooked the last John and going by what she had said about his success in the casino, this one would be very lucrative to roll over. They might only break his nose, rather than his arms, but it depended upon how much resistance he put up. If he didn't show up they would direct their frustrated violence towards Veronika, with a k.

All the Saints

Blackwood had used the Christmas recess to review a mountain of paperwork in his newly-refurbished home office. It had been a welcome break and he and his family had enjoyed some respite from media attention. The twins were getting to an age at which they were more interesting. They were engaging with him, and their personalities were starting to come through. They loved rough and tumble play and once they were wound up it was impossible to calm them down until one of them had a full, bubbly-snot, red-faced tantrum caused by the other. As much as it was fun, it was also tiring, and he was pleased to be walking back to his desk in Westminster, fresh, a few kilos heavier, and with new vigour to tackle his department's expenditure.

The noise around Jenny Foxton had quietened and the story was now lining the floors of domestic pet cages and wrapping the valuables of people moving home. He had kept in contact with the Foxtons. Christmas was particularly challenging for them, and they had been invited to his parents' house over the festive period. He had been invited to join them but declined the invitation.

Blackwood had acted without his usual careful political acumen when he pushed for the sacking of Anker. It was a knee-jerk reaction and Southall had warned him against it, as it was something that could come back to bite him. The publisher might view the action as favour to be called against or be used as a bargaining chip in the future. He was in no doubt that he had stepped over the line with the coroner, but that was definitely the lesser of his two actions. In fact, the coroner had been very understanding and had agreed to the verdict without much persuasion.

The press and the Opposition had moved on to other news and recently the focus had been on the mauling to death of the Welsh couple by their large dogs. The Opposition had been calling to see the Dangerous Dogs Act of 1991 further tightened and said the deaths were the result of slack policy under Blackwood's watch and it was a sign of the incumbent government's ineptitude. Sitting in Opposition was so much easier: if rain caused flooding, if inflation soared, if winter came late or summer was too dry, it was the government's fault. In Opposition, all you had to do was challenge and point the finger, and he was learning how much harder it was when he was truly accountable. However, he relished that challenge and today, with his piles of paperwork with pages neatly tagged with multicoloured index flags and sections of reports highlighted, he was prepared and ready for his meeting with the Director General of MI5.

Sheila Wilkinson was in her late fifties and had had a notable career in public service, working as a diplomat overseas for many years before joining MI5, where she moved around various clandestine departments, increasing her profile internally. It was a formality that she would receive a Royal Honour and would likely be a Dame in the next year or so. Her appointment as Director General was made by Blackwood's predecessor and whilst he found the department to be evasive in its dealings with him, he liked and respected Wilkinson greatly for her proven track record and she spoke with a directness he appreciated. She walked in confidently, dressed in a well-tailored navy trouser suit, with natural grey short-cut hair. She was angular, neat, and efficient in appearance.

'How have you been, Peter? I have quite an agenda for you. I am afraid the enemies of the state don't usually take a Christmas break,' she said, sitting.

'Very well. Thank you for sending me the report and I appreciate that your department isn't usually exposed to this amount of scrutiny. Times are changing. Our secret services need to step out from the shadows and be accountable. You know, "who watches the watchmen"? When Thames House opens, it will be the opportunity to have you step into the light, Shelia.'

'The eventuality was explained to me before my appointment, and I am comfortable with it. We will be very much in the public eye on the banks of the Thames and, as you say, we are in a different era. The days of vast numbers of agents spread out internationally, working locally to gather data, is coming to an end. Technology is helping us to be far more efficient in both collection and interpretation of field data. Our shadow wars will become digital battles. I have grave concerns with the freedom and speed of access those that would do us harm will have to some of the information that, perhaps, used to be harder to come by.'

'Have you and Graham been talking?' Peter asked rhetorically. 'I don't disagree, perhaps I need more education around the subject. But that is for another day. I am talking with my department heads about expenditure and how we need to reduce it. The government was elected with a manifesto of cost cuttings and the PM believes that we are in a period of relative international and internal stability. Therefore, perhaps we can review the direction and extent of our spending in certain departments.'

'Our talks with the paramilitaries are very early, Peter. I admire the PM's optimism, but we saw only last year the extent of the determination and the lengths they will go to achieve their goals. Whilst we will obviously engage positively through our channels, we both shake with one hand and in the other hold a gun. Beyond that situation, we are watched with envious or hateful eyes all the time, and those watchers change and the reasons for the anger or jealously alter. If we step back from our diligence, we let them come closer and that simply makes us more vulnerable,' she replied.

'I don't disagree, however, my role is to bring about the will of the people, which I have the mandate to do. I don't want to clip your wings, but we need them to be spread more efficiently. Using technology more, reducing our man-hours. The Met Commissioner has started to look at our CCTV network and how we can access private systems to give us eyes in areas where they don't have coverage currently either because of risk or location. That seems to be a forward-thinking approach, which has been signed off, and it's gathering pace.'

'That is good, but hardly new. GCHQ has been operating this for some time and we have shared its benefits with many departments, so it is rewarding to see that these ideas are being picked up. Just because technology is advancing it does not mean we need fewer boots on the ground. The chatter on the internet is growing at pace. Already, we can't keep up with it. So where once we needed an agent to be in, say, Chennai, to report, we can now do much of that from Gloucester or London, but it still takes a seat and, of course, if action is needed, we need those boots on the ground.'

'You are saying we need MORE?' asked Peter.

'Certainly,' came the reply.

'Well, you need to absorb the costs through savings and then find some additional savings. I have tried my best to understand the report, but it is confusing. I mean...' Peter opened his folder. Running his finger down the colourful array of index tags on the edge, he settled on one and flipped the prior pages. 'Operation Black Widow, redacted entries, cost £456,735. Fruit Pie, redacted entries, cost £1,387,669. Great Bear, redacted, cost £4,567,121. Redacted. Redacted. Much of the report is black block.'

Wilkinson shifted in her seat and made a slight cough. 'Peter, much of what we do is secret.'

'I understand, but I am the Home Secretary and I have security clearance, do I not?'

'Yes. Even so, the less you know of much of what we do, the better for you. I can say that Black Widow was successful and has been discontinued. Fruit Pie relates to operations in co-operation with our friends across the pond and is very much on going. Great Bear is our friend to the East, do I need to go on?'

'Bluntly, yes. Corkscrew?' Peter turned his folder around so that Wilkinson could see the entry. She didn't move from her position and her expression remained deadpan. Peter didn't understand how she did it, but other people who obstructed him would push him to anger, however, he enjoyed their exchanges. She was far more intelligent and quicker-witted than he and he admired her achievements and capability. He felt there was some degree of genuine mutual respect.

'Corkscrew is ongoing work we are undertaking with Customs and Exercise around illicit importation of quality wines.

We are assisting with the identification of the network, as it seems there are other goods being conveyed under the cover of this activity. We traced the import of Eastern Bloc decommissioned arms that were being transported to Liverpool for onward delivery to Ireland and we have infiltrated the criminal gang that is shipping from the Czech Republic to France. We strongly believe that the weapons are released with the knowledge of the Kremlin—another attempt at destabilisation.'

'There we go. That wasn't hard, was it? What about these here?' Peter turned some more pages and pointed to a largely redacted sheet with only the four headings "Order of Saint George", "Order of Sinjon", "Order of Saint Andrew", and "Lesdix".

'They are expenses of the Crown.' She acknowledged Blackwood's inquisitive look. 'There are various costs for the Crown that are directly for the Crown's benefit, managed by the Crown but paid for by various state departments.'

'And what do these relate to? The costs are significant.'

'That I am afraid I cannot share with you, Peter. I have tried to dance around this, but you are not permanent; let's assume that your party loses the next election, or there is a reshuffle, and you move on. You will take with you all the information you have gained since being in office. How many Home Secretaries are alive today, do you think? Ten? Twenty? More? If each Home Secretary knew everything, then what would be the chances of a serious breach of security, deliberate or accidental? You are told what you need to know to do your job and we get on with ours.'

Of course, Blackwood appreciated the point, but, his instinct told him that this redirection of royal expenditure was an issue, a deceit, and also a challenge to his cost-cutting exercise, if he was looking to impact the royal purse. 'The royal family are supported by the Sovereign Grant and the Civil List, so how much more do they cost us, beyond what is declared?'

'I cannot comment any more on these costs because I don't know. I would suggest you direct your questions to Stowe and Arc, the Crown's legal representatives. These are legitimate costs that relate to our monarchy and are therefore essential for our constitution and establishment. I will consult with my department heads, and we will see what additional information it would be possible to share, and we will review our budgets.' Wilkinson stood and offered her hand, clearly indicating that the meeting was at an end regardless of Blackwood's intentions.

He shook her hand and smiled. 'Shall we continue this next week?'

'I shall count the days, Home Secretary,' replied Wilkinson.

She left the room and Blackwood nodded, ending another meeting with the Head of the Secret Services where he was none the wiser as to the outcome. She would have made a formidable politician. He had time for a coffee, a quick review of his emails and an opportunity to retrieve his voice messages before he had his next meeting with Jenks. Whilst they had spoken at length over the telephone, he had not seen Jenks since their lunch meeting in his club. Today he would be visiting Jenks in his office at the Yard, and the man was even more intolerable when he was in the security of his own territory. Unfortunately, none of his messages gave him the opportunity to cancel his meeting. Blackwood stood and loaded his briefcase and left for the short walk to Scotland Yard's offices. He moved with the enthusiasm of a pupil returning to school after the summer break.

***

His meeting with Commissioner Jenks was as awkward as he expected. During their meeting, Jenks had sat behind his laminated desk, dunking his way through a variety of beige biscuits and drinking his insipidly coloured tea, probably sweetened with a generous helping of white sugar. To Blackwood, Jenks summed up the 70s in all its polyester and nylon, *Carry On* movies, and Cinzano commercials. He was still living in the age of *The Sweeney* and *The Professionals,* but he lacked the charm to be forgiven as nostalgic. He was simply a worn-out relic that had been in sight for so long that people were by now blind to him. The man was a dinosaur and the more time he spent with him, the more clearly Blackwood could see the prejudice and bigotry. It was proving to be a very challenging relationship as they came from different backgrounds, different generations, and very different ends of the political spectrum.

A strong, freezing winter's wind gusted against Peter as he walked from Scotland Yard to his club. It ricocheted off the buildings as it danced its invisible whirligig down the street, mischievously inverting umbrellas, blowing open loosely held coats, and ruffling carefully quaffed hair, its mocking whistle heard as it squeezed tightly through small gaps as it rushed past towards its unknown destination. Peter didn't mind the rain, snow, or ice, but the wind annoyed him. It was often cantankerous, opposing progress, and when it rained, it assisted its damp conspirator to squeeze through undiscovered gaps in outdoor clothing. He had his head down. The next turning would take him off the street that was acting as the wind's funnel and he couldn't get there quickly enough.

He liked to walk between meetings when he could, and with many government buildings and his club in such proximity, it was a simple luxury afforded regularly. It gave him an opportunity to reflect on conversations had and plan conversations due. In that walk, Blackwood decided that Jenks would need to go and a replacement that he could work with step up. Jenks' management during his tenure was best described as adequate, so Blackwood would need time to build the environment that would lead Jenks to resign. Perhaps retirement would be better suited; he was eligible. First, he needed to identify who would be a good fit for the role. The decision timed well with the conclusion of his journey, and he pushed the heavy glossy black door inward and walked into the warmth and comfort of his club.

As he took his seat in one of the drawing rooms and ordered a drink, a tall, older gentleman approached. His wiry grey hair was cut short, his charcoal grey suit looked expensive with its pocket square that matched his tie, and he had a warm smile as he introduced himself.

'Mr Blackwood, I hope you don't mind the approach. I am Jeremy Stowe of Stowe and Arc Solicitors. I had heard that you were a fellow member, but I have not had the opportunity to meet you before. May I join you?' His accent was public school, boarding on plummy.

'Of course.' Peter waved for him to sit in the armchair opposite. 'I have heard of your firm. Pleasure.' The drawing room had varied clusters of high-backed maroon, tan, or dark green leather Chesterfield armchairs arranged around low coffee tables, inviting discreet discourse.

'I am flattered, and I trust the commentary was positive. We are a small discreet firm and we do not actively seek new engagements. We tend to represent family interests, acting in a wide range of matters for our discerning international client base. I have long been a supporter of your politics and have followed your progress with great interest. It is indeed a pleasure to have the opportunity to make your acquaintance. Perhaps we may speak for a while?'

'You are the Crown's legal representatives?' asked Peter.

'We do not disclose or discuss our clientele, Mr Blackwood. Discretion is a much-underrated commodity, and it gives our firm great value. Perhaps one day we may be able to offer you counsel. How are you finding your position?'

'I take my responsibilities very seriously and it is challenging, but I wish to serve and the office I hold is one of the most significant in our democracy and I will do all that I can to fulfil my obligations.' He spoke with passion.

'I believe that to be true. Do your ambitions exceed your current position?' asked Mr Stowe.

Peter laughed. 'I am Home Secretary and I give this role my full attention. Perhaps one day, should the circumstances arise, I may have the opportunity to take the premier position in government. I will not hide from or apologise for my ambitions—it would be untruthful not to acknowledge them. However, I support the Prime Minister and do not see a situation where I would not.' It was a well-rehearsed response. Of course he wanted to be the leader of his party and Prime Minister. Few kids play football to be the keeper—they all want to be the striker. Politics was no different.

'Very good,' nodded Mr Stowe.

A waiter came and took an order. 'May I refresh your glass, Mr Blackwood?' offered Mr Stowe.

'Please call me Peter, Mr Blackwood is my father's name. Bushmills, please, Mr Stowe.'

'Thank you. My friends call me Jeremy, and I believe that would be appropriate. Irish not Scotch?' Mr Stowe raised an eyebrow.

'Whiskey doesn't belong to Scotland. Although I enjoy a Scotch, I find Irish to be less peaty, sweeter, and more mellow. I am afraid I take mine with ample ice so I would accept that I am far from a connoisseur. It's similar to sparkling wine and champagne—I find the former to be dismissed as inferior where often it can be comparable if not superior to the latter and therefore can offer much better value. I trust you will treat this secret with the discretion you are famed for, otherwise everyone will switch.'

'Quite so, I am a bastion for confidence, I shall keep mum.' Mr Stowe tapped his nose. 'Personally, I like an aged malt, the darker and peatier the better, with a dash of spring water just to bring it alive. But then, I was raised conservatively. "Conventionally predictable" would be an accusation I would find hard to refute.' Mr Stowe raised his glass.

'There is a lot to be said for being conventional, Jeremy. You appear to have done well by being so.' Peter received his new drink and took a sip.

'Being conversative in nature does not necessarily oppose change and progress. Us conventional thinkers just pull on the reins of those at the front that are driving forward. Progress and change are like vehicles travelling downhill. Left unchecked, they gain momentum until they become dangerously out of control and eventually crash. Us conventional people are the foot brake that helps control the speed the vehicle travels. That is why I enjoy my role: through law, I am guardian of established principles, which have been stressed and tested over hundreds of years. Changes to these principles should be challenged, not to hinder progress, but to ensure that they remain relevant. We must protect what we have built to bring us to where we are.'

Peter nodded. 'A legal chameleon. One eye on the past and one eye on the future?'

'I have been called many types of reptile in my career, but chameleon is a first, Peter. I shall receive it in the manner that I perceive it was made.' Jeremy leant forward subtly, inviting Peter to do likewise. 'I shall confess that our meeting today was by design. One of my clients has been particularly interested in your career and progress and I am representing them.'

Peter sat back and raised his guard. 'I am approached regularly by pressure groups, corporations, and organisations who lobby me. This is not the channel for that.'

'You will find my approach to be quite in order, I assure you. A position has become available, which would not detract from your current office and my client would like the opportunity to discuss this with you. You have an impeccable record; I have seen many people come and go but few show a decision path as clear as yours. My client has been impressed with your professional and personal conduct and believes that you would a great asset. The role is sensitive, and I will just remind you of your obligations under the Official Secrets Act.' Mr Stowe paused, and this raised Peter's interest.

'I have Emerald clearance status, Jeremy. I have passed my background checks and of course, as I am sure you realise, our intelligence services report into me.'

'Yes, you have greenlit all our checks.' Mr Stowe continued, 'This position is one of the most established in the country and probably one of the most discreet. I would like to invite you to our offices in Lincoln's Inn Fields where we can speak more freely. I have already taken the liberty of speaking with your secretary and proposed a date. You will understand that this requires your utmost discretion.'

'It is intriguing, but I really need to know some more before I commit my time,' Peter said.

'Of course. The position is in Lesdix and it involves the management of the ancient Order of St George. I am led to believe that you will be familiar with these titles. Again, I will remind you that this a matter of state secrecy. The appointment is recorded in your diary with my office, which would be quite normal considering our clientele, so no-one will question it.' Mr Stowe had finished his drink and stood. 'It was a pleasure to meet you, Peter. I will look forward to our further discussions.'

High Roller

Marcus had researched and collected the addresses of the twenty-one casinos in London and his plan was to work them all over the next few months. He had taken a short-term tenancy of a penthouse in Thames Quay, in the Chelsea Harbour development. The agent that met him for the appointment looked him up and down, heard his Welsh accent, and wanted to cancel the viewing. Marcus bribed him with two thousand pounds in cash and paid the rent by bank transfer that day. Others may have thought it expensive, but he would make that money that evening on one roll of the dice.

The five-bed apartment had generous terraces that looked out over the river, giving an elevated view along the Thames and into the harbour below. The floors were polished white marble, while all the kitchens (there were two) and bathrooms (there were five) were decorated in shiny black granite and chrome. He had a private lift that opened into the main reception room and the furniture was Italian, minimal, monochrome, and leather. There was a twenty-four-hour concierge service in the main reception and what seemed to be a regular queue of black taxi cabs waiting for a fare.

He had been looking for short-term rents in the Evening Standard and had been quickly bored, ringing for a viewing of the apartment mainly out of curiosity. The location was convenient to the West End and its casinos, and he wanted to see what a top-end apartment was like. The agent's attitude had got under his skin, and he took on the tenancy mainly to show that he could. It was another world to the one he had grown up in and a mighty step up compared to the Ambassador that had been his home for his first few nights in London.

He had travelled outside Central London, visiting smaller casinos. It had been quickly apparent that the more provincial casinos ran a much smaller cash line, with relatively low maximum table bets. He had spent the same amount of time, carefully winning just enough to seem lucky, but he came away with much less cash.

After the returns on his first night, he didn't have the patience to waste time on those smaller venues, so he decided to focus on the higher profile central casinos, where the 'money' went, and he would leave with it all. He still had to work out his identity issue. It was necessary to join these establishments, and although he was a novice, it was obvious to him that word of a lucky Welshman would quickly spread amongst the clubs and he would find himself excluded. His plan was to source some identity documents in the next few days and in the meantime keep to the less salubrious casinos around North and East London.

During the day he would practice his spells and incantations, fine tuning his card, dice, and dial manipulations. He was trying to improve his connection with *Mamddaear*, but with so little of nature's environment around him it was weak. Being by the river and elevated appeared to help, but once he was at street level and in the throng of people and traffic, it was almost impossible. Without the timeless environment of the cave, practice time seemed limited. A day would quickly pass and he would make little progress. Being in London not only limited his connection to *Mamddaear*, it also limited the scope of his practice, as he was confined to spells that he could devise or rehearse within the walls of his apartment.

He had visited London Zoo during the week, and it was a banquet of energy that he feasted on. There were so many creatures in such a small space that the zoo acted like a transmitter, and he felt connected and safe. He had initially paid little attention to the frustrations, fears, and boredom that were being felt from the animals held in concrete cells and behind iron bars and railings. There were strong sources of *Grym*; lions, tigers, polar bears, elephants—he was turbo charged whilst sitting on a bench, being anonymous. He had found it easy to connect with the chimpanzees and had taken to sitting near their enclosure, and when visitors stopped and took an interest in the chimps, he would make one of them throw excrement at them. It never got old.

It was dark by four in the afternoon and from his penthouse window in the winter's night, the city's streetlamps and headlights sparkled like stars. The river cut a black meandering line through the centre of the artificial universe, like it had been torn in two, with London's bridges being the last strands of sinew desperately holding the two sides together. Marcus had bought himself a new black suit from Hugo Boss which fitted as though it had been tailored. He wore a crisp white shirt and new shoes. He had a fresh haircut now, with his hair swept back and cleanly shaven; he liked himself in the mirror and he was enjoying the lifestyle he had created for himself, but he had to remain focused on his task. He headed to the reception and had the doorman flag him a black taxi for the journey to that night's target casino.

Marcus made his way to the tables, past the rows of slot machines that flashed bright and velociously, vying for attention. It was nine in the evening and the venue was busy, but the gamblers were largely recreational—the more serious and habitual players would start arriving around eleven. He glanced to the bar, looking for a seat to have a soft drink before taking a place at a table and a familiar figure caught his eye. He instantly recognised her walking away from him, her tightly fitted long dress accentuating her lithe build, her pale bare shoulders and arms contrasting with the bright red material of her dress. He almost called out, but stopped himself. He walked rapidly toward her and gently tapped her shoulder.

'Hi, Veronika, what a pleasant surprise to see you here.'

As she turned and he could see that her make-up was poorly covering a bruise to her cheek, and as he looked her over, he saw bruises on the inner side of her arms. He recognised them as finger marks.

'What happened to you?' he asked. He had a strange emotion in the pit of his stomach that he had not experienced before. It wasn't fear, or anger.

Her initial expression seemed to be fearful, then her eyes welled slightly, and it changed to relief.

'Hello, Lucky.' She feigned a smile, but Marcus could see that her eyes didn't change their expression. She glanced over to her left, towards the bar. He followed her eyeline to see two men leaning against the bar, seemingly engaged in conversation. 'Do you want to buy me a drink?' she asked and slipped her arm into his. She led him to the far end of the bar, away from where the men were standing, and the duo sat on bar stools.

'Are they with you? Are you OK?' asked Marcus, who was still trying to understand the emotion he was feeling. He ordered drinks.

'You are the first person to show me kindness for a long time, Lucky, and my heart warmed when I turned to see you. I have decided that I will tell you the truth. I think I am less scared of your reaction than I am of those two men.' She took a sip of her drink and then a deep breath. 'My job is to pick up targets, like you, that are spending lots of money, and get you to come back to a hotel room we have booked and then you are robbed.' She hung her head down, seemingly ashamed. 'I paid three thousand pounds to come to the UK. I was told it was a fee for a modelling contract. When I arrived, they took my passport and told me I owed them thousands more. I am held in a house with other girls who come and go. They are horrible, the things I see happen to other girls. When we first met and I booked a room, it was to rob you. When you didn't show up, I was relieved because you were kind to me, but they hit me and did other things to me that I can't think about. I am scared. I have no-one and nothing.'

He could see the fear in her eyes, but Marcus' emotion didn't change. He thought he should be angry, he wanted to be angry, but he wasn't and seemingly couldn't be. He had an overwhelming desire to help. Then it all became clear to him.

'I am a very powerful person, although I may not look it. There is much I can do, and I will help you, because I believe you. But you will have to do things for me.'

'I understand,' she said and she slid her hand up his thigh towards his groin.

'No, not that.' Marcus recoiled. Surprised by the action and stumbling with his words, he said, 'Not that I wouldn't want that. If that is what you were suggesting. I mean, you know. If you wanted to. I do. I would. Damn. I don't want you to give me that for this. I mean. Oh, shit.' He felt stupid.

'What do you want then, Lucky?' she asked, almost impatiently.

'First off, please stop calling me Lucky, call me Merlin,' he said. 'I will take you away from here tonight. You will be safe, I guarantee it. I want passports. I don't care what they look like, so long as they are genuine. If you can get me those, I will give you freedom. You can stay with me, leave, whatever you want.'

'We have those. In the room upstairs. We have credit cards too, if you are interested? They sell all that stuff on; they only want cash.'

It felt right. Marcus was certain this was right. They discussed plans and he waited as she left towards the toilets. As she passed the two men, one of them stood and followed her out of sight. After a few minutes, she returned and said, 'It is all set, I have said that you have a lot of cash with you, and you wanted to pick up where we left off last time. They believed me. They have left to wait for us. Are you ready?'

Veronika and Marcus took the lift up six floors to the room.

'When we get to the room, I will open the door and you will go in first. By the time you realise I am not behind you, it will be too late, they will be waiting in the bedroom. Usually the guys give in immediately and give them everything. I wait out here, as a look-out, in case someone comes along the hall,' she explained.

'Got it,' said Marcus as they stood in front of the door. He had been thinking about what to do, and decided they needed to be taught a lesson. 'OK, let's do this.'

Before she swiped the card key, she gave him a light kiss on his cheek, then shrugged and winked. The light on the door lock changed from red to green, gave a little beep, and clunked as the electronic mechanism released the door. Marcus took a breath and stepped into the unknown.

As he passed the bathroom door to his left, the main chamber came into view, and he saw them. He realised at that moment just how large these two men were and they looked like they were capable of violence. The younger one of the two, probably in his late twenties, had a tattoo peeking out from the top of his black t-shirt.

'You thought you were going to fuck Veronica, but, my friend, we fuck you.'

Marcus smiled at them, 'I didn't know it was going to one of those parties.'

The other man grunted and stepped forward. Marcus shook his head and took a step back. The sound of flatulence filled the room, long and loud, and the man stopped and looked down as his bowels evacuated fully and rapidly. Marcus looked to the other man and winked. He immediately disgorged powerfully over his partner's back, the jet of vomit spraying in all directions on impact. The two were looking at one another in confusion and embarrassment, temporarily forgetting their intentions. The older one turned back to Marcus, anger radiating from his expression.

The younger man picked up the telephone from the bedside table and swung it with all his might, bringing it crashing down on the other's skull. As the older man fell to the ground, he hit him again and again. With each impact, the phone went 'ting'. Ting! Ting! Ting!

'NE! NE! NE!' he was shouting with each impact. He could not stop himself. It was as though he was possessed. The phone shattered, leaving the older man lying insensible, bleeding from his head and ears.

Marcus pointed to the younger man and then to the mirror that was fixed to the wall over the dressing table. He threw himself, with full force, headfirst into the mirror. The glass shattered. He fell down upon the dressing table, and as he slid unconscious to the ground, the table toppled on to him. Blood was flowing from his head injuries, mirror shards embedded in his face and forehead.

Marcus stepped forward. He was fully aroused, the power exciting him, and was thinking how to end this when Veronika came into the room.

She stopped in her tracks. 'Pane Bože!' she said quietly as she saw both men prone and bloody on the floor, surrounded by broken glass. The air smelt of vomit and excrement. 'Merlin, are you hurt? What? How did you do that? You made too much noise. We need to leave.' She was still assessing the sight before her, her two brutish abusers beaten and broken.

'I need the passports. Where are the passports?' he snapped.

Veronika jumped at the tone. 'Over there.' She pointed to a large, soft bag on the bed. 'Take it and let's go.'

Marcus picked up the bag and started to leave. He paused and turned back—he wanted to finish the job, but Veronika tugged his jacket. 'We need to leave.'

They calmly left the building and stepped into a black cab and headed home. He was breathing quickly; adrenaline was still pumping through him. It was exciting. He felt powerful. He felt totally in control.

Veronika moved next to him and, placing her hand on his thigh, she felt his full erection. She was undecided over this skinny man. He was shy and awkward, but he was also confident and clearly physically competent, and this made her nervous of him, which she found exciting. Opening up to him was an act of desperation and she was still trapped, hundreds of miles from home, without means and in the company of another violent man who apparently only had one thing on his mind. She completely misinterpreted the source of his arousal. The immediate threat had passed for now; she had no other option than to see where this led.

The journey back to his apartment was swift—much of the traffic had disappeared, and without obstacle the true, small size of central London was apparent. The lift doors opened, and he stepped into his reception room and, walking to the dining table, threw the bag down. Veronika walked in behind him and was looking around the penthouse in amazement, 'This is where you live?'

'Yes,' Marcus replied absentmindedly. He unzipped the bag and tipped the contents on to the table. Out tumbled passports, wallets, loose credit cards and rolls of cash in denominations, bound with elastic bands. He turned to Veronika. 'Make yourself at home, I need the bathroom.' As quickly as he could, without running, he made his way to the nearest toilet, where he collapsed in emotional agony as once again his sense of joy turned into his torment of cursed pain and appalling apparitions.

He returned to main living area a few minutes later, exhausted and looking pale. 'I am tired. You may pick any room you choose. If you do not wish to stay you can take what you want of the money on the table and leave.' *Damn it*, he thought. 'You are welcome to stay, though. As I say, pick a room.'

Veronika had walked the sizable apartment whilst waiting for Marcus to return. It seemed too good to be true. She hadn't expected to be freed without condition. She watched Marcus walk away down a corridor towards a bedroom. She looked at the table, which had upon it more than enough resources to give her the opportunity to go home to Prague. It was around midnight, where would she go? She only had the very thin clothes she was wearing. She still had no passport. She hadn't been coerced or forced into sex. She hadn't been beaten. This situation was as good as it could be for her right now so she would stay and see what tomorrow had in store. She found the bedroom furthest away from Marcus' room and, locking the door, she undressed and climbed in between the clean, crisp sheets of the most comfortable bed she thought she had ever laid in. She felt the most secure she had for months and was soon in a deep sleep.

When she woke, the apartment was silent. She called out but was not answered and the clock on wall showed it was 11:30 in the morning. Lighting a cigarette, she explored the spacious, light apartment. She was struck by how anonymous it was; the walls were devoid of the usual photographs that accumulated over time, and most of the drawers and cupboards were empty. His wardrobe had very few clothes hanging. A Sega Mega Drive was wired into the large television in the main living space and a laptop sat on the desk that stood against one of the floor-to-ceiling windows that overlooked the Thames. It chimed to life but was password protected. The huge Wolf American fridge in the stainless steel and black marble kitchen chilled a single milk carton, a tub of butter, and three eggs.

On the dining table was a note that read:

Morning Veronika.

There is some money in the envelope on the table for you. There are some baggies and coats in my wardrobe. They will be too big, but they are warmer than your dress and will do for now. I had the concierge arrange for some trainers in your size, which are in the bag on the table. You can use the money to buy some more clothes. I have told the concierge that you may be staying here for a while so they will help you if you need it. I am out for the day. I will back around 4 PM.

M

Joseph Allen

Marcus was pleasantly surprised that Veronika was there when he came back that first day. He had expected to return to an empty flat, with both her and the cash long gone. He was relieved and a little confused as to why she hadn't left. However, he had mixed emotions about her staying as he hadn't thought the consequences through when he helped her. If he was being honest with himself, it was the brain in his pants that had called the shots that night, his ego and libido getting the better of him. She was beautiful and he enjoyed watching her and wanted her more each day. As she padded around the apartment or sat curled up on the sofa, with her blonde hair tied up in a scrunchie, her slender neck bare, watching trashy daytime TV in her jeans, crop top, and oversized hoodie, he still found her mesmerising. She was easy company, polite, and quiet, which was a blessing as she had only left the flat for brief periods, cautious not be seen by an associate of her captives.

Quite quickly she adopted the role of housekeeper and cook, and he was grateful that he didn't need to think about such things. They seemed to have an unsaid agreement not to ask about each other's previous lives. She was undemanding. Marcus did not mind if she took money as he was making plenty and he hoped that soon she would come to him during the night. He thought it would be a fair exchange. However, with a house guest, he was limited to practising his wizardry in his bedroom, and the lack of freedom was beginning to grate. He was spending much of his day walking in the great parks of London or in London Zoo and most evenings visiting casinos, working his way through the list.

He was growing tired of London; the initial colours and excitement of the city was a thin façade he now looked past to see the real face of humanity that lay underneath. Unconnected and uninterested in the world that hosted it, mankind took what it wanted without consideration of the consequences. It had become a parasite

[handwritten: Time out for state of the world for author]

feeding off the planet at an ever-faster pace. People were obsessed with the superficial; the size of their home, the clothes they wore, the perpetual lust for pleasure. They were controlled by the need for money that saw many of them fill their days completing meaningless tasks that were only for the gratification of humanity, to give them enough money to carry on consuming those things that they were told they needed. The process that most people went through was entirely pointless and inconsequential individually, but collectively this vast swarm of humanity was devouring all around it, like a global locus swarm. The animals held captive in London Zoo were placed behind bars or isolated by deep moats in the name of 'Conservation', and the irony offended him.

He was finding his wizarding progress slow going without the Great Library and it had taken him much practice to recreate the *Gorlois Englyn*, the spell which Merlin used to disguise King Uther so that he could sleep with his rival Gorlois' wife Lady Igraine in Tintagel Castle. From this deceit was born Arthur, who would become king. The incantation had proved tricky because he was enchanting himself, and his dad hadn't taught him shapeshifting. Early attempts simply didn't work, but as he progressed, he started to be able to make small changes to his features. The first significant result was hideous—his facial extremities prolonged, giving him a fin-like nose and long, drooping ears. Much to his relief, after a few minutes the effects wore off.

It was the arrival of spring and its warmer, longer days that was the timing of his breakthrough. He was then able to shapeshift his appearance to any of the images from the passports he held and revert in the time it took the lift to drop from his apartment to the main foyer. The change that he had not been able to overcome was the colour of his eyes and they remained stubbornly pale blue despite all his practicing. He impatiently dismissed this detail as unnecessary; he was not making masterpieces. He only needed to fool clerks in the dark, subterranean rooms of London's casinos.

So far, he had seven active aliases he had used to join eight casinos. These aliases increased his opportunity to work each casino before each alias became blacklisted. So far, he had avoided raising any undue attention to any of his personas, managing his winnings, and if he became bored, he would leave, shapeshift and return. To keep himself amused he had started building personalities around his personas. Roger Dame, who, according to his passport, was born in Kettering, was forty-five years old and had a slight lisp that Marcus thought suited the round-faced, grey-haired man in the picture. He had given Roger a limp, from a motorbike accident. It was obvious to Marcus that Kevin Bannister had to be a barrister. He had a long, pointy, mean-looking face and short-cropped hair. Marcus enjoyed speaking with his prim, public school accent.

Tonight, however, he was Joseph Allen, born in St Albans and thirty-three. Joseph looked athletic; his hair was that finger combed just-tidy style that rugby players had, and Marcus thought he was handsome. He decided that he was a sales rep for a pharmaceuticals company. It was Joseph's second outing, and he was already ten thousand pounds up, having been playing blackjack for an hour. The table had quietened, and he had pocketed his chips, deciding to play one more hand before moving on. The tables of a casino seemed to have waves of gamblers. They washed up like an incoming tide, then receded again. Marcus could sense the rhythm. As with all things, it was the cycle of *Mamddaear*, the ebb and flow which led to harmony. Even in this artificial, sterile environment in the basement of a building of brick and steel, *Mamddaear* was still present, and Marcus was now finding the connection that evaded him when he first arrived in the City.

'Hey, man!' The man taking the seat next to him gave him a slight nudge as he tossed some large denomination pound notes to the croupier. 'You headed straight to the table then?'

Marcus looked over, attention gained by the contact. The man was in his early thirties at a guess; he looked slightly clammy and smelt of alcohol, with his shirt collar undone and tie loosened. He had probably been out drinking straight from work and his eyes had a slight drunken glaze to them. Marcus didn't recognise him. He nodded.

'You didn't get me a drink, ya bastard. It's your round, too.' The stranger grumbled as he accepted the small tower of chips and placed one on the felt in front of him.

'There's table service here,' Marcus replied, as he tried to gauge the situation.

His new companion wasn't paying him much attention as he was looking around the room. 'I saw Dan as we walked in and that bird from Finance and few of her mates are coming along in a bit. That was a good session in Spicers and good on you for coming back here, after, you know, you were mugged. Let's make some MONEY!' He glanced back at Marcus. 'You alright? You look weird, man.'

Shit. Marcus suddenly realised. 'I'm just going for piss.' He said as little as he could. He stood and headed to the bathroom. As he walked, he scanned around anxiously—he didn't want to meet someone else that recognised him as Joseph.

Joseph was standing at the urinal, one arm against the wall, propping himself up, emptying his bladder. He was thinking that he should have had something to eat. The mix of alcohol was taking its toll, and he was feeling lightheaded and slightly distant from his surroundings. He didn't like to drink too much, and since he had been robbed, he was wary of the vulnerability that being drunk gave him. He heard the bathroom door open, and someone go into a cubicle, locking the door behind them.

As Marcus locked the toilet door, his heart was racing, but he was breaking a smile. As much as the situation was tense it was also amusing. He took another passport from his other internal jacket pocket. It was Kevin Bannister. He muttered the *Englyn* as he looked at the photograph. Flushing the toilet and placing the passport back in his pocket, he unlocked the door and walked into the bathroom.

Joseph was refreshing his face by splashing it with water from the sink. Another drink or two and he would call it a night. He looked up as he felt someone standing next to him and nodded a greeting. The other man started laughing, patted him on the back, and then left the room. Joseph looked at his reflection. He couldn't see anything out of place or amusing. 'Wanker,' he said to himself as he dried his hands and headed back to the casino floor to find his companions.

Marcus was still smiling as he left the club, adrenaline subsiding. He needed to revise his plans, as that could have been disastrous. It was essential that he remained under the radar and anonymous as he had much ahead to do. He decided to stop working for the night and thought he would walk a while. The evening was pleasant. The sun had set, but it was still relatively early for him. He walked into one of the many twenty-four-hour convenience stores that lit up the dark streets with their multi-brand, illuminated advertising and clinically white lighting. He picked up a soft drink from the chill unit by the entrance and then noticed the blue lottery display unit. It was so obvious, perhaps it hadn't occurred to him before because he had lacked the confidence, but, what a quick solution. The jackpot that week was over eight and half million pounds, whilst he was doing well working the casinos it would take much more tedious work to accumulate that sort of capital.

As he paid for his drink, he asked for a lucky dip ticket, so he didn't even have worry about selecting the numbers. He left the shop and then paused, checking his emotions. He didn't want to feel joy because of the pain that would bring. He clenched his fists, closed his eyes and prepared. He concentrated on *Mamddaear*, reaching out for anything. He connected with a pigeon that was roosting quietly in one of the few trees that stood sparsely along the street. It was just a moment, but it was enough. Marcus opened his eyes and relaxed. Perhaps he had already beaten his father's curse. *Just goes to show what a weak wizard he was*, Marcus thought.

Tenth Dan

The cottage that the Merlinis had previous occupied had been redecorated. The floral wallpaper that looked like it had been there for many decades had been replaced by magnolia paint, new carpets had been laid upstairs and the ground floor's stone tiling had been cleaned, sealed, and polished, removing any traces of recent events. All the Merlinis' belongings—what there were of them—had been removed, donated to charity, or destroyed. It had been necessary to refurbish the kitchen and much of the old furniture had been replaced, which had required an enjoyable spending spree for the Davies.

Amy had taken the position of Farm Manager, and the cottage came with the position. It was now Amy's home, and it was fresh, light, and newly proven to be warm during the cold winter months. Both properties had recently been fitted with modems and separate lines to access dial-up internet, which had been a godsend for Amy. As much as she was engrossed in her new vocation, she was missing her life in London and her friends, whom she kept in contact with by landline and increasingly by email. She was also given a mobile phone, but there was scarcely any signal in the valleys, and even up on the peaks, she would have to hold the phone high in the air to see a single bar of signal, making the use of the phone impractical.

She didn't mind living alone as her days were full and her family close by. Her farming duties were quickly dispatched with the help of her father, who was increasingly enjoying the responsibility. He maintained the livestock and kept the flock in the cave supplied for the dragon, meaning that she was only required to round up the herd and bring it in from the hills each night, which she found easy. The sheep responded well to her and would follow her lead willingly. The Guardian said it was because of her positive *Grym*.

This freed up her day, which she would spend visiting the cave and in the company of the Guardian and the dragon. The time lag in the cave meant that she had almost a year's worth of study complete already. Since becoming the Guardian, Dafydd's knowledge of the Great Library had become absolute, and Amy's thirst for knowledge and natural academic leaning meant that she was progressing rapidly under his tutelage. She had learned that the dragon's name was Adar Llwch Gwin and her ability to speak with Adar had developed to the point that they could converse freely. They were becoming friends, as bizarre as that was when she stopped to think it over.

The Guardian had said that today she was going to learn the *Math Englyn*. This was the incantation that turned Math ap Mathonwy's nephews into deer, boars, and then wolves, and would be her first step to learning shapeshifting. She and her father met at the entrance to the barn and made their way down together.

'I must be crazy agreeing to this. Your mum asks if you can turn me into Jason from Take That,' groaned her dad.

'Really? Jason? I thought she was more of a Robbie fan. Even then, I thought she'd have gone more classic—Robert Redford or Paul Newman.' She stopped and looked at her dad, eying him up and down. 'Yeah, Jason would be an improvement.' She laughed. 'Dad, you're perfect as you are.'

'I'll take that. So, please try not to muck up what little I have, eh? I've done some pretty out there things in my time, but this is a first and I don't mind admitting I am little nervous. What if you turn me into a donkey or something and can't turn me back?'

'That wouldn't be the end of the world. You'd still be you, just a little hoarse.' Amy smiled at her own quip.

'Tell you what, you stick to the magic, and I'll crack the jokes. Deal?'

'Deal,' she agreed.

Adar was already circling above as they entered the meadow and walked towards the Keep. 'The Guardian says no-one seems to have made a connection with a dragon as strong as you have, since Uther himself. You appear to have a pet dragon,' said Tom.

'He is remarkable, dad. His memory goes back long before Uther. It's a jumble of pictures, moments and they can't all be his. He talks of great battles over vast plains where dragons fought alongside humans, deserts and sand dunes, high mountains constantly covered in snow. The hunting and killing of his kind, old and young being trapped and speared. It is as Dafydd—I mean, the Guardian—said. Adar has all the memories from all his kind, like a shared consciousness. I don't understand why he doesn't feel trapped or resentful towards us.

'It seems that dragons were not uncommon, but, as the number of people grew and became more organised, they started to compete for resources. There can be only one apex predator. Dragons were feared and then became a pest as they ate livestock and protected their territory and their young. It was conflict over resources initially, and mankind kept coming, hunting and fighting in ever larger numbers. Eventually the purpose of the hunt changed to simply be a sport and the kill became a prize. Adar's memories include young dragons, half-starved because their parents had been hunted, being killed as they were too weak to fly. It's like he doesn't have the emotion to hate.

'I guess with such history and life behind him, a year passing is only a moment. He accepts that the present is quickly passing. He feels safe and has all he needs, so has no reason to feel remorse, fear, or anger. He has fond memories of Merlin and Uther. There have been others that were close to him, but they were the closest. I think they were the first that really connected. He speaks like a grandparent, you know? Knowledgeable, reflective, circumspect… but he does seem to be tired.'

Adar looped the loop high above and swooped down low over their heads, the rush of wind blowing Amy's hair, and he came to rest by the Keep in a spot which he seemed to favour, his tail twitching, betraying his pleasure at seeing Amy.

Dragon voice

'Hello, my Amy. I miss you when you are not with me.' Adar's thoughts were being heard in Amy's mind as clearly as if he was speaking them aloud. 'Scratch my chin,' he requested as he lifted his great head up slightly. As Amy did so with both hands, she could hear contentment. It was a unique sound, like a purr, but much deeper and slower.

'Adar, I must spend more time with the Guardian and then we can sit a while and talk. Okay?' said Amy. Adar gave a short sigh and then laid back on the grass. 'You spend too much time sleeping,' said Amy as she patted his side and headed into the Keep.

'I meet others. I don't sleep,' he replied.

As they walked into the Great Library, the Guardian appeared. His hair and beard were both long and braided. He was wearing an ornate black gown, with a subtle triquetra pattern embroidered.

He gave a theatrical twirl. 'What do you think of this one then? This looks even more the part, huh? I copied it from a design that Oras the Great wore. He thought quite a lot of himself to add the suffix "the Great", but I think he had an eye for fabrics. I suppose Oras the Great does sound more auspicious the Oras the Tailor.'

'You look like ZZ Top's bedtime,' said Tom.

'I like it,' said Amy.

'Tom, be nice, or I will turn you into a pool of piss.' The Guardian winked.

'If you two don't stop it, I will knock your heads together!' said Amy.

'Interesting concept as I have no form,' said the Guardian, and as if to prove the point, he sunk to his waist in the floor and then rose again. 'Ah, it's good to see you both. Eternity is an extra long time when you only have Adar to talk to, and dragons are not renowned for their rapier wit. Right, are you both ready?' he asked. 'Tom, you will be safe. It won't hurt and you will keep your consciousness throughout. If we turn you into a dog, try to avoid the temptation of licking your balls. You won't be thankful when you are back to yourself.'

'Don't rush to that conclusion.' He looked over to Amy, 'Sorry, you probably didn't need to hear that.'

'Ewww. Dad. Seriously.'

The Guardian whispered the *Englyn* into Amy's ear and stood back. 'When you are ready,' he said.

'Wait!' called out Tom. 'You're sure you know what you are doing?' He looked to both Amy and the Guardian for reassurance.

'Honestly,' said The Guardian. 'It usually works fine.' He glanced at Amy, who had started to whisper the incantation.

Tom's clothes fell to a heap on the floor. Amy gasped. The Guardian gave a brief clap. From the heap was jettisoned a small piglet. Oinking loudly, it ran past Amy, out of the Library, and towards the main door.

'Fuck! Stop it!' called Amy as she started off in pursuit.

'How?' responded the Guardian. 'No physical presence and all that.' He was speaking to an empty room. Amy was already in hot pursuit of the deft piglet. As she caught up, it would dart in a different direction. It was weaving and dodging towards the woods and the cover of the ferns and other low vegetation. 'If it gets in there, I will never find him! Come on, Dafydd! Enough now!' she shouted, breathless.

The piglet disappeared into the undergrowth, Amy could hear the rustle of leaves as it continued its rapid progress into the security and cover of the woodland. 'Fuck,'. she said as she stopped running and caught her breath.

'What now?' the Guardian asked as he appeared next to her. 'It could take hours to find him in there,' he nodded towards the woods. 'Of course the *Chorts* could get him first—nice, plump, tender bit of boar would be a welcomed change for their palette. I do wonder why Adar et al don't get bored with lamb all the time. I suppose he can catch some fish in the lake, but that's hardly a substantial meal. Imagine, the same food day after day for years, decades. It's quite like marriage,' mused the Guardian before realising he was digressing. 'Sorry, back to now. So what next?'

Amy was beginning to get frustrated and then she had an idea. She paused, took a deep breath to calm herself down, closed her eyes, and cleared her mind. She reached out for her dad. She saw undergrowth rush past, she felt the mossy, leaf covered woodland floor under her bare feet and the brush of fern fronds against her cheek, she smelt the damp, cool, woody air. Her heart was beating in time with her piglet father. It was thumping quickly, excited. She stopped by the roots of a great tree. The base had large, plate-like mushrooms growing. She was smelling the rich earth, taking in all the scents of soil, digging. 'GOT HIM!' she said excitedly. She muttered another incantation, which would return her father to his form, and turned to the Guardian. 'Well, aren't you the sly one. Next time you want to teach me a lesson, can we do it with a little less drama?'

The Guardian was hovering, legs crossed, hands in his lap as if in meditation. He was smiling 'The greatest teacher, failure is. Hmm.'

'Yoda? Seriously? You are such an arse,' said Amy.

A rustling of leaves announced the arrival of Tom. He was standing amongst the ferns. His faced was mudded, he was naked, and he was fortunately only visible from the waist up. 'Do you think you can magic me my clothes, please?' He held up his hand. 'Look what I found! Truffles! Scrambled eggs and truffles for lunch, everyone?'

The Guardian rejoined them once they had finished eating. They sat at the table by the jetty, lunch plates cleared. 'You learned an important lesson today. All we do, all our knowledge, is part of us and you must now accept it as just a part of you. You don't think about writing a letter, driving a car, cooking those eggs. You use knowledge that you have subconsciously, without effort.

'You do not need to force it. Of course, what you have left to learn is vast, but have the confidence to do without thought and you will surprise yourself. All of our *Englynion*, incantations, spells are simply the thoughts of our predecessors put down to paper—a proven recipe, if you will—so that others can use the knowledge and learn faster. It is record of their connection with *Mamddaear*, but you have your own. You can make your own magic, and you are learning the language, so don't be afraid to practice.

'We shall, of course, continue lessons, but you have learned much, and you now need to relax. Think of it as becoming fluent in another language—eventually you don't need to think of the words to strike a conversation. However, as you speak more, you learn new words and phrases that express yourself more strongly, more quickly. This is the same. Do you understand?'

'Yes, I think I do,' Amy said. With that there was a small crack and, in the air above where they sat, a multicoloured starburst blossomed and faded like a firework. 'Like that.'

'Like that,' the Guardian agreed.

'Best not be doing that in London, though, eh?' said Tom. 'What time are you leaving?'

Amy had received a letter from Stowe and Arc, inviting her to London as part of her appointment to the Order. The invitation was very welcomed as it gave her a chance to visit her friends and reconnect with the city that she loved. She had made plans to stay in Limehouse and she was going to spend some time with Kieran, with whom she had been in regular contact by phone and email. 'I'm all packed, off tomorrow, and I'll be back in three days. I'm staying in Lucy's flat as she and her flatmate are both away.'

Monkey

Amy had underestimated the distance between Baker Street Tube Station and London Zoo. She checked her watch; she had agreed to meet Kieran at 11:00 AM at the entrance and even if she ran all the way she would not be on time—that was assuming that she managed to run that distance and not get a stitch or pass out. If she could get there in one piece, she would turn up sweating profusely, unable to speak, and probably collapse. A crowd might form. They might call an ambulance. A TV crew might arrive. Her parents would happen to be passing. Her father would say, 'I told you'd let yourself go.' Thinking it through didn't take too long and she opted for the safer alternative of flagging down a black cab. The driver snorted contempt that his fare was going to be minimum charge rather than a profitable journey along the Westway to Heathrow Airport.

To distract herself from checking her watch to see the minutes speed up as every sixty seconds past eleven she was late, Amy looked out of the window as the cab made its unrushed progress along the Outer Circle, taking in all the huge, white, stucco plaster buildings that lined the street opposite the great park. She hated being late and especially today. She hadn't seen Kieran for months and her absence had made her realise her feelings towards him. It was not love, but she had missed his conversation and the way he made her laugh even though they had spoken on the phone and exchanged emails. Her meeting with Stowe and Arc was late afternoon, so they had agreed to be tourists for the day with a few hours at the Zoo and then something to eat at an Italian on Great Titchfield Street. Amy would head to her meeting and then they planned to meet up in Narrow Street in East London, near the flat where she was staying.

Kieran had bought the tickets and was reading the small print on the reverse to kill time while he waited. The sound of squealing, worn-out black cab brakes caused him to look up and he smiled broadly when Amy stepped out. 'Good to see you,' he said as they exchanged a brief kiss.

'Sorry I was late,' replied Amy.

'I didn't notice,' lied Kieran. 'Right! 99 first. Or tigers, chimps, then 99?'

'99 immediately. Then chimps, polar bear, hippos, lion, pub?' she countered.

'99, chimps, polar bear, then pub?'

'Pub?'

'I would have said just pub, but I've bought the tickets now.' Kieran waved them. 'Sprinkles and chocolate sauce?'

'Of course, wouldn't have it any other way. What made you suggest London Zoo? I haven't been here since I was in Brownies, or perhaps it was a primary school trip,' Amy asked as they headed through the football stadium-like turnstile into the zoo.

'Dunn—a bit more romantic than Tower of London, or HMS Belfast, and that's all I've got when it comes to touristy London, I'm afraid. I came here with my parents when I was a kid. I got a white baseball cap with a logo; I think it was a panda. Anyway, I lost it on a boring Thames cruise that afternoon and I cried all the way home.'

'What a terrible childhood. You still carry the trauma?'

'Well, you don't see me wearing baseball caps, do you?'

'True,' said Amy.

As they walked, Amy was distracted; now that she was receptive and aware, the *Grym* of the animals around her connected with her own. Her sensory acceptance had been improving whilst in her new home in Wales, but, here amongst such varied and numerous other sources, she felt energised. Even though it was a typical English summer's day where the sun was stubbornly shielded by a high, light covering of cloud, the colours shouted to Amy with Mediterranean vividity. She could sense all the animals' emotions: hunger, boredom, loneliness, curiosity. Some watched uneasily as strange predators filed past, staring at them. Others took no notice. Some viewed their observers as prey, hoping for an opportunity to strike. Above all, there was an underlying melancholy which unsettled her. It was not something she had considered before, but they were all aware of their captivity.

They walked and talked, losing track of the time, and eventually found themselves by the chimpanzee enclosure. A moat separated the enclosure from the viewing public and its inhabitants were lying around, disinterested and relaxing as Amy and Kieran approached. A larger animal with a whiting beard looked up and took interest in the couple as they came near. 'Relative of yours?' asked Amy.

'Not that I know, but he does look pissed-off,' replied Kieran as the chimp started to energetically climb the framed platforms of the enclosure and swing between the ropes with increasing vigour. 'Seriously, he looks properly angry.'

The chimp ran up to the edge of the moat and looked to be preparing to jump and then stopped. It rose on its legs, beat its chest and bared its teeth.

'I think we should move,' Ssid Kieran as the chimp suddenly crouched, expelled faeces into its hand, and threw it at them, catching Kieran and sticking to his chest.

'JESUS!' he shouted, stepping back. The chimp called out in celebration and attempted to repeat the action, but Amy and Kieran had retreated away from their vantage point and the animal's excrement hit other onlookers who had been laughing at the spectacle. Several passers-by had stopped to watch the events and a stranger came forward and offered Kieran a pack of tissues. 'Thank you,' said Kieran.

'You're welcome, butt,' said the round-faced, grey-haired man. 'I work here—well, just finished my shift. I am thorry. There are notitheth.' He pointed to a sign on the perimeter fence. He pulled out a t-shirt from his backpack. 'Here, thith is new. It was for my next shift. I can get another tomorrow. We look about the thame thize.'

Kieran took the white t-shirt and opened it up. On the back, it said 'London Zoo', separated by a big red heart. He glanced at Amy, who was trying her best to remain straight-faced.

'Thank you, but I really I can't take it from you.'

'I insist. Tell you what, buy me a scoop—call it a fiver. It's cheaper than in the shop, and you can just change now and throw that one away,' said the man.

'Okay. Thank you. If you are sure.' Kieran took out his wallet, gave the man a note and carefully removed his soiled top. By the time that he had changed and thrown his top away into one of the waste bins nearby, the man had gone on his way.

'That was an unusually kind thing for someone to do,' commented Amy as she watched Kieran change tops, noting with approval his physique. 'It was either karma, making up for your childhood loss, or the chimp had discerning taste and was making comment on your frankly unfashionable Fred Perry,' said Amy with a smirk. 'Come on. I'd say that either way, it's a sign we're done here. Should we head over for lunch?'

Amy and Kieran had only to wait for a few minutes for the familiar rattling diesel engine song of a black cab and made their way to Great Titchfield Street. Amy insisted on paying the fare because Kieran had bought the zoo tickets, and he reluctantly conceded.

The restaurant had been a regular haunt of Amy's parents when they both worked in London before Amy was born. They would meet on payday, and it was their monthly extravagance, whilst they lived on modest incomes and saved to buy a home. After a while, the flamboyant owner recognised them and started to treat them with a free drink, or 'the best table in the house', which changed each visit depending upon which tables were vacant. On their rare trips to London, they would make a point to dine there and the owner, who was omnipresent, would welcome them back as if it had only been a week since their last visit.

Amy had adopted the habit of visiting a few times in a year and was never sure that he actually remembered her, but he always warmly welcomed her in—as he did with every other diner that she observed. It was part of the appeal. The food was traditional: not a drop of cream in their carbonara, pizzas as good as those served on the shores of Lake Como, and her favourite thin, delicate veal marsala that melted in the mouth.

The walls were covered in photographs of the owner posing with celebrities that had dined there, famous faces going back to the 1960s: Richard Burton, Clint Eastwood, Faye Dunaway and many others smiled broadly throughout the restaurant and down the stairs to the additional subterranean seating and the great water tank that housed multi-coloured exotic fish and provided lighting in the otherwise dimly lit lower space. The restaurant had full-length windows that could be folded back in the summer months, giving street seating and an all'aperto dining experience. Amy and Kieran were seated on one such table.

'Ciao, bella signora. Molto bello rivederti? Questo è il tuo ragazzo?' said the short, white-haired man that approached, clutching menus. The owner was probably in his late sixties and walked with the confidence of a king in his domain, and he radiated charm. His white shirt was unbuttoned sufficiently for a tuft of white chest hair to be visible, along with a thick gold chain. His skin was leathery brown and sun-weathered, and his sleeves were rolled back up his forearm to show his gold Rolex.

'Sto molto bene, grazie,' Amy replied, and without thinking added, 'È il nostro primo appuntamento, ma finora tutto bene.' Amy looked to Kieran, 'This is Lorenzo, the owner. My parents have been coming here for years.'

Kieran nodded and smiled.

'Your Italian is very good—takes me home to Turin.' Lorenzo looked to Kieran, 'Non sono impressionato dalla scelta dei vestiti.' He winked at Amy who gave a slight laugh. 'You are a fan of London Zoo, I see. You must like it very much.'

Kieran felt slightly embarrassed, 'There is a story behind this, but hell yeah. Who doesn't love a zoo?'

'Molto bene.' Lorenzo passed them the menus and talked through the daily specials. They ordered and were left alone, whilst their bottle of rose was opened and their food prepared.

'You have many talents, Amy. I never knew you spoke Italian,' said Kieran.

'I have plenty of time on my hands on the farm, so I am just putting it to good use,' she said. The Guardian had warned her to be careful with her new abilities, but, like the coin trick when they last met, she could not stop herself from playing just a little bit. She was being careful, but it was amusing to her. 'Do you speak any other languages?'

'I struggle with just the one,' he replied. 'My school wasn't the best and I was far from the best student, which explains why I do what I do for a living. It's been alright for a while, but I am starting to get itchy feet. I would like to do a bit travelling while I can. I've saved up some money. I thought I might head over to New Zealand and Australia, then have a look at Thailand. It's not been the same in Wimbledon, now that you lot have moved on. It feels like it's time to make a change. I was surprised that you decided to stay in Wales. I mean, you have so much to offer and, well, it's a sheep farm in the arse end of nowhere. I mean, I didn't expect it. It was a shame to see you move.'

'It's not what you think it is. The area is beautiful and full of history. I've learned so much, and it's not "the arse end of nowhere" by any means. It's not city living, and it doesn't mean that I'll be there for ever. Other circumstances led to my current situation, but I'm enjoying it. I'll carry on until circumstances change again or I stop enjoying it,' she replied.

'I didn't mean to offend you, sorry. It's just… I thought that we were going somewhere. Just selfish of me.'

'I'm not offended and we're good. Let's just enjoy ourselves, and see what happens,' Amy said.

'Cheers to that!' Kieran raised his glass, and they chinked in toast.

They talked without an uncomfortable pause and time passed quickly until Amy needed to leave to attend her next meeting. Kieran insisted on paying for lunch, to which Amy agreed, provided that she would pay for dinner, and the bill was brought to the table.

After a brief moment, Kieran said with alarm, 'I've lost my wallet!' Then it dawned on him. 'The toe-rag stole my wallet! He must have lifted it when I changed my top earlier.' He stood and rechecked his pockets and looked at the ground around them in a vain hope that he may have dropped it nearby.

Amy burst out laughing. 'I'm sorry. You're not having a great day, are you? Let me get this, and you can pay for dinner. What have you lost?'

'Cash, a few cards, driving licence. Nothing I can't replace, it's just annoying. I need to cut and run to the bank to cancel my cards and sort out some money.'

'Sure, I understand,' she said.

Kieran went to leave and then returned to give Amy a kiss. 'I'll make up for it later, I promise. If this was the first time you met me, you'd think I was a complete loser!' He turned to set off.

'The way your luck is going, I feel I should say be careful crossing the road,' she said.

Kieran paused and turned back. 'Erm, do you think you can lend twenty quid, just until later?'

Amy laughed and handed him some cash. 'See you in the Grapes around 7 PM!'

Kieran gave a backward wave as he disappeared around the corner. Amy settled the bill and set off towards Holborn.

Lincoln's Inn Fields

The offices of Stowe and Arc were in a five-storey narrow white town house squeezed between two substantial buildings overlooking the Square, which had recently seen wrought iron fencing and gates installed that were locked during the night. It was the largest public square in London and the homeless of the city had used the space to rest and sleep in relative safety. The installation of the fencing was designed to remove these unwanted vagrants from the area, not by providing a solution but by sweeping them on to the next forgotten area of London waiting for gentrification. There was an atmosphere of excitement and prosperity in the city following a long period of austerity. Redevelopment and rejuvenation projects were blossoming across the tired Great Wen, bringing new people and their money to reignite the embers of the fire that fuelled ambition and success for many.

The efficient-looking receptionist dialled an extension number, announced Amy's arrival, offered her a drink, and asked her to take a seat in reception. She was promptly collected by man of similar age who looked bookish and meek, and she recognised him as Mr Heaney, who had visited them all those months ago. He led her up several flights of stairs to another, smaller, reception where he asked her to wait once more.

A door opened and Mr Stowe walked out and greeted Amy. 'Miss Davies, Jeremy Stowe. Delighted to finally meet you. Please come this way.'

She followed him into his office. Two tall sash windows looked out over the Square, ornately framed portraits were on several of the walls, and a large mahogany desk with a green leather top sat with dominance in the room, in front of which was a low coffee table with four leather tub seats. A well-dressed black man stood as they walked in. She guessed he was in his late thirties. She recognised his face.

'Please allow me to introduce Peter Blackwood. Peter, this is Amy Davies. She is in our employ, and I thought it would be beneficial for you to meet. She will join us for the next part of the meeting. She is aware of most of what I have told you, but the first few items on our agenda were for your ears only, and must remain so.'

He continued, 'Miss Davies, you may well be aware of elements to the *precis* I shall share, so please entertain me with your patience. This great nation of ours has its origins so very deep in history that our earliest references predate common written archives. Our roots were planted by the ancient Britons, and we are a nation that has been shaped by thousands of years of conflict and conquest. Much of our early history been lost completely or passed in songs and poems through lore. However, it is possible to trace our origins through generations, spanning the rules of ancient kings such as Brutus, Jago, Cherin, Lud, Eudad Hen, Uther and Arthur, and many others.

'We have a great wealth of culture that other, less mature countries can only view with envy, and this has been protected and kept sacred over the millennia. Lesdix was created by Constantine III, who ruled after Arthur died in battle. It was a secret brotherhood whose role was to protect the jewels of our land that Arthur and Uther had unified, during their magnificent reigns. These jewels define us, drive us, and give us our unity of purpose and belief. They are not just objects to be admired. They are the very essence of our being. It was believed that if they should fall then all we know would be lost. All that has evolved would fade and our island nation would be no more.

'Lesdix was Constantine's reimagining of the Round Table, the legend of which I am sure you are both familiar. There were ten positions. One was held by the King, and the others were trusted members of the Court. Lesdix were separated into three orders—the Orders of Saint George, St John, and St Andrew. Each of these Orders took responsibility for a specific jewel of the nation. As the years turned into decades and centuries, the Lesdix and its Orders were set aside and eventually lost in what became the huge administration of the Crown. The Monarch lost direct contact with the Order, rarely calling upon it.

'The last reference we have in the brotherhood of direct monarchic influence was from Charles I, who appealed to the Brotherhood to rescue him from captivity–'

Amy interrupted with enthusiasm, pleased that she was up to speed. 'I have read the report of Wyllyam.'

'Very good, Miss Davies,' nodded Mr Stowe patiently, 'The attempt to rescue the king would have been foolhardy indeed, ending a thousand years of secrecy and jeopardising the very entity that he was sworn to protect. The events coincided with the dragon's last cycle, and it was too weak to assist. As history shows, when the reign of Charles I ended, we faced a period of great uncertainty— some would say tyranny of a different kind. However, during his rule, Charles I was quite a prolific legislator, and when he wasn't introducing new taxes, one of his Charters was to formally recognise our entities and provide a royal endowment for perpetuity, and in doing so, the Order of Draic was renamed at his request. You will still find reference to Draic in older literature, and traditionalists among us prefer the original title.'

Blackwood raised his hand, like a pupil in a classroom, 'But what is it, exactly, that the Orders do?'

'The preamble is necessary.' Mr Stowe continued. 'Let me give you an example; you both know of the legend that says if ever the ravens leave the Tower of London, the Crown would fall?' Both Peter and Amy nodded.

'Very good. There is some truth to this, but the ravens are misdirection. Britain was once ruled by Bran the Blessed, and upon his death he ordered his head to be buried under the White Hill of London, which is where the White Tower stands today. He said that as long it was in place, Britain would be safe from invasion. It is said that Arthur exhumed the skull, but as I say, this is misdirection. Over time, as the story was retold, it was deliberately altered. You see, *brân* in Welsh, Cornish, and Irish means crow or raven. The adaptation of the tale from a skull to birds was subtle, quite creative I think. So you see, myth is also reality, of a kind. People now fuss around black birds and enjoy the tradition, unaware that the skull is held under great security by the Order of St John beneath the castle they stand in.'

Amy now raised her hand. 'But we've been invaded by Saxons, Normans, and Vikings. So, didn't work, did it? Just saying…' She trailed off, realising the contrary nature of her comment.

'That is a valid point,' replied Mr Stowe. 'We have learned much since the creation of our brotherhood, and in our early days, we took many things very literally. The world we knew was smaller, and the challenges we faced were different. Even great thinkers can be limited by their imagination—if you believe the world to be flat, you will limit your thoughts around that truth, even if it is flawed. In those times, "Kingdom" was everything. You see, we now understand that there is no divine connection between these things we protect and our Crown. The power these objects hold is not limited to kings or birth rights and is quite indiscriminate for those that are open to it. So, we need to protect ourselves from others accessing and abusing the power that could be unlocked.'

Mr Stowe stood and walked to a window, looking out over the square. 'I understand that you are particularly gifted in this regard, Miss Davies, and that is why you have taken on the role of protector, with your father, after the tragic death of Mr and Mrs Merlini.'

'Peter, you will be aware of the Merlinis. They were the couple that were mauled to death in their cottage in Wales last year. I recall there were questions around dangerous dogs—quite a media circus. At the time, my neighbours had a police visit because another resident had reported their French Bulldog as a dangerous animal—quite absurd, the frenzy that we can create and how we can act.'

'Yes, I do remember. It was terrible. They are connected to this?' asked Peter.

'The Merlinis and indeed the Davies families have been active members of the Order of St George for several generations. We were all very moved by their terrible passing. Their son was quite troubled by events, and we accepted his standing down. Amy was identified by Mr Merlini as a talented individual, and we had given permission for her to be invited in before they passed away. It was an extraordinary appointment, but as it was recorded in the minutes of Lesdix, we need to move forward and evolve.'

Mr Stowe turned and looked to Amy. 'I would like to you explain what it is you do, what you care for, if you would.'

'Sure,' said Amy. 'Our role is to provide for and protect Adar Llwch Gwin.'

Peter Blackwood sat, waiting for more. After a moments silence he asked, 'Okay, what is Adar Shook Gwin?'

'That's close enough.' Blackwood's pronunciation fell awkwardly on Amy ears. 'He's a dragon.'

Peter laughed. 'Sorry. Forgive me.' He apologised for his uncontrolled reaction.

'Mr Blackwood, I can understand your incredulity, but this is absolutely the truth,' said Mr Stowe. 'Miss Davies, can you please tell Mr Blackwood a little more about your role, insomuch as your other duties, aside from directly caring for Adar?'

'You mean, me being an apprentice wizard?' she asked.

'Absolutely,' nodded Mr Stowe. 'Perhaps a little something to help Mr Blackwood's progress along the road to acceptance? Mr Merlini would, on occasion—generally towards the end of the evening of one of our longer appointments at your parents' home— do a few things to entertain.'

'No card tricks, please,' said Peter. He was trying to keep an open mind, but what he was being told was incredible.

'It's not a performance.' Amy was annoyed by the suggestion.

'I apologise. Of course, I am not saying you are a magician. Just something for Mr Blackwood's benefit—a practical demonstration?' Mr Stowe quickly replied.

Blackwood shrugged challengingly.

'I will do this exercise once only. I will do two, no, three things that should "progress you along the road to acceptance".' She glared at Mr Stowe, then turned back to Peter. 'Are you ready?'

Peter nodded.

'May I hold your hand?' she asked. She took Peter's hand. 'When you were eleven, you were playing in the living room. It was a small room with a chimney breast that had been opened to create a shelf. There was an award—glass—some sort of industry award. Medicine. Yes, it was for your mother. She was really proud of it, and you broke it. Knocked it over by accident, but you blamed your cleaner, and she was sacked. You never owned up.'

Amy was flying through his memories as though they were her own. It was like being coupled with Adar, but far less exhilarating. Being coupled with Adar was a technicolour, Imax, Leicester Square sound system experience; being connected to Peter Blackwood was twenty-four-inch colour television by comparison. 'On your wedding day, your dad came and knocked on your door. He was alone. He gave you the cufflinks that he wore on his wedding day, and you lost them that night. You have never told him.'

Blackwood pulled his hands away; he had never told anyone these things. 'That's enough. I am uncomfortable,' he said. He was baffled and worried as to what else she may have seen.

'Just one more,' said Amy. She had only been warming up, unsure as to what was expected of her. *Just something small and inexplicable*, she thought. She snapped her fingers and created a flame burning above her—this was easy, basic. The flame rose and turned into a small bird of flame that flew in loops over her hand, then multiplied: two, four, eight. Each time the number grew, their size reduced, and their speed increased. Quickly, they turned into a spinning loop of flame, four feet in diameter. It rose up towards the ornately plastered ceiling and then, suddenly, it was gone. 'Will that do?'

Both Mr Stowe and Peter sat in silent amazement. It was quiet pedestrian to Amy, but she was not given much notice.

'I think that will do for today,' said Mr Stowe. He pushed a button on his desk phone and it crackled to attention. 'Would you please bring my guests' coats. There's a good fellow.' He addressed the pair, 'I have made arrangements for Mr Blackwood to visit you, Miss Davies, so that Mr Blackwood may meet your charge. There are other government interests in the area, and, if questioned, his visit will be a PR exercise to meet those impacted by the dangerous dogs and the unfortunate events of last year. It won't be a public appointment, of course, but it will not raise questions as a follow-up, personal interest appointment. Miss Davies, I have made arrangements with your father. Good day to you both.'

They parted company. Peter took out his mobile phone and called Rachel. The phone diverted to voicemail, and he left a brief message. He decided to walk back to the office to give himself time to digest events of the afternoon.

Dinner Date

Amy was pleasantly surprised by Lucy's flat. It stood on Narrow Street in the London Docklands and was in a converted wharf which overlooked the Thames. Narrow Street was a chronicle of five hundred years' architecture; sixteenth century buildings stood shoulder to shoulder with Edwardian, Victorian, and modern contemporary constructions. Somehow, their differences brought them together to tell a story of longevity and endurance. Lucy and her flatmate worked in Canada Tower, which stood imposingly on the skyline. The decor was bare brick, steel beams, and wooden floors, which gave it a heavy industrial feel, softened by extravagant leafy plants and accoutrements. It was jumble of styles and ages, and the interior's eclectic furnishing reflected the diversity of its surroundings. A small park sat opposite the flat and the Grapes was only a few minutes' walk away. Even so, Amy was late, walking into the narrow pub with its green ceramic tiles and black wooden exterior fifteen minutes after 7 PM.

The bar was already crowded as she made her way through the throng looking for Kieran and found him sitting smugly on the riverside balcony.

He waved when he saw her. 'I daren't get up. I had to kick the crutches out from the guy that looked like he was going to get this table before me. I've had six people come up in the last twenty minutes and ask me to move because they felt more worthy for a range of reasons. I've never been here before and when I walked in, I wondered why you wanted to come to an old man's pub. This is alright, though.' Kieran stood and kissed Amy on the cheek. 'You sit here, don't let anyone steal the table, and I'll get you a drink. What would you like?'

'Jeez, take a breath and hello to you,' said Amy. 'Something long and cold. G and T, VAT, surprise me.' She sat down and was looking out over the river. She had imagined a more picturesque view, not the modern boxy housing estate on the South Bank. To

either side were unremarkable riverside apartments. The Thames'
dark water was retreating east, outwards to the estuary, its pace
revealed by the wake left as it advanced past old silvered mooring
posts that had stood a century's sentry.

Kieran returned and handed Amy a drink. 'How was your
meeting?'

'I saw the Home Secretary in the reception of the law firm,
that was odd. You know, seeing someone famous.' She realised that
perhaps she shouldn't have mentioned that, but she felt relaxed and
comfortable. It was just natural conversation and not entirely the
truth. 'The meeting was dull—just to do with the farm, meeting with
the trustees. I could have probably had a phone call.' She raised her
glass. 'Cheers!'

Kieran met her glass with his. 'Cheers. I enjoyed this
morning. I know London Zoo was not perhaps the best of locations
for a date, but this is hardly the most remarkable of locations, is it?
Shall we go somewhere else? I mean, it's a bit OLD here,' Kieran
asked as he glanced into the dim interior of the pub, with its wooden
panelling covered in horse brasses and photographs of 'Ol' Laanden
Taaan'.

'In my defence, I don't know this part of London. Lucy
suggested it. It was close to the flat and apparently it's like five
hundred years old,' agreed Amy.

'That would explain the taste of the nuts,' said Kieran. He
pulled out a coin from his pocket and said, 'Heads, we head west.
Tails, we pick up a takeaway and go back to yours.'

Kieran tossed the coin, and it spun over the table, coming to
a rest on tails. 'Well, I hope you haven't left dirty clothes all over
the floor and dishes in the sink.'

'Don't judge everyone by your own shabby bachelor
standards,' replied Amy. 'I've not stocked up, but there's an off
licence next to the Chinese down the road.' She was relieved that
she had cleared up before heading to the pub, but she had expected
him to come back tonight, and she had made the coin land on that
decision.

'Perfect. My turn to pay,' Kieran replied, holding up his wallet.

'You found your wallet? Where was it?' asked Amy.

'Oh, yeah. I called the zoo, just in case, and I am glad I did. It had been handed in, so I went back and picked it up. It must have fallen out my pocket, probably when I gave that guy the cash. It was all there, including my folding. Drink up. I can taste crispy duck and sesame prawn toast!'

They left the pub and made their way back to the apartment. As they plated up and poured a drink, Amy said, 'You don't ever talk about your family. What's their story?'

Kieran looked at Amy for moment. 'It's not a very interesting story. My dad died when I was young, and I was the oldest of family, so I had to help mum with the farm. I would get up and do the chores that I could, like feeding the chickens and chopping wood, before I would go to school. It was tough. Some years the crops would fail. We never had much money, but Dad had made me promise to help out. So that was my life until my mum died, and I came to London. Been here six years, moved around a little, took the job I do now because I needed to work and just haven't got around to doing anything else.'

'Sorry about your parents,' said Amy. 'So, do you have brothers, sisters?'

'I had a sister; she was killed in a car crash with her boyfriend in Barnes. They were in a mini. They probably would have lived if they were in another, larger car.' Kieran looked away and took a drink.

Amy put her hand against his face, turning him back to look at her. 'I am so sorry. You've never talked about it, any of it—I had no idea.' She looked at Kieran. It was the first time she had noticed his striking pale blue eyes. She leant forward, they met lips and kissed. 'I wasn't sure you were interested; you almost fell into the "Friend Zone".'

'I wasn't sure if *you* were interested. Do you know the scale?' asked Kieran, Amy shook her head. 'Under the rating systems, you are an eight, in my view. Now, before you get all prickly, that is a high score. No-one gets a ten, other than perhaps Bo Derek in that movie. Nines are like Cindy Crawford, Naomi Campbell, or any of the others in the *Freedom* video. I rate myself as a seven—a strong seven, but still a seven. You can date up or down a level, but more than that is doomed to failure. Here's a bet: look at Whitney Houston—she's like a solid eight, maybe a nine. Bobby Brown? Come on—on his best day, with his best clothes and shit, he's a six. Watch, it will be a car crash. Charles and Diana, there you go. Diana, with her pearl necklace, cashmere jumper, blonde hair, GTI, the whole Sloaney thing going on, she had to be an 80s nine, right? Then you have Charles—well, if you ignore his lineage, fabulous wealth and international celebrity and just go on his looks, what, a four? Maybe a five? It was never going to work. So I wasn't sure. About you—us, I mean.'

'Only an eight?!' Amy punched his arm. 'It's okay, I would give you an eight. Weirdo. Do you lot sit in the pub on rainy days, rating women?'

'Damn straight!' nodded Kieran, laughing.

'Is it sensible that we start something? Long distance relationships don't really work, and I am not sure I want one anyway. You're also thinking about going travelling.' Amy was thinking aloud, weighing up her choices. Sleeping with Kieran would break a long dry spell. She enjoyed his company, but sex could make everything complicated.

'You think too much. Live life as it comes. It is a gift—that's why it is called the present. We only exist now, in this moment.' Kieran moved closer to Amy and gently placed his hand around the nape of her neck, drawing her in for another kiss. Amy responded.

'Actually, you kiss quite well. For a boy,' said Amy, smiling. 'What else you got?' Amy stood and held out her hand. 'Come on. The rumours are that the Chinese is shit from there, anyway,' she said as she led him to a bedroom.

The first time they made love, it was disappointingly quick. Amy was just finding her stride when Kieran finished his race. It had been quite a sprint from start to finish; clothes trailed from the hall to bed. Bed sheets were cast aside. Although brief, Amy thought the boy showed promise. They lay and talked for a while, and once they were sufficiently recovered, they took to the starting line for what proved to be a longer distance run, and they passed the finishing line as a team. And again. Then they slept.

Kieran woke and the illuminated hands on the old-style wind-up clock by the bed said it was 1:30 AM. He rolled over and looked at Amy, who was in a deep sleep, breathing shallowly. It was the first time he had studied her face. Her expression was relaxed, her complexion was clear, her mouth was open, and her lips looked soft. For the first time, he was struck by how attractive she was: a natural beauty. He lay and watched her for a long moment, thinking about moving closer and instigating intimacy once more, now his confidence had grown. However, he pulled the quilt up over her shoulder. She made a slight murmur and rolled on to her other side.

He was thirsty. He carefully slid out of the bed and gathered up his clothes from the floor as he walked through to the kitchen, dressed, and poured himself a glass of water. Looking around the living room, he found a notepad and pen next to the phone. Smiling to himself, he left a note for Amy that read:

Thank you for a funky time, call me up whenever you want to grind.

He was sure she'd understand the reference, and he left, quietly closing the door behind him. He had lost his virginity that night and smiled when he thought about who he had lost it to. At first it was a rush of breathless adrenaline, testosterone, dopamine, and endorphins; a pounding heartbeat, a surge of sensation that was incredible whilst it lasted. Which wasn't long at all. He imagined it must be similar to the chemical high that people sought through synthetic drugs. He had wanted more, and fortunately Amy had also been willing. He had quickly found some measure of control and the sensation had lasted longer, but he had quickly tired.

He had to walk to Tower Bridge before he found a black cab with its light on, and he wearily flopped in the back as it headed across the near-deserted streets of early morning London towards his home.

After The Beep

Anker had received a reasonable severance payment, which afforded him some time to enjoy not working. He had indulged in sleeping late into the day, he had caught up with several colleagues and friends that he had lost touch with, and his darts and pool skills had improved significantly.

It was before midday, and he was sitting in his local mass-market, low-budget pub chain of the type that had started appearing in high streets across London. They were large and new but decorated in the busy carpet and dark wooden chairs and tables that made them feel traditional and familiar. They stocked their own-brand, low-cost lager and beers, which were enjoyed by their regular patrons, many of whom would arrive at opening time and remain until closing, smoking thin hand-rolled cigarettes and making their drinks last long after they became tepid and flat. Two of the regulars walked in. Both were skinny and slightly hunched, as though life had been pressing them down since birth. One was wearing a vest and Adidas three-strip tracksuit bottoms, the other what looked like a nylon Hawaiian shirt and jeans that sagged from his hips like a slightly dirty, deflated balloon. Both saw Anker and made their way over to him.

'Morning, Will! Fancy seeing you here! Fancy a quick one?' the one in the tracksuit asked.

'Just the one, Mrs Wembley,' said the other. They snorted in unison with knowing approval.

In that moment, life smacked Anker across the face; they were his Jacob Marley, and their lives would be his future unless he escaped immediately. A sense of dread punched his stomach, motivating him to stand up, and he left without saying a word or giving a backward glance, leaving Tracksuit and Saggy Pants in bemusement.

Tracksuit raised his middle finger and shouted, 'Rude cunt!' towards the exiting Anker.

Saggy Pants downed the remains of Anker's pint and burped, 'Cunt,' contemptuously. The pair high-fived.

When he returned to his flat, Anker called Brown. 'Plod. I've got an idea. Let's join forces and share resources. There are so many stories out there that we can find and sell. Do you know the story of the two bulls on the hill?'

'No, go on,' said Brown down the phone.

'There are two bulls on the top of the hill, looking down at a herd of cows, and one says to the other, "I'm horny, lets charge down, grab the first cow we can and fuck it." The old bull says, "No, son, we'll walk down there calmly and fuck 'em all". Do you see?' Anker was excited. 'We can turn our information gathering into a quiet factory, and instead of grabbing hold of one story and pushing it out, forever looking for the next, we constantly work everyone and, gradually, we get them, we get them all and sell the information on to others. They write the stories, but we make them. We make them all!'

It was not too much of leap for Brown. It was almost like being handed the last part of a jigsaw puzzle he had been looking for. 'Will, this has legs. Let's meet and discuss it further–'

Anker interrupted, 'Sod that. Let's just get on and do it. I have some ideas.' He took out the tracker that had been transferred from pocket to pocket with his change and keys since he last saw Brown in the Chippy and flipped it in his hand. 'We'll start with my friend, Peter Blackwood.'

Anker Brown Research Limited was born.

They invested equally to form the company and took a small, tired, but discreet office in Shoe Lane, off Fleet Street, close to newspaper publishers and, more importantly, to the pubs and bars where the journalists and editors drank. The office was on the first floor of a converted eighteenth-century workhouse, and its small sash windows looked out over the narrow lane, which was undergoing renovation; old dark brick buildings were being demolished and replaced with huge glass and steel offices that reached up and stole the sunlight from the street below. The sale and development of their building was being negotiated, which was why they were able to steal a bargain on their short lease.

Brown glanced at the north-facing hands on the wall clock over the office door. 'Glad you could make it,' he said sarcastically. The smell of warm bacon and fresh ground coffee filled the office with Anker's entrance. 'Thanks for the coffee, but you can keep the butty. I had breakfast at breakfast time.'

'Mrs Plod helping you diet again? All the more for me, then. Here.' Anker dropped a well-thumbed tabloid paper onto Brown's desk and bit into his floury bap. 'I've finished reading it. Four of our stories in there today. Some lucky bastard's scooped eight and a half million on the lottery this week and chose to remain anonymous. There's no money in finding out who he is, but I'd love to know what someone does with all that money.'

Brown dusted crumbs off his desk, 'If it were you, I would guess at a huge house, a car, a boat, cocaine, and hookers. We've just invoiced for six other stories across three publications, and your old boss has been true to his word—they are buying our leads as soon as the Factory can generate them.' Brown sipped his coffee and nodded at the flavour with approval.

'What have we got on today?' asked Anker through his mouthful of bacon roll, taking a seat at his desk.

Brown stood, and, using a retractable pointer, started tapping against names on the list made on a large white board that filled a wall. It was split into columns with names and CV rankings. Brown had a colour-code system that Anker didn't have an interest in learning, but he understood CV ranking because it was his idea. Column Value was a simple way to commoditise their leads based upon press interest or coverage. 'We had eyes on a Belgravia hotel last night and are waiting on the photos of the Right Honourable Crispin Urquhart and his aide. Shame he's only a back-bencher.'

'Nice,' said Anker. 'Don't worry too much, I've sold the second and third lead this morning to McHenessey, and he's loving our work so far. I am meeting them later at the Wig and Pen to give them the paperwork. What's with the ones in blue?'

'You really don't listen, do you?' Brown tutted as Anker shrugged. 'Blue is Sports. Footie players are starting to chuck their money around—booze, tarts and drugs. We're looking into the doping rumours around that up-and-coming Aussie cyclist. It's all low CV at the moment. Slow burners, but where there's money, there's dirt, and cash is pouring into sport thanks to BSkyB.'

He tapped on the next column. 'The Factory has picked these new people-of-interest's phone numbers, and we're into their voicemails and messages already. Most are TV media, and, apparently, five of the accounts had no security and another eight were passwords like "password", "1111" or "0000"! I've picked up a couple of new geeks in the team, who are cracking emails, and that is looking fruitful.'

'The Factory is working well, and the pipeline is getting busy. I was out last night, networking, and I am going to need some cash for later.' Anker emptied various receipts from his wallet and pushed them into a jar on his desk.

'You're spending our money almost as quickly as Carol can invoice it,' said Brown.

'It's rolling in—I don't see a problem. Anyway, I do the same thing as your network of nerds and cost a lot less. Mrs Plod is keeping a tally on the money from your *des res* in the suburbs. I can hear the cash register ringing from here. She's not complaining, is she? You and her seem to be getting on better lately—happy wife is a happy life, and all that.'

'Yep, keeping tabs on your spending is keeping her busy, and we are getting on better than we have for years. I haven't told her that we're not using her logo design, though. She was really pleased with it, and I don't have the courage to tell her.'

'She's a better bookkeeper than graphic designer, that's for sure. I mean, a brown anchor is a bit literal. I am glad Carol is on board—I don't want to do the money side, it bores me, and if it keeps Mrs Plod out of the office, then we're all winning.' Anker pinged an elastic band across the office in no particular direction, watching it bounce on Brown's desk.

'No-one comes here but us. Ever. We're offline for a reason, and whilst we've taken proper advice on security, we can't have what's in here seen by anyone,' said Brown as he picked up the elastic band and put it in his desk tidy.

'I know, I know. Well, at least, not seen by anyone who hasn't paid.'

'Final item, as always, Will. Blackwood,' said Brown. 'At last, I think we have some interesting developments. The tracker we had installed in his bag by our friend at his club has given us a pretty solid record of his movements. He left his wife, Rachel, a voicemail, which has been flagged. At the time he was in Holborn. It's pretty interesting. Listen to this.'

Brown pressed play on the cassette machine on his desk.

'Hi, its me. I have just been to the most incredible meeting. Seriously, you would not believe the things that go in in this country that no-one knows about. I am going back to Whitehall for an hour—I have a meeting I that need to attend. But I will be home early. After that, I will tell you everything. You will not believe it, I promise you. I have to go to Wales later this month and have a follow up meeting. It's insane. Love you, bye.'

'We know that the recording was made in Holborn. Blackwood had a meeting with at Stowe and Arc, an established senior law firm retained by the State for activities that benefit from not being under public scrutiny. I came across them once, dealing with a counterfeiting ring. They are one of those badly kept secrets in certain circles. The Factory has accessed his diary, and I suspect the appointment he refers to is next Thursday, as he has the day blocked out. We have a week to find out some more, but this is very much eyes on. Whatever this is, it is big.'

'I want it. I will go,' said Anker with enthusiasm.

'I thought you might.' Brown smiled. 'I have some bits and bobs for you to take with you. I've hired you a car.' Brown passed over a purple rucksack. 'Car hire paperwork, GPS, camera, data cards, mobile phone—it's all in there. Sorry about the colour, it was our Kevin's DofE kit. I think it was only used once, but it was the only thing I had at hand at home this morning.'

'Well, I guess no-one I know will see me. Thanks, man.' Anker took the rucksack and put it over one shoulder, as though he was trying it on for size.

'Yep, you could pass as Hillary or Fiennes,' commented Brown.

'So long as it's not Scott, I don't mind,' Anker replied.

.

Cauldron

Veronika was bored. Merlin was out and had said he wouldn't be back until the morning, which was his way. They had had a conversation earlier that day, when he explained that he wanted to move on and had been looking at buying a home in Scotland. He had played the casinos as much as he could for a while and needed to lay low, which was a professional gambler's risk. He said being too successful made you unpopular, and if they don't let you through the door, you can't work. He had shown her details of remote, old Scottish castles, standing on the edge of lochs, or sitting high above woodland. They all looked cold and dull to her. He must be worth a small fortune as the price of the properties were all over a million pounds. He had asked her to go with him. He said that she would be safe, and, in a year or so, she would be forgotten by those that wanted to harm her, and she could go home. He would help her.

The months she had been staying in their apartment had given her time to emotionally repair and recover from her ordeals. She felt less at risk. She had started to think about her future rather than her immediate survival. She was feeling better. Merlin had been generous with his money, and she had saved a small rucksack full of rolls of fifty pounds. It was heavy and valuable, but she had left it in her wardrobe with no intention of leaving, and it grew fatter and heavier as each week passed.

She had grown to trust that he wasn't going to harm her, and she could see that he was attracted to her. However, the feeling was not reciprocated. He was wiry, almost skinny. She had seen him without his top on. His back and torso were covered in swirling tattoos that would probably be attractive on a man with a more athletic physique. He was awkward company—not unpleasant, but conversation dried up very quickly, and he had showed very little interest in her background and gave very little away about his. All that said, there was something, a magnetism, that kept drawing her in, and, perhaps, she was starting to grow some feelings towards the funny little Welshman, but didn't want to admit it to herself.

Merlin's announcement had brought those thoughts to the forefront of her mind, and she needed some distraction, away from the apartment, to give her time to make some decisions. She decided that some long-overdue retail therapy was in order, so she called down to the concierge and asked them to call her a taxi. As she sat in the back of the black cab that rumbled its way towards Selfridges, she felt a surge of joy run through her. It was the first time in a long while that she had felt free, almost happy.

She slammed the taxi door and looked up at the ornate, sculptured clock above the entrance to the shop. It was the same air and the same city, but she took a deep breath in, smelling car fumes and the fast food stall that was busy serving customers across the street; this air was different. It was freedom. People were milling around; some were walking with intent. Parents with children, friends, individuals, life was passing by all around her. She felt normal and free. Veronika walked through the various designer concessions. She tried on dresses, tops, jeans, and hats. She browsed through accessory stalls and tried on shoes. She found herself on several occasions wondering if Merlin would look twice at her in various of the outfits.

Time passed with speed, and she had amassed a clutch of varying sized branded bags when she decided to treat herself to a facial from the in-house beauticians. She was given a tall glass of cool, sparkling wine whilst the beautician set to work, and Veronika relaxed and revelled in the attention.

A member of staff approached and interrupted her daydreaming. 'May I arrange for your shopping to be delivered to your home this afternoon, madam?' asked the polite young female. She had a European accent that made her question sound like a song.

'Thank you, that would be great. How much is it?' She was thoroughly enjoying being treated with such attentive service.

'Madam, it is complimentary. It is clear you have been very busy with us today, and it is the least we can do. If you can give me your address, then I will take your bags off for dispatch and bring you another drink,' she sang.

Veronika gave her address and enjoyed her next glass of wine. When the beautician had finished, she paid in cash and decided that, as she wasn't weighed down with her cumbersome shopping bags, she would walk across Hyde Park and take in the people and sights that she had missed for so many months, and then hail a black taxi home once she was in Knightsbridge. Her thoughts were to follow her funny little Welshman to see where that may lead, as well as for the adventure. Her alternative was to head away from London, on her own, to uncertainty. Her cash would buy her time, but not the security she had been enjoying. There seemed to be no strings attached to her invitation, and, perhaps, actually, she might see Merlin in a different light.

When she arrived back at the penthouse, she drew a hot bath. Her bathroom had glass doors out onto a balcony, and she slid them open wide, letting in the summer's evening air and the faint noises from the street below. She would bathe and then maybe go out for a late dinner at one of the river-fronted bistros that ran along the ground floor of the development. Tomorrow, she would tell Merlin that she would go with him.

The intercom buzzed impatiently, and Veronika tied up her bath gown and padded to the handset in the living room. The concierge said that her delivery from Selfridges was waiting, and asked if they could send it up. Veronika agreed and, putting down the receiver, pressed the green button that unlocked the lift doors so that they would open on arrival. She walked to the kitchen and poured a glass of water.

She turned as the lift doors shooshed open. Her heart stopped, and the glass fell from her hand, shattering on the ceramic tiles. She didn't recognise one of the men, but the other had a tattoo on his neck, his face marked with red scars that were still healing.

'Hello, Veronika-with-a-k. We have been looking for you.' Both men dropped the bags, and the man with the tattoo started to run towards Veronika. She turned to run but slipped on the water and broken glass beneath her feet. She landed heavily, and caught her head, knocking herself out.

When she came to, her head was pounding. She tried to move, but her arms were constrained. As her vision began to clear, she saw blood stains on her white bathrobe and the silhouette of a man who looked over as she made a slight groan.

'Je vzhůru!' he called out.

gerup / (v)zuru

The lights were on. The sky outside was the light purple of dusk or dawn.

***

Marcus exchanged pleasantries with the security guard that worked the concierge desk during the night, swiped his keycard, and called the lift. He was weary and had a headache. It was 4 AM, but his long day had been more successful and rewarding then he could have possibly expected. It had been a very positive week; his lottery claim had been processed, and he had declined every one of the next steps the company had recommended. He refused publicity, and he had had to be rude to the recommended financial advisor, who had been persistent—almost to the point of harassment—in trying to convince him to take his services. He declined their accountancy recommendation and their private bank introduction. He just wanted the money with no ties so that he could disappear into obscurity until he was ready. It would take another few weeks for the funds to be released, but they had given him one million pounds 'to keep him going'. He had viewing appointments of some promising properties in Scotland lined up and had made arrangements for a stopover in Wales on his way north. The only part of his plans that remained insecure was whether Veronika was going to join him.

As the lift doors opened, Marcus' *Grym* surged through him like a lightning bolt, but before he could act on it, the impact of the baseball bat caught his temple, instantly knocking him unconscious.

He came to with a sharp gasp as cold water was thrown over him, forcing him into consciousness. He was tied to a chair, and opposite was Veronika. Her face was bloodied, and she had swelling around her split lip and above her left eye, which was almost closed. She looked over to him. He could see fear in her eyes.

Two men were standing relaxed and smoking beside her. He recognised the one with the tattoo. The other was shorter and stocky, with closely cut hair. His neck was thick, and Marcus noticed his hands looked disproportionately large. Marcus thought he looked like a rugby prop, and it made him briefly smile to himself.

'Hello. Veronika tells me your name is Merlin. What sort of name is that? Your dad liked magic?' Tattoo walked toward him as he spoke. 'You'll need a fucking miracle to get out of this.' Tattoo punched Marcus. The force spun his head, rocked the chair and stunned him momentarily. He could taste blood in his mouth. 'We have been looking for Veronika for a long time. And you, of course. Veronika belongs to us. You stole from us. No-one steals from us. You also have to pay me for this.' He pointed to his face and the pink scars.

'How is your buddy, the fat one?' asked Merlin. He couldn't help himself, but he braced himself for the likely outcome of his question. He was hit again, in the same place. Pain seared through his head, the sound of the impact seeming like an explosion in his cranium.

'Matka kurva,' spat Tattoo. He could not remember what had happened in the hotel. He had woken in a bed in one of their houses, their third crew member—the driver—having found them after they had failed to report in. He was not allowed to go to hospital and was cared for by an old doctor who smelt of alcohol and had white, wiry hair protruding from his ears and nose. His stitching skills were terrible, and it meant that his scarring would be permanent. His partner on the night had not been so lucky. He had been taken away.

It was said he was going home to be cared for, and he knew that he would never see him again.

'You are in no place to make jokes. I am not going to kill you. I hurt you enough so that you will not be able to walk again, like Tomas. You can eat through a pipe and shit your pants for the rest of your days. That is the price for stealing from us, and I also pay you for Tomas. It will be fun ,I think. For me.' He went to hit Marcus once more, who flinched, and he stopped and laughed. 'Veronika has no value to us now. I think you will watch us as get rid of our rubbish. Jan over there likes Veronika, I think. Don't you, Jan? You can watch as Jan fucks her.'

Jan nodded and pulled Veronika's head up and back by her hair. 'Teď vypadá ošklivě jako pes!'

Tattoo laughed. 'He says he not like her anymore, and she looks like a dog. You see, her face is fucked up. Watch this, Merlin.' He nodded to Jan.

Marcus was still trying to recover; he noticed the knife too late. Jan ran the blade across Veronika's neck, left to right, her flesh opening. The cut was deep and severed her artery, sending a pump of red blood that splashed against the white tiled floor. Veronika's struggling tipped the chair backwards, and she landed with a crash on her back, still tied in the chair. Marcus could see she was haemorrhaging blood rapidly and her life would drain away quickly.

Rage exploded within him. A huge pulse of power shot out from his core, sending a shockwave that knocked both men to the floor. As it travelled outward, it knocked objects from tables, moved furniture, and hit the triple-glazed windows with a boom that came reverberating back. Marcus was up on his feet, unaware of how he had freed himself from his restraints. He was acting almost instinctively. He pointed to both men, lifting them up into the air. They were shouting but he was not listening. He could hear no sound, see nothing other than the two men floundering in the air. He twirled his fingers, and both men began to spin, faster and faster, until they were whirling with so much momentum that they were a blur. Then it stopped. The two men had been changed into rats that were suspended in the air as though they were being held by their tails. Their legs were moving and they were squealing. Inside the rats' bodies were the two confused and now frightened men, only their form had been changed. Marcus walked forward and stood between them. He started to laugh as he decided what his next course of action would be.

He walked to the kitchen island, the two rats suspended in space by their tails in front of him. They were struggling in the air, trying to right themselves and escape. Merlin nodded at the deep stainless-steel sink, bringing the waste disposal to life with a whirl.

'You lose,' he said.

The squealing rats were dropped one at a time into the throat of the disposal unit. The tone of blades changed as they met the temporary resistance of the small bodies. Within a few moments, the disposal unit stopped gurgling and clattering and returned to its monotone buzz. He nodded and the sound stopped.

He turned to Veronika. She lay pale and lifeless. *So much blood*, he thought. He had a flashback to the cottage in Wales, but he forced that out of his mind. He knelt down, gently moving the body on to its side so that he could untie her arms. He picked her up, being careful not to slip on the large pool of congealing blood, and carried her to the nearest ensuite. He ran a bath—being cautious that the temperature was right—removed her gown, and placed her body in the water. He knelt and started his *Englyn*. He closed his eyes and repeated the poem, time and time again. He knew of *Bran's Cauldron*. His dad had told him of the spell and how it was used to bring soldiers back to life, although he had stopped short of teaching him the incantation. Marcus closed his eyes and chanted his version of the spell over and over.

There was sudden splash and Marcus looked up. Veronika was staring at him, startled and coughing. She was unharmed. There was no sign of the violence she had endured. She looked confused and scared. 'Relax,' said Marcus. 'Let me get you a clean gown. Stay there. Rest.'

Veronika went to speak, but no sound came. She clutched her throat. Marcus braced against the bath to stand, and she grabbed his wrist, giving him a look of plea. He put his other hand over hers.

'It's OK. It's over. Let me get you a robe and then we can talk. I will be a moment.'

As he walked to another bathroom, he looked to the living area, Veronika's blood had disappeared. Only the two chairs remained, discarded on the floor, and a few items that the two men had left: a cigarette packet on the counter, a black, soft sports bag, and the baseball bat.

Marcus returned, he held up the robe and looked away as Veronika stood, dressed and stepped out the bath. She leant on him, weak, as they walked into the main room, and he led her to the sofa to sit. Veronika tried to speak again and was unable to. She looked to Marcus and pointed to her throat.

'I can explain. But I need to know what you remember. Do you remember me coming home?' he asked, and she nodded. 'Do you remember what happened next?' She nodded. 'All of it? What they did to you?' She nodded again, and her breathing faltered. Tears welled up in her eyes.

'It is time that I told you who I am.' Marcus held her hands in his. He knew this moment was important. It would set the legend, his truth, from this day forth. 'I have powers. The things I can do are unimaginable to most people. I come from a long line of gifted people. I grew up in Wales, where my abilities were honed in secret from an early age. I was orphaned from birth and raised and taught by a great wizard who only the gifted can see. I completed my apprenticeship and have been sent out to find my place in the world. My casino wins are not chance. I make them happen. I am building wealth so that I can spread the word and teach people the truth. I used my powers the night that I freed you and again today. That should show you what I am capable of.

'When I saw you, that night in the casino, I knew we were to be together. Your path led to me, and mine to you. That is all in the past. What has been and what will be are unimportant. We only exist in the present. Today, I brought you back to be with me because it is meant to be so. The gift of life I have granted you comes with two conditions. You will never speak again. That was the exchange for your life. This I cannot change. The second is that you will have life as long as you remain with me. If we part company for too long, my magic will wear off and your life will end.' The last condition was a lie which came easily to Marcus—he didn't want to lose Veronika, and this untruth would be sure to tie her to him. 'Come with me, and I will give you everything you could wish for. I will protect you. You can help me spread our message, and we will save the world. You have gone through much tonight, and you need to rest.' Marcus touched her temple, and she relaxed back into the sofa in an instant and deep sleep.

He sat and watched Veronika whilst she slept. He had acted instinctively as events had unfolded, and it was effortless for him. He knew that his abilities were improving, and he was starting to realise his potential—his future was limitless. The power was exhilarating. He felt himself become aroused as he looked at Veronika's chest gently rise and fall underneath her white bathrobe as she breathed, the shape of her neck, smooth and thin, at how vulnerable she looked. He thought of how he had dropped the two men to their death, to be minced like cattle meat, of the control he had over their death and now Veronika's life. He rubbed himself. His heart rate was rising. He unzipped his trousers and took himself in his hand.

The intercom buzzed, interrupting him. 'Sorry to disturb you at this time of the morning. But we have had a power outage in the building and in an event such as this we need to notify all our residents. We have the matter under control, of course. Contractors have been called, and we will update you as soon as we have some news,' said the voice down the phone.

Marcus thanked them, assuring them that he had been awake. He hung up, picked up the sports bag, and inspected the contents. Inside were a set of pliers, bolt-cutters, a Stanley knife, plastic ties, a ball gag, plastic sheeting, and a towel, under which he found a small handgun that had a star embossed on the grip. He held it in his hand. It felt comfortable. He had never seen or fired a handgun and wondered its worth to him, but he would keep it. It might serve a purpose in the future.

Convergence

It was late morning when Blackwood's black Jaguar XJ12 pulled up on the gravel drive outside the Davies'. He and his driver had set off from his home at 5 AM, and they had made steady progress, not that Peter noticed particularly. He had been working his way through the reams of documents that had been carefully labelled, categorised, and neatly organised in his briefcase for him. He had arranged several telephone meetings and received a great many more calls. He liked the convenience of his car phone, but it was relentlessly demanding of his attention. Not that long ago, the time he spent travelling gave him an opportunity to consider important matters and, occasionally, catch up on some valuable sleep. Having accessible mobile communication was a mixed blessing.

A story had been broken by one the tabloids around a routine Met Police stop and search on a black man in his early sixties. The incident had quickly become ill-tempered, and a crowd had formed. The officers restrained the man, handcuffing him, and during the event he incurred minor injuries that needed treating in hospital. It transpired that the man was a human rights solicitor. The reasons for the stop were extremely tenuous and the story was growing into a wider debate around the sus laws and police prejudice. The man was a known activist for many causes, and it was for both of these reasons that Peter had been made aware of events. He was reading the report prepared by MI6, as there was intelligence to suggest that the incident was conspired to cause social unrest. This could be the opportunity to move for the replacement of Commissioner Jenks. It could also be a time to address the sus policy, which he knew was abused.

He stepped out of the car, his leather-soled shoes crunching on the gravel. The air was fresh and smelt of summer, and the light was different—somehow clearer, sharper. He paused and listened to the silence and took a deep breath, as if he was taking in the environment to his very soul. He was struck by how peaceful it was as he looked around at the cottage and its collection of ramshackle outbuildings.

The door to the cottage opened and Amy stepped out, followed by her parents, and they greeted one another.

'This is one of the most bizarre meetings I have attended in my career to date,' said Peter. 'I am not expected back in London until tomorrow, and my most pressing matters are dealt with. So I have the time to be able to acquaint myself with you all and, the, erm. Well, the, erm.' He could not quite bring himself to say it.

'Dragon,' finished Claire.

'Yes, dragon,' repeated Peter, still very uncomfortable with the truth he was about to experience.

'His name is Adar,' said Amy. 'He knows you are coming.'

'Please, come in. You must need to freshen up, and we can talk some before we go down. I am sure you have plenty of questions,' said Tom as he gestured Peter into the house.

***

For most of the journey, Anker had managed to wedge his GPS unit so that it was on the dashboard. However, for the last hour and a half of the journey, as he had wormed along twisting rural roads, it had kept coming loose and repeatedly rattled down into either of the front footwells. If he wasn't stopping to retrieve it or trying to resecure it, he had been watching the little icon blink its way ahead of him, taking his eye off the road, which very nearly saw him crash into a dry wall or off the mountain several times. He could not see the concept catching on, regardless of whatever Mercedes might be doing, and was relieved when the GPS signal finally came to a stop.

He had parked the hired Ford Fiesta in a small layby that was close to where the signal had become stationary and started on foot with his rucksack over one shoulder. He had opted for the shortest route and very quickly regretted his decision. The climb was far steeper than he had expected, his training shoes gave little grip or support, and progress was slow. He quickly built up a sweat, and he stopped for two cigarettes on the way up whilst he caught his breath, flicking the cigarette butts down the slope behind him. He reached the first peak only to see a second further away. He had looked back and considered returning to the car and parking closer, but the car looked conspicuous enough parked in a layby. It would just seem abandoned if he left it on the road.

He carried on for over an hour before he could see the buildings from which the GPS signal was coming. The point-to-point distance he had covered was not far, but he had had to ascend for most of his journey. His legs were tired, and he sat down, opened a can of Coke, and lit another cigarette. It was the first time that he had paused to look at his surroundings, and he thought that they were beautiful, if you liked that sort of thing. He delved into his bag once more and took out a packet of crisps. A crow landed ten feet or so away and stared at him, its head twitching from side to side.

'Hungry?' he asked, and he threw a crisp towards the bird which flew off.

Anker took out his camera, fitted with a long-range lens, and looked down towards the collection of farm buildings. He could see Blackwood's driver leaning against the rear of his Jaguar, smoking a cigarette. He scanned the farmhouse and other buildings. A door opened to the main building and Blackwood and two other people walked out and through the farm. He did not recognise either of the people Blackwood was with. One was a younger girl, in her twenties, with a dark bob, and the man was probably late forties. They made their way to the barn at the back of the property and stopped for a moment. The shutter on Anker's camera was tick-ticking away as he tried to zoom in to get a clear view of their faces. Unfortunately, the distance was just beyond the power of his lens. They went into the barn.

He changed the memory card, looked around to make sure he was alone, and started down the hill, cautious to keep low as there was very little cover. He stopped towards the bottom of the slope, behind a small pile of rocks, and waited. The crow came back and watched him intently.

'Just fuck off,' said Anker as he threw a badly aimed stone in the bird's general direction, sending it off into the sky. He watched as it flew down and perched on top of the barn. 'Fucker,' said Anker under his breath. He sat and waited. Time passed and his impatience and curiosity grew. He moved forward again. The ground levelled out and he quickened his pace towards the barn.

The crow cawed and flew down and through the part-open barn door. Anker quickly moved to the side of the barn and out of view. His heartbeat was raised, and his mouth was slightly dry. He waited again, but there was no sound coming from the barn, so he worked his way around and peered into the darkness. It looked unremarkable, just a barn full of old shit, but there were no people. He stepped in and waited a few seconds for his eyes to adjust to the lower light.

The interior had objects covered with tarpaulin and general long-forgotten tools. He noticed that there was another barn door to the rear that was too close to be the back of the barn, and in front of it was a black holdall. As he walked forward, the crow flew past him and out of the door. Anker dropped his camera.

'Fuckity-fuck,' he said.

He picked it up and looked it over, checking for damage. Anker walked past the bag and cautiously peeped through the gap in the barn door and saw a rock face. Though he hadn't seen them leave, he was alone in the barn. He opened the bag and looked inside. He found a handgun and some sort of necklace made of leather with a dull, misshapen stone hanging from it.

'What the fuck?' he said to himself.

Picking both up, he was surprised by the weight of the pistol. Instinctively, he tried to pull the top back, as he had seen in the movies, but the weapon resisted him. He looked it over and noticed that a small button by his thumb had a red and green dot by it, and it was pointing to the red. He took that as being the safety and put the weapon in his pocket. He rubbed the stone necklace between his fingers and thumb while he considered what to do next. Turning back to the rock face, he now saw a tall, slender opening, which he had not noticed before. It was pretty obvious that Blackwood and his companions had to have gone through the opening, as he had not seen them leave. His journalistic curiosity made him squeeze through the opening.

***

They were sitting in a motorway services canteen. Marcus sat back and took a sip from his black coffee. He looked over at Veronika. The sadness in her eyes had faded lately and she seemed more relaxed. He was getting used to the silence. It suited him, but he did miss what conversation they had had. He had newfound confidence and had decided that on their first night in his new home, he would make his move. He felt that she was becoming warmer towards him, so he would surprise her with candles and flowers, the whole shebang. He had been thinking of casting a spell to take her, but he wanted her to come to him freely; it was her submission to him that excited him. The waiting was a sweet pain.

She was wearing headphones and listening to a mix tape he had made for her. She caught his eye and gave him a brief smile. She was wearing her hair down and one side was tucked behind her ear, showing a small golden drop earring. The other side hung down slightly over her face. He wanted to brush it backward and feel her soft hair. She was dressed simply, understatedly even, but he could feel the other men in the cafe looking at her. He glanced across the room and met the stare of a grey-haired man in a white shirt and tie, who quickly looked away. The man had been staring at Veronika. Marcus thought how effortlessly he could pop one of the dirty fucker's eyeballs without even needing to stand up.

He returned to the crow.

He had watched the black car pull up and the Davies greet a stiff in a suit before they all went inside. He waited. As the crow flew in high circles, he noticed the stranger stumbling his way up from the valley. The stranger was clearly no man of the outdoors— he was dressed for a trip into town, not over a mountain. He worked his way up to the ridge and things became interesting when he stopped above the farm and took out a camera. Marcus flew down to have a closer look. Whoever he was, he was also interested in the same people. Marcus smiled. This had potential. Veronika smiled back, returning the gesture, thinking it was intended for her, but Marcus didn't see it; he was with the crow.

He watched the man clumsily make his way down towards the barn and crouch behind some low cover, though he was still very conspicuous. Marcus watched as the man waited. *He could be there for ages*, thought Marcus, so he flew down and into the barn. The man was bound to follow. Then the opportunity became clear. He could set in motion events that would really mix things up. It was too good to miss.

Marcus took another sip of coffee and a deep breath as his next spell would take concentration. His efforts made him jolt in his chair, knocking the table and causing their drinks to spill slightly. He opened his eyes. He had done it. He had done it!

Veronika tutted and mopped around her cup using one of the flimsy paper napkins from the plastic container on their table.

The crow flew out of the barn, startling the man as he deliberately flew across his path. Marcus had moved the black sports bag to a place where the man would be bound to see it and look inside. He did not think it necessary to wait to see events as they unfolded. He was confident he had set an unavoidable path, so he uncoupled from the crow and returned his consciousness to the canteen.

'Change of plan,' Marcus said to Veronika. 'We don't have to go to Wales now. Once you have finished your coffee, we'll just carry on up the M6 and get to Glasgow before the end of the day. It's a long drive—you can sleep, and I will drive.'

They left the service station in the Mercedes they had hired for the journey and joined other travellers heading North. Marcus pushed the cassette tape into the deck and Patches by Clarence Carter started to play. 'I know it's cheesy, but I love this, I do.' He started to sing along, 'In the mornin' before I went to school, I fed the chickens and I chopped wood too...'

***

Amy had gone ahead to meet Adar. Tom and Peter made their way down the passage, into the open plain of the cave and towards the Keep.

Aware of the silence between them as they walked, Tom spoke. 'The first time I came down here it was impossible to accept, even though it was there, in front of me. It is surprising how quickly we accept change, once we have adjusted to it.'

Before Peter could respond, they could hear the sound of wings beating against the air, a slow and deep *whomp* beating rhythmically. He looked up as they emerged from the darkness. Huge, magnificent, regal, Adar was flying down in a wide spiral, and on his back sat Amy. She was positioned at the base of his neck, above the shoulders that bore his great wings. She sat with confidence, her arms free as she waved down towards the pair. They landed near the Keep and Amy dismounted, patting Adar.

'Nice entrance,' said Tom.

Blackwood was hesitant and dumbfounded.

'Come,' said Amy. 'He knows you mean no harm because of the charm you wear. You need to come and touch him, connect with him, and you will know all that you need to.'

Amy encouraged Peter to step forward. He reached out and touched the dragon. Adar's skin and scales twitched around the contact, turning red. Peter's knees gave way as if in a faint. Neither of his companions were able to assist in time and he collapsed to the floor. They helped him stand, his legs still weak as he regained his senses.

'Incredible. I need to sit down. Do you have any water? Incredible,' he muttered.

They escorted him to the bench by the jetty, where a tall crystal water jug stood. Amy took one of the four glasses and filled it before passing it to Peter.

'Welcome,' came a voice, and the Guardian came forward from the Keep. He counted the glasses and the number of people present, dismissing the slight inaccuracy of his spell. 'You must be Peter Blackwood. I have a few names. You may call me the

Guardian.' The tall, robed man stood back and didn't offer to shake hands. 'There is no need to speak just yet. There is so much to take in. It is best to allow the events to flow around you. You have time to contemplate them later. I see you have made the acquaintance of Adar and he approved. I have learned that he is an unimpeachable judge of character.'

Peter was still staring at Adar. 'Unbelievable.'

On the edge of the woods, some distance from the Keep, just hidden within the ferns, sat Anker. He had been glued to the eyepiece on his camera, his shutter click-clicking in rapid spurts. He was not thinking about what he was witnessing as he was recording it, his journalist training and instincts taking over. The memory warning light flashed on his eye display. He tried to change the card and keep track on events; he had to take his backpack off, and he frantically rummaged around for the pack of additional memory cards.

As the cover on the memory dock clicked shut, he looked back towards the building, and standing in front of him was a man who appeared to be wearing a kimono. He was smiling and waving at Anker. Not sure what to do, Anker waved back. Without warning, the man dropped his kimono, turned around, bent over, and pulled his buttocks apart. A bright light shone out, momentarily blinding Anker and leaving a black spot in his vision, as if he had stared at a light bulb.

'FUCK!' howled Anker in surprise and mild disgust as he wiped his eyes.

As he stepped back, his rucksack fell off his shoulder, spilling and scattering its contents—phone, the rock necklace, cigarettes, his last can of Coke, and camera paraphernalia—over the ground. The strange man picked up his clothing and, giggling, ran past Anker, knocking his shoulder and running naked into the woods behind him. A small beam of light from his buttocks jiggled a trail of his progress away through the undergrowth. Adar suddenly looked up, held his head high, sniffing the air, and, with one huge beat of its wings, set off up into the sky.

Confusing where + who we are with

'There *were* four people,' said The Guardian to himself.

Amy also sensed the presence of another, and she looked over towards the woods. Without the protection of the *Hudcloch,* Anker's presence was felt by all but Blackwood and Tom, who followed Amy's sight line to see Anker bending over, picking up his belongings some distance away.

Adar's scales turned bright flame red as he soared high in the air above, scanning the land below. He spotted movement in the ferns and started to dive down towards it. Anker looked up, lifted his camera, and pressed the shutter button for another burst before his sense of self-preservation came to the fore. He dropped the camera and started to run out of the woods, across the plain, towards the Keep, towards people, perhaps safety. He was suddenly very afraid.

Adar let out a burst of fire which shot down and exploded on the ground, just missing Anker, sending a shower of soil and grass out like a shell impact. The energy knocked Anker off his feet and some distance through the air. He landed with a thud and rolled several times. As he scrambled to his feet, he fumbled in his pocket and pulled out the pistol. He turned, raised it towards Adar, and squeezed the trigger.

'NO! STOP, ADAR, STOP!' Amy called. She knew that Adar was acting instinctively and defensively, and she couldn't connect through his intense focus on his target.

The pistol's trigger remained firm, and Anker realised that he had not flipped the safety off. He stared up, frozen, as the beast closed down on him. Adar swooped, one of his claws engulfing the man, and he took him up into the air. With his other claw, Adar grabbed at a limb that was protruding from its clenched claw-fist and pulled. Anker screamed as his leg was torn from its socket with a pop audible from the ground and Adar discarded the limb, which fell to earth like a soft toy dropped from a baby's stroller. Adar squeezed. From their vantage point, the onlookers could hear the crunching and snapping of bone. Adar relaxed his grip, and the crushed and lifeless body dropped to the ground, landing like a soft sack with a thump. Adar landed next to it and gave the cadaver a brief sniff before picking it up in his jaws, flipping it up into the air and swallowing it in one snap. He then sniffed around and, finding the limb, finished consuming his prey. Adar beat his wings up, and he dived down through the lake.

Blackwood retched, the clear vomit catching his shoes and speckling his trouser hems. Tom passed him a packet of paper tissues from his pocket and pointed to Peter's chin, helpfully indicating an area to be dabbed.

The Guardian spoke. 'You don't see that every day.'

'Who was that?' asked Tom.

'Jesus, I need to sit down,' said Blackwood. Amy placed her hand on his shoulder and led him to the bench table whilst Tom walked towards Ankers' belongings, collected them up, and returned. He sat at the table and opened the wallet.

'William Anker,' said Tom as he placed a business card on the table.

Blackwood looked up, 'Did you say William Anker?' He picked up the card. 'This is not good. I know Anker. He's a journalist. We have had run ins in the past. Why was he here? Did he follow me? This is not good.'

'How did he get in?' asked Amy.

Tom threw the *Hudcloch* on to the table, 'This is how, but how did he get it?'

'That stone was Kath's, I recognise it,' said The Guardian. 'She lost it some time ago and it is now found. It was the only one unaccounted for. How this man came to own it is of no consequence. He was alone and no-one will find this place. Besides, there is no body, Adar has seen to that.' He turned to Blackwood, 'I sense you are torn. You feel you have a responsibility to do something more. You do not. It was the man's time to return to *Mamddaear*. How he made his journey is not relevant, he is back at the beginning. His flesh has gone but he still exists. No crime has been committed; he wasn't murdered, he died as a natural consequence. It is not murder when an abattoir takes the life of a lamb so that it can feed a human.

Adar saw prey and fed on it. It is the order of things: there is balance.'

'But people will come to look for him,' said Amy.

'Where will they look?' asked the Guardian. 'There is no natural entrance to this subterranean oasis. They will be walking the slate and soil of the ground above for eternity and find nothing. The Order will deal with any short-term inconvenience that may arise—it is far-reaching and more powerful than any of you realise. You should all leave for now. It is clear that these events have affected you all and you need to find peace within yourselves.

'Peter, accept what you have seen. Much of what you believed has been challenged, and you will need to come to terms with the reality that you are now facing. Be assured everything is in balance and unfolding as it should. I see a clear path for you, which you will find rewarding, but it will not be without difficulty. Today is perhaps the first test you must overcome. Tom, please remove these things and destroy them–' the Guardian gestured to the items scattered on the table, '–but save the weapon, as that will serve you in the future.'

'I don't know how to use that. I've never even loaded the shotgun in the house. Hang on, what do you mean it will serve me in the future?' Tom looked at the weapon on the table.

'It is in one of your futures. Now, you must all leave.' With that, the Guardian faded away into the ether.

Later

Amy had surprised herself by how little the death of the journalist had affected her. After the first few nights, she was sleeping normally, and now she found a few days would pass before it would come to mind. She didn't feel responsible; she didn't murder him. In fact, she wasn't remotely involved in the circumstances around his death. She was a bystander, an innocent witness. At the time, she had tried to intervene. However, guilt still sat within her stomach. He was a person, a someone—he lived a life—although an unpleasant one, from what Blackwood had said about him. But he must have had a family, people who cared about him, who wanted him to come home, or at least would want to know what happened to him.

About a week after he died, the police arranged a search for him. The local mountain rescue team assisted and there was a brief media circus covering the story. Anker's hire car had been found abandoned a few miles away and the search had covered a wide area of the rugged terrain. Sniffer-dogs and helicopters were called in, but to no avail. The police had visited and asked if they had seen him or heard anything, but they didn't stay long—it was a cursory single visit.

She had not fully appreciated the new clandestine world she had found herself in. The events in the cave would simply not be discussed ever again. The Order would see that the story went away, and, judging by the lack of police activity, they had been true to their word.

Peter Blackwood seemed to have been the most affected by events. Amy had never witnessed Adar hunt, or be aggressive, but she knew and understood him. Anker was a stranger, an intruder in his territory—a threat—and Adar had acted instinctively. For Blackwood, it must have been too much to take in at once.

Kieran had been playing on her mind more than Anker. At first, she wasn't sad, more disappointed and confused. Amy had left

What about Brown? What would he do his mate's just vanished

messages and sent emails to Kieran and had not had a reply. He was not some random guy that she had at met a party and had a drunken tryst with—she had known him for more than year. She had considered him a friend before they became lovers. Fortunately, she was not in love. She was not so naïve to fall so quickly for someone, but it had had potential. She thought that it really could have led somewhere. If she allowed herself, she could feel a little used, but he did not seem to be the shag-and-run type. Quite the opposite, in fact—she could tell from his clumsy awkwardness that he was not very sexually experienced.

The night that they had spent together, she had woken briefly and heard him leave, but she hadn't thought much about it; he had to work the next day, so of course he needed to get home and shower and change clothes. Perhaps the bed wasn't comfortable. Maybe she snored. God forbid she had farted. It was considerate that he didn't wake her up when he left. She found his note and that had made her smile. It was kind of dorky and *Purple Rain* was one of her favourite albums.

But a few days passed, then a week, then another week. None of her friends had heard from him. Then she received the card in the post. It was cheap card, the type that would be bought last minute from a convenience store or petrol station by a forgetful grandchild, or husband. All it said was:

Decided to go travelling. Send you a postcard. X

to Wales
or Lucy's ?

Perhaps she could have seen it coming.

She may well have moped around for a while, mourning the loss of possible relationship, but that wasn't the only thing on her mind. Her mum had always said that troubles came in threes and, following her discovery today, the trilogy was complete. Amy was sitting in her parents' kitchen, waiting for them to come in. Her mum walked in.

'Hey, cariad. When did you come in? I was about to put the kettle on. Your father will be back soon. Do you want to stay for dinner?' She was busying around the kitchen.

'Always have time for a cuppa, thanks. I need to talk to you and Dad,' said Amy.

'That sounds ominous,' said her mum.

Amy's dad came through the front door, called out and after kicking off his boots came through to the kitchen.

'Hello, butty. I wasn't expecting to see you today. That's a nice surprise.' He sat at the table and Amy's mum distributed mugs of steaming tea.

Her mum looked serious and asked, 'What's up, my love?'

Amy took a breath, 'I've not been feeling myself the last few weeks. I've felt sick and bloated and I have been late.'

'Late?' repeated her mum.

'Late,' confirmed Amy. 'I had a feeling, you know. I can't explain it, but I knew. So, I bought a kit and...' Amy put the pregnancy test result on the table. The two blue lines were visible on the slim, white, plastic stick.

'Oh,' said her mum.

'Oh,' said her dad. 'Are you sure?'

Amy put down two more test results. Her mum picked each one up in turn and looked at them.

'Jesus, Amy. You're twenty-three. How did that happen? I mean, I know how IT happens. Didn't you take precautions?' Tom was trying to hide his anger.

'Of course. Well, I thought we did. To start with anyway,' she replied.

'TO START! For heaven's sake! Spare me the details! Who? Tell me you know who the father is!'

'TOM!' said Claire.

'Of course I do!' said Amy indignantly. 'It's Kieran. He's a friend from London..."

'A FRIEND!' interrupted Tom

Claire punched him in the arm, 'Let her speak, Tom. You can see this is difficult for her.'

'I've known him for a while. We were friends from Wimbledon. When I went to London last month, we met up and spent most of the day together and one thing led to another. We're not serious, I like him, but we're not a couple.'

'Well, that's OK then, isn't it? We haven't met him, where is he? Why isn't he here?' Tom was still struggling to keep calm.

Claire moved around the table and sat with her arm around her daughter. Amy's initial bravery was ebbing, and the fear and concern was starting to emerge. 'I don't know. We haven't spoken since London. He sent me a card to say that he was going travelling, which was his plan. He doesn't know, Dad. We haven't been in touch.'

'It just gets even better!' exploded Tom. 'An absent father! I can tell you how difficult it is to raise a child as couple—you reduce the resources, money, time, and love by half and it must be nearly impossible to bring up a kid as a single parent. This is life changing; you are going to have to become an adult immediately. You have flicked the life switch from "free" to "fucked". These next years should be your best—young, free of responsibility, money in your pocket to go do the things you want, and the opportunity to taste life before you get bogged down with commitments and family. You've just leap-frogged forward ten years, missing so many life experiences. I didn't think you were this irresponsible.' Tom stood and left the room, as Amy finally gave in to her tears.

Claire squeezed her daughter and Amy put her head into her mum's breast, seeking the security and reassurance of a parental hug. 'Ignore your dad. He's just a man. I can imagine that you are scared. You haven't had time to think this all through.' She paused and looked Amy in her eyes. 'There are options, you know?'

'I am not going to have an abortion. That is not even a consideration. I would expect Dad to come up with that!' snapped Amy.

'OK. Sorry. It was just an option. We are here for you. Both of us. Ignore your dad's reaction. He still sees you as his baby girl. He will be kicking stones in the garden for a while until he calms down and sense prevails. He loves you. We love you and we are here to support you. You know that?'

'Thank you, mum,' said Amy.

Tom walked back into the room and sat down at the table. 'Sorry for my reaction. This is happening to you, not me, and I just forgot myself. You are still my baby, but I need to accept that you are an adult. We'll work through it. Together. If I am going to be a granddad, I need to buy some cardigans from M&S.' He winked at Amy and reached out for her hand. This was her life, and he needed to support her, not berate her. One of the lessons he had learned over the last ten years was that life would just happen: it was the reaction to it that mattered.

There was a knock at the door. 'We'll carry on this conversation in a bit,' said Tom as he stood.

***

Peter woke with a start. His heart was pounding, and he thought he might have just spoken in his sleep. He looked over, and Rachel was still asleep. The nightmares were less frequent, but they were no less distressing. Through the darkness the digital display on his clock announced it was 3:30 AM. He walked, naked, downstairs and, pouring a glass of water from his Sub Zero fridge, sat at the kitchen island and looked out over his garden. The moon was high and bright, casting shadows on the monochrome landscape, and he watched as an urban fox explored the shrubs, unaware it was being observed. It was beautiful in its peacefulness. The world didn't care about Peter Blackwood's worries. He was inconsequential. The fox sprang into the darkness behind a tree, emerging briefly through the shadows with its small quarry hanging from its mouth. It bought back the memory of Anker being held in the dragon's grip and he shuddered.

He had stopped short of telling Rachel everything after his first meeting with Stowe and Arc; by the time he arrived home he had regained his sense of duty and discretion, simply explaining that there was a unit of special interest in Wales, and he wasn't able to say anymore. Rachel had noticed he was troubled when he returned from his trip. He said he had been an observer on a special ops training event which resulted an accidental fatality, and that, again, he wasn't able to discuss the details. Peter tried to hide his emotions. He never wanted to look weak with so many hyenas stalking him and he was the rock of the family—unflappable, dependable. If the rock foundation were to show a crack, it could bring everything crashing down, even if the crack were only superficial; perception is often more important than reality.

Stowe and Arc had offered counselling, which he had initially been too proud to accept, but he decided that he would call that day and make an appointment. He realised that he would benefit from having someone he could talk to, although what he would be able to say would be limited. Even if he was not bound by the Official Secrets Act, who would believe him?

The deceit troubled him. Although he was assured there would be no fallout from events in Wales, he had an anxious few weeks watching news coverage and waiting to see if any tenuous connection was made. He knew that any link to Anker, no matter how slight, would be jumped on and exhausted by the press and the Opposition. If the truth of events came out, the impact would be cataclysmic.

In the short time since Blackwood's introduction to the Order and Stowe and Arc, he had been introduced to many new people of influence, lords, and business leaders. Jeremy Stowe's reach and contacts list was already proving to be vast, and Blackwood's ambition could sense great opportunity. He had received a call from Jeremy Stowe a few days ago, suggesting a social lunch with the Chief Constable of Surrey Police, Angela Francis, who had been gaining political popularity and had been showing steady helmsmanship for some time. Blackwood had already mentally shortlisted her as a potential replacement for Jenks. The coincidence of the invitation was perfect timing. He had already set matters in motion to move against Jenks and was waiting for a legal opinion before he met with Jenks to discuss his early retirement. He was on the cusp of another satisfactory manoeuvre.

He walked downstairs and carefully opened to the door to his sleeping twins' bedroom. He could hear their soft breathing, the nightlight showing their haphazard sleeping positions. He wondered how they could sleep in positions that he doubted he could achieve awake. He carefully straightened them up and covered them with the light blankets that had been discarded and crumpled at one end of their toddler beds.

There was no point in going back to bed, so he made a coffee, dressed in a hoodie and jogging bottoms (which were in a pile waiting to be washed), and headed to his desk to prepare for the day ahead.

***

Brown's unremarkable 1930s, three bed, semi-detached home was on the border between Kent and South London, in Beckenham. He and Carol had bought the house after they married. It was the only house they had been able to buy, and it was close to where both of them had grown up. It filled up with their children quickly, and was cramped and noisy for two decades, during which they had frequently discussed moving, but just never got around to it. Their children had now moved out and where once the house buzzed with the sounds of family, it now stood quiet and empty, like a mausoleum to childhood. Neither of them was particularly house proud, and it was conspicuous amongst the rows of well-maintained properties with short-clipped lawns that surrounded it.

The dining room had become Carol's office. Grey metal filing cabinets stood next to the mahogany sideboard that had been a wedding gift and displayed a black and white photograph of Colin at his police Passing Out parade, their wedding photo, and his Queen's Police Medal. Carol was busy keying numbers into her Excel spreadsheet, and Colin was sitting in the living room rubbing his hand. He had just slammed down the handset on his phone with sufficient vigour that he caught a finger between the handset and phone base. He didn't swear; he was at home.

He had reported Anker missing after five days of no contact and it had been a frustrating four weeks waiting for news. It was not uncommon for Anker to disappear off-grid; he might have been following up on his story with Blackwood, or he may have stumbled on something else. There was always the chance that he was drying out and recovering from one of the various vices that may have distracted him. Brown had stopped dialling Anker's number and had cleared his mobile voice mail several times since his disappearance. As unreliable and annoying as Anker could be, this was not like him, and as time passed Brown had become increasingly concerned for his friend.

He had provided the last GPS location that had been recorded to the police when he made his report. It transpired that the hire car was only a few miles away from the last ping, but neither the police nor the mountain rescue units could find any trace of him. The last known location of the GPS signal appeared to be in a lake. The detective running the search had said that the GPS units were notoriously inaccurate, and it took all of Brown's persuasive powers to convince the Inspector responsible for the case to arrange for a diving unit sent from Manchester to sweep the lake. They found nothing. The conclusion was that his body was further afield, and the GPS unit had either been switched off or run out of power. There were around eight deaths a year in the area, but these usually happened in winter, not late summer. Even so, the police seemed to be relaxing into the idea that Will had become another statistic, highlighting the dangers of mountainous areas and inexperienced day-trippers.

Colin had been researching, and he had found the story of the Merlinis' deaths in the previous year. They had worked for a sheep farm in the area where Will had gone missing. He also knew that the Home Secretary had attended a meeting on the same farm. He hadn't told the police why Will was in Snowdonia specifically, and he knew that all these things were connected. Their ineptitude staggered him, and his mind was set: he was going to Wales himself.

He picked up his holdall.

'Right, I am off then. I will give you a call later, once I have checked in.' He paused. 'I love you, Mrs Brown.' It was the first time in many years that he had said that with true sentiment; working with Carol over the last months had been refreshing. For many years, they had become obstacles to one another, immoveable objects that they each had to work around every day. Anker Brown Research had given them new common ground, and he had remembered why he trusted and valued Carol. He had started being thoughtful rather than thoughtless, and it had created the same reaction in return. He had started using the business cards she had designed, appreciative of the time and thought that she had put into it.

Carol stood and gave him a hug. 'Have a good journey, and I will miss you. Speak later.'

Brown threw his overnight bag in the boot of his car and headed off to find Anker. The journey was uneventful and long. It was early evening by the time his Ford Mondeo pulled up on the Davies' drive. It took him a several steps before his back allowed him to stand and his legs could reach full stride. He knocked on the door to the farmhouse and took out a business card in readiness.

Tom opened the door. 'Good evening, can I help you?'

Colin offered his card. 'Yes. My name is Colin Brown. I am an independent investigator. I was wondering if I could ask you some questions?'

Tom looked at the card and instantly recognised the anchor logo. He did his best to look neutral. 'It's not a great time actually—we were about to sit down for dinner.'

'It won't take too long, or perhaps I could come back in the morning. I am staying at the Black Lion.' Colin stepped forward far enough to see past Tom and through into the hall. It was just enough to make closing the door inconvenient. 'I was hoping you might remember seeing this man.' He took out a professional photograph of Anker that he used for his work profile and showed it to Tom.

'That's the journalist, the one that has been missing. Tanker? Lanker? We have had the police come and ask us questions too. I am afraid none of us recall seeing him,' said Tom.

Colin could see the hall coat stand crammed with coats and surrounded by an assortment of scattered shoes. On a bench was a purple rucksack. He didn't flinch. 'OK, thank you. I am sorry to have bothered you. Will is my business partner and his wife is really worried over his whereabouts. The police don't seem to be getting very far, so I thought I would come and have a look around. It is getting late, so I should leave you in peace. Besides, I don't want to miss the kitchen in the pub.'

'You'll have a long wait for a hot meal at the Dirty Dog. They only serve food at lunchtimes on a weekend. I would invite you in, but we have a family thing going on,' said Tom.

'Oh, that's not necessary and thank you for heads up,' said Colin. 'My wife packed me a lunch I haven't touched, so I won't starve. Before I go, I am looking to speak with the son of the Merlinis, Marcus? He lives in the cottage in the next valley, right?'

'He is travelling. Our daughter lives there at the moment. She has also spoken to police and was of no use, I am afraid,' replied Tom.

'Sorry to have troubled you, again. My number is on the card if you think of anything.' He nodded and returned to his car without waiting for a reply.

Tom watched the car complete a three point turn on the drive, and Brown gave a brief wave as he headed away. He closed the door and headed to his office. He called out to Claire and Amy, who were sitting in the kitchen, 'I'll be back with you both in a moment. I just need to call Jeremy.'

Colin's mind was racing. That had to be his son's rucksack. He knew he had been lied to. He just had to work out why and what was really going on. He dialled his home number on his mobile. The phone gave three short beeps and clicked. He looked at his phone to see there was no connection and tutted to himself.

'Hi Jeremy. It's Tom. Can you call me when you pick this up? I think we have a problem.' Tom put the receiver down on his phone.

Epilogue: Murphy's Law

It was 3:35 PM by the time Kieran found a branch of his bank, and it had just closed. He could see the tops of the heads of the staff ignoring him from inside as he knocked on the huge black door. He kicked the bottom of the door in frustration and headed to the nearest tube station to make his way home. He made it with just enough time to allow him to shower and change out of the ill-fitting and embarrassing 'I Love London Zoo' t-shirt. He had some emergency cash in a coffee jar. He was always having to replace the money; he seemed to have many cash emergencies.

As he closed the front door to his one-bed flat behind him, he pressed the play button on his answer phone.

'Hi, son. It's me. Your mum wants to know if you can make it this Sunday for lunch. Posh plates because it's your sister's birthday. You may not remember her, because you haven't seen your family in ages, but to remind you she's the one with blonde hair, always takes hours in the bathroom. Your mum's cooking one of her roasts and your sister's bringing her mate, the one you say you don't like but really you do. Anyway, give your mum a call and let her know that you are coming. It will make her day and therefore mine. It would be good to see you. Over and out.' The machine beeped the end of his messages.

Kieran rolled his eyes. He had moved from Southampton to get away from his family, but they didn't seem to get the message. He should go. He hadn't seen them since last Christmas. Perhaps he would ask Amy if she would come. It was a bit presumptuous, but aside from being covered in monkey shit and having his wallet stolen, the Amy part of the day had been going well. He was confident that tonight was going to be the night he had been waiting for since he first met her. He had had a few previous relationships, but after the initial physical attraction they soon petered out. But Amy was different. She made him laugh and she knew shit about shit he liked and that was a new experience for him. He was aware that if something didn't happen soon, he would be 'friend-zoned', and it was all to play for. He needed to up his game tonight.

He opened his emergency cash stash, and it was empty. Kieran groaned. Murphy's Law, he thought. If it could go wrong today, it would. He had a back-up to his back-up; a credit card, untouched, still stuck to its delivery letter, in a drawer by his bed. He had even prepared for his own lack of preparation. He congratulated himself.

He was about to undress when there was a knock on his front door. Kieran opened it to a tall man, who had a long, pointy face, he thought he looked a bit grumpy. 'Can I help you?'

'Mr McShane?' The man held out his hand. 'David Connor, London Zoo.'

Kieran frowned. 'OK.' He shook David's hand. 'Erm, how can I help you?'

David's grip on Kieran's hand slackened suddenly and he started to falter, as if to faint. Kieran stepped forward to steady the stranger.

'Oh, I don't know what's come over me. Could I have a drink of water, please?' David's face was ashen and clammy.

'Of course, come in,' said Kieran without hesitation as he helped David through and into his open-plan apartment. 'You look terrible. Sorry, I mean, are you OK? What happened?'

'I really don't know. It's been a long shift, and I haven't eaten since this morning.' He took a sip of water, seemingly collecting himself. 'Where was I? Ah, yes. I work at the Zoo. Your wallet was handed in, I saw your address and it was on my way home, so I thought I would just return it. I am afraid there's no cash in it.'

Kieran laughed. 'That would be about right.' He took the wallet and looked through it. 'Well, all my cards are here and my driving licence. Thank you. You are lot are really helpful. Above and beyond. One of your workmates gave me a t-shirt earlier too.'

'Monkeys?' asked David.

'Yes. Shit throwing is common, then?' asked Kieran.

'We've been having a problem with a couple of chimps, although some think they are just very decerning when it comes to people.' David finished his drink and glanced around the room.

'You're not the first to make that comment today.' Kieran started to laugh but noticed that David had remained quite straight-faced. 'I don't mean to be rude, but I am in a rush. I am really grateful that you would go to so much effort, but if you are feeling better…'

'You were on a date today? With your girlfriend?' David's tone had changed.

'Something like that.'

'Lots of couples come to the Zoo. Have an ice cream, stare at the lions and polar bears. I don't get it, personally. It's a place of science. We preserve endangered species and further our knowledge of the nature that surrounds us. You wouldn't take your date to a laboratory,' said David.

'I've never looked at it like that. You don't get ice cream and gift shops in a lab.'

David carried on, ignoring Kieran's reply. 'Visitors seem to enjoy winding up the chimpanzees. Throwing food or stones at them or making monkey noises. Did you do that? Did you throw stuff at them?'

No. I didn't.' Kieran stood. 'Really, I do need to get on.'

'How long have you known Amy? She's pretty hot if you like that sort of thing.' David gave a little smirk.

'You know Amy?' Kieran felt his heart rate rise and face blush slightly with anger.

'Are you fucking her? I bet she's a good shag. Mmm.' David licked his lips, his smiling broadening.

'Right mate, you better fuck off now. I don't know who you are, but in about ten seconds you are going to get to know my fucking boots really well.' His temper was cracking.

'Are you going to bark all night, little doggy? Or are you going to bite?' David sneered.

***

Marcus had arrived at the zoo earlier than usual and was sitting in his favourite spot, meditating and honing his Grym. His connection was growing more each day, and he was starting to see the strings that bound all things together. It was like a vortex spinning skyward from everything, a countless mass of whirling ether. Over time this incomprehensible, impenetrable forest of flow began to take shape and Marcus could see his surroundings. He could walk with his eyes shut, seeing the world in another dimension of light and colour, creating shapes and shadows. There were still places that remained dark to him, due to either his lack of strength or a lack of Grym; centres of humanity where the man-made environment suppressed nature's force. Each connection was unique, like a human's fingerprint, and he had been practicing finding and following people. He had to have touched them—that way he picked up their signature—but once connected, he could reach for them whenever he wished.

He was beginning to be able to trace where they had been—everything leaves a trail of Grym. Well, it was more like the wake of a boat or the exhaust trail of a jumbo jet, which he was learning to follow like a dog could follow a scent. He had looked for Veronika and knew that she was out, heading to the West End. He kept a trace of her whereabouts. She had been the first that he had been able to find.

He was suddenly drawn to a new, yet familiar Grym that pulled on him from nearby. It was strong and danced brightly and with a vigour he had not seen before. He opened his eyes and saw Amy standing with a tall young man by the chimpanzee enclosure. She wouldn't recognise him; he never went to the Zoo as himself. Today, he was Roger Dame. This was serendipitous. The familiar tug of resentment yanked in his stomach and the next action was as obvious and it was amusing. He tuned his mind to the older chimpanzee, which he had found was the most susceptible to his calling. The male chimp reacted immediately, and Marcus watched with glee as the turds started to fly, hitting Amy's companion with sharpshooter precision.

check why Amy didn't clock N was Marcus as Roger

Bolstered by his success, he was recklessly brazen and approached the couple. How he enjoyed the expression on the twat's face as he looked down at his shit-soiled top. Amy looked amused and concerned. He could feel the connection between them. He took the money that was offered him for his 'help', and it was a simple spell to move the wallet from other man's pocket to one of his.

Marcus was bitten with curiosity and was sure that this was a path he had to follow. He watched the couple leave. He overheard they were off to lunch, and he would follow, changing his persona so they would be none the wiser. There was no rush; now he knew Amy's Grym, he could wait and see where they ended up. As he walked towards the exit, he stopped at a quiet spot, out of CCTV camera sight, and, in a moment when he was alone, he became Joseph Allen. Joseph was his favourite. Marcus thought he was handsome; he felt good in that body.

He sat alone in the same restaurant, inside but in plain view. He toyed with the idea of having their food spilt or souring their wine, but just stalking them was excitement enough for now. He had to look down and put his face in his serviette to hide his amusement when the moment came for Kieran to search through his pockets in panic and embarrassment, looking for his wallet. He followed Kieran as he left the restaurant, and as he turned the corner on to a side street, about fifty feet behind Kieran, he took the opportunity to morph once more. He was now Kevin Bannister.

Kieran's converted flat was in a terraced row of houses, unremarkable and small. Marcus thought of his light-filled penthouse and scoffed to himself as he knocked on the door.

When he took Kieran's hand, a pulse of energy shot through his body. An avalanche of memories flooded him; he saw grazed knees, he felt the sting of being punched on the nose, anticipation as he hung high from a climbing frame, excitement of turning a key in a car ignition, nerves from kissing a spotty-faced girl. It was like having a flipbook of memories thumbed through in an instant. He felt Kieran's heartbeat. He saw himself standing in front of himself.

It was all instantaneous. His vision started to funnel and darken, and he would have collapsed if Kieran hadn't steadied him.

As he regained his senses, he realised he had almost coupled with a human. The connection had been lost when he had let go of Kieran's hand. It was an immense step. He knew that Kieran was going back to meet Amy. He knew where and he knew why, or at least what Kieran had hoped for.

'You know Amy?' asked Kieran. Marcus could see the subtle changes to Kieran's expression.

'Are you fucking her? I bet she's a good shag. Mmm.' This should get things moving, Marcus thought, licking his lips. He did not hear what Kieran said next. It was not important; the immediate future was set. 'Are you going to bark all night, little doggy? Or are you going to bite?'

He was surprised by Kieran's lack of hesitation and speed as he came forward. He didn't move. He just squeezed his right fist as tightly as he could, and with that, Kieran dropped to the floor mid-step, crumpling forward with the momentum of his movement. He was limp and already dead when his head thudded against the carpet floor. Marcus had stopped Kieran's heart. It was instant, silent, and clean. He nodded with satisfaction. 'You've had a fucker of day,' he said as he looked down at the lifeless body.

If he cleared up, he would risk being late, so he decided he would come back later and pick up what he needed. He stood in front of the bathroom and muttered the Gorlois Englyn and in that instant took on Kieran's appearance. He turned his face from side to side. Kieran was quite a good fit, though he still couldn't adjust his eye colour and they remained pale blue. It would have to do.

Stepping over the body, he left the flat to meet Amy. A new persona had been added to his growing repertoire, and there was some sweet revenge ahead.

PART TWO
COMING SOON

THE
DRACO GRIMOIRE

Chapel

Duncan had always been big. As a child his father had hoped he would be a rugby forward, a flanker or lock, maybe. But it was clear as he grew that his intimidating size was not matched by his temperament. He would have another calling.

He stretched as he stood up from his bed. His lower back ached and it took a few seconds for his eyes to focus as best they could. He had the body of an eighty-year-old, which was a disappointment for a man of his mid-fifties, so he tried not to dwell on it. It took a few minutes for his body to realise his mind was awake, so, like a car on a cold day, he needed to tick over and warm up before setting off. Rather than exercising, Duncan adapted; he sat on a dining chair to breathlessly put his socks on, he wore slip-on shoes, and he accepted that anything that fell on the floor was lost to him. As he made his way down the creaking, narrow staircase, he heard his wife snoring from one of the other bedrooms, where she would probably remain until after his first service. She had got so drunk during the previous afternoon that she had passed out in the downstairs bathroom and soiled herself. Duncan had cleared up, helped her shower, and directed her into what was becoming her permanent bedroom. She would have no recollection of events when she finally woke up.

The walk from the rectory to the chapel took him through the ancient village that had been built in the shelter of the glen. The cold air and relentless rain helped to clear his head of the brandy-induced fog that wrapped around his thoughts at that time of the morning. In the next few weeks, the rain would change and drift down silently as snow and he would, no doubt, be called upon to be Santa at the Christmas fair. His dean did not approve of the conflicting message that Duncan's festive role might convey, but Duncan did not much care for the dean, or the politics of the Church. That was probably one of the less obvious reasons why he had been moved to this parish, so far from where he had preached for nearly two decades.

The chapel was freezing as Duncan started the old oil-fuelled heating. It always took a few attempts. It needed replacing; like many things in his parish, it had been forgotten and left to decay. The austere interior would soon be temperate enough for the few regular parishioners that would show up, provided they kept their coats on. Next month, the pews would be full as December brought out the Christian in everyone. However, once they had sung their favourite hymns and had a glass of mulled wine, they would forget the Holy Spirit and disappear until next year.

Mrs Henderson was the first steward to arrive. She bustled around filling the water urn and setting out the slightly soft biscuits for after-service refreshments. Stuart Morrison, retired teacher, was next and placed the hymn books out, always optimistically setting for a full chapel. His early-stage Parkinson's made his progress slow, and he would spend much of his time picking up the books he dropped. As the congregation drifted in, the usual greetings and polite conversations were conducted.

Always the last to arrive was Wallace McKenzie, who would sit alone on the pew closest to the entrance, his musty, smoky aroma filling the air around him, guaranteeing his solitude. He lived by himself on a croft, away from the village, next to the loch. He would be seen mumbling to himself on the rare occasions he came to the village. He seldom bought from the local store, never drank in the pub, and therefore was widely ignored by all, bar Duncan. God was within everyone, regardless of their sins, a belief in which Duncan took daily solace.

The reverend was closing the main doors when another worshipper approached. He was not familiar to Duncan.

'Good morning and welcome. Come in, out of the rain. We are about to start.' He smiled and held out his hand. The hooded man accepted the greeting and held Duncan's hand a little longer than Duncan felt comfortable with. The man looked up and his blue eyes pierced through to Duncan's very soul. He shuddered as he withdrew his hand. 'You are new around here?' he asked.

The man pulled his hood back, revealing a lank-looking ponytail, and shook off rain droplets from his coat. He walked past without comment and sat on the pew on the opposing side of the aisle occupied by McKenzie. The service was the regular, well-rehearsed format. Duncan had performed so many he couldn't recall much of the detail, but whenever he scanned the congregation, he was met with the same penetrating stare from the stranger. The post-service tea was stewed and needed sweetening to be palatable, and the sugar and biscuits raised Duncan out of the last of his hangover as he smiled and nodded his way through amenable discourse with the lonely, needy, or elderly that remained for company and conversation.

It was approaching one in the afternoon as he returned to the rectory, walking through the never-ending rain. He dreaded returning home to face Audrey, who would be drunk, listening to bad music very loudly, or drunk, cooking with the kitchen in mayhem whilst listening to bad music very loudly, or drunk, sitting in the conservatory in quiet anger. By 6 PM, she was often vacantly staring at the television or passed out in an alcoholic stupor on the settee. He managed to plan most days so that he would be out until the evening. Today, however, he had no appointment in the afternoon, so his intention was to finish off the bottle of brandy from yesterday and find peace in his own drunken haze. He took a breath and braced himself for Audrey Roulette as he crossed the threshold and entered the house to the sound of convivial conversation coming from the formal reception room.

'Duncan, we have a guest.' Audrey was sitting in an armchair clutching a large glass of wine. Her pupil dilation betrayed her insobriety, though her rounded greying bob looked finger-combed and she was wearing fresh clothes. 'I opened the bottle of wine for Mr Merlin, you understand. But he prefers tea, so there we are.' She shrugged.

Duncan glanced at the near-empty bottle of white wine on the coffee table. It was one of the labels from the bottom shelf of the

Co-Op: New World, vinegary, nasty, less than a fiver. Their guest had managed to dodge a bullet.

Merlin was sitting in the other armchair. He didn't stand. He nodded and took a sip of tea from the cup and saucer he held.

Follow the author at www.jsalderidge.com for updates and to order your pre-release copy of **THE DRACO GRIMOIRE** when available.

Printed in Great Britain
by Amazon

41588269R00142